"What the hell do you think you're doing?"

C.J. whispered.

Tamara sagged against the wall. C.J. would have none of it. He pressed his body against her more tightly.

"Are you following me?" she asked.

"Damn it, Tamara, if I were you, I would start talking now. And I'd tell the truth. Got it?"

"How is it you manage to show up every place I am?" she whispered fiercely. "Are you stalking me?"

"You stubborn, ungrateful fool. I'm not stalking you. I'm worried about you! I went back to your hotel and, lo and behold, I found you sneaking across the parking lot in a trench coat. Have you seen too many movies, or what?"

"Maybe." He had been worried about her? When was the last time anybody had worried about her?

"And then I discovered you breaking and entering. So you'd better start talking, Tamara, because I may have worried once, but I only play the fool so many times."

Dear Reader,

Any month with a new Nora Roberts book *has* to be special, and this month is *extra* special, because this book is the first of a wonderful new trilogy. *Hidden Star* begins THE STARS OF MITHRA, three stories about strong heroines, wonderful heroes—and three gems destined to bring them together. The adventure begins for Bailey James with the loss of her memory—and the entrance of coolheaded (well, until he sees *her*) private eye Cade Parris into her life. He wants to believe in her—not to mention love her—but what is she doing with a sackful of cash and a diamond the size of a baby's fist?

It's a month for miniseries, with Marilyn Pappano revisiting her popular SOUTHERN KNIGHTS with *Convincing Jamey*, and Alicia Scott continuing MAXIMILLIAN'S CHILDREN with *MacNamara's Woman*. Not to mention the final installment of Beverly Bird's THE WEDDING RING, *Saving Susannah*, and the second book of Marilyn Tracy's ALMOST, TEXAS miniseries, *Almost a Family*.

Finally, welcome Intimate Moments' newest author, Maggie Price. She's part of our WOMEN TO WATCH cross-line promotion, with each line introducing a brand-new author to you. In *Prime Suspect*, Maggie spins an irresistible tale about a by-the-book detective falling for a suspect, a beautiful criminal profiler who just may be in over her head. As an aside, you might like to know that Maggie herself once worked as a crime analyst for the Oklahoma City police department.

So enjoy all these novels—and then be sure to come back next month for more of the best romance reading around, right here in Silhouette Intimate Moments.

Yours,

Senior Editor and Editorial Coordinator

Please address questions and book requests to:
Silhouette Reader Service
U.S.: 3010 Walden Ave., P.O. Box 1325, Buffalo, NY 14269
Canadian: P.O. Box 609, Fort Erie, Ont. L2A 5X3

MACNAMARA'S WOMAN

ALICIA SCOTT

SILHOUETTE BOOKS

ISBN 0-373-07813-7

MACNAMARA'S WOMAN

Copyright © 1997 by Lisa Baumgartner

Published by Silhouette Books
America's Publisher of Contemporary Romance

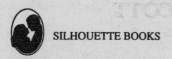

SILHOUETTE BOOKS

ISBN 0-373-07813-7

MACNAMARA'S WOMAN

Copyright © 1997 by Lisa Baumgartner

This edition published by arrangement with Harlequin Books S.A.

® and TM are trademarks of Harlequin Books S.A., used under license. Trademarks indicated with ® are registered in the United States Patent and Trademark Office, the Canadian Trade Marks Office and in other countries.

Printed in U.S.A.

Books by Alicia Scott

Silhouette Intimate Moments

Walking After Midnight #466
Shadow's Flame #546
Waking Nightmare #586
*At the Midnight Hour #658
*Hiding Jessica #668
*The Quiet One #701
*The One Worth Waiting For #713
*The One Who Almost Got Away #723
†Maggie's Man #776
†MacNamara's Woman #813

*The Guiness Gang
†Maximillian's Children

ALICIA SCOTT

recently escaped the corporate world to pursue her writing full-time. According to the former consultant, "I've been a writer for as long as I can remember. For me, it's the perfect job, and you can't beat the dress code." Born in Hawaii, she grew up in Oregon before moving to Massachusetts. Recent winner of the *Romantic Times* award for Career Achievement in Series Romantic Suspense, she spends her time chasing after two feisty felines, eating chocolate and running around the globe.

Alicia loves to hear from readers! You can reach her c/o NEC, P.O. Box 1667, Framingham, MA 10701-1667.

In memory of my grandfather, Fritz Baumgartner, for teaching us so much about family and community.

Acknowledgments:
Special thanks to Patricia Stancliff, PT, for breaking my heroine's bones, then teaching her to walk again. And thanks to SCCA drivers Anthony Ruddy and Jim Biondi, as well as Dick and Bob of Shine Racing Services, for attempting to instruct me on how to race. As always, all mistakes are mine.

Prologue

They called him Spider, but that wasn't his real name. He'd been born Frank or Bob or something generic like that. It had never suited him, so Spider worked well enough.

He'd been a small, scrawny kid who'd grown into a small, scrawny man with overly long arms and legs. When he ran, his limbs bounced around like disjointed attachments, ungainly and awkward. He didn't run often.

Mostly, he tended to his graveyard.

It wasn't *his* graveyard, per se. Really, it belonged to the dead souls who'd been laid to rest here. He supposed it also belonged to the fine people of Sedona, as one corner of the cemetery was maintained by the Historical Preservation Society. In that corner, all the hundred-and-fifty-year-old slate tombstones and wooden crosses were tumbled together. Some of them had been scoured blank by the dust and wind. Others still bore morbid little rhymes such as "Abe took six in the shoulder, now he ain't gettin' no older."

Spider made sure he dusted these tombstones every night; otherwise the thick red dust made the inscriptions hard to read. He also checked the integrity of the black wrought-iron fence bordering the cemetery. Finally, he inspected the markers themselves for any fresh nicks or chips—you wouldn't believe what people tried to take as souvenirs these days.

Spider took great pride in the fact that during his twenty-five years as caretaker, there hadn't been a single incident of vandalism. Something like that shouldn't mean much, but it did. Time had made people crazy, and these days there wasn't nothing people wouldn't do to a cemetery. Young kids covering loving inscriptions with spray paint. Drunken teens pelting century-old mausoleums with empty beer bottles. Sneaky tourists trying to hack off a piece of history.

As far as Spider could tell, not even dead people were safe. And it was up to him, as the caretaker, to provide the last bastion of protection to those who could no longer help themselves.

Graves were important. People came to remember the past, and they came to seek comfort from the ones they'd loved. Walking through the cemetery late at night, a man could hear the strangest things. A son telling his departed father about the birth of his first child. An old man passing on the day's events to his wife, dead five years now. A mother swearing to her recently buried child that she wouldn't forget, would never forget. Graves were like confessionals. Spider had read once that the FBI even used them to trap killers seeking forgiveness from the ones they'd harmed. Spider knew a thing or two about that. Over time, he'd overhead things he shouldn't have. Over time, he did his best to forget those utterances.

Now he was trying to uncover the nine-year-old riddle of the cognac bottles, which was why he was still up after the time polite folks had gone to bed. The moon was big and clear in the sky, perfect for a midnight vigil. He could hear crickets as he huddled behind Sedona's first mayor's tombstone. He could hear the dry, sandy rustle of the lonely wind.

He waited to hear more.

He waited, as patiently as he could, to hear footsteps.

It was October 15. The night the cognac bottle always appeared.

It had taken Spider until five years ago to put that together. Once a year, he'd find a bottle of fifty-year-old cognac next to this group of three graves. The first year, he'd thought nothing of it. He'd figured some of those white-bread, preppy brats from one of the resorts had left it. Seeing that most of the bottle remained, he'd commandeered it for himself. He wasn't much of a cognac man, the stuff could burn a hole in your belly, but if the rich folks could drink it, so could he.

The next year, he'd been surprised at finding the same bottle in the same spot. He'd marked the date on his calendar.

The third year, he'd been curious. The date had held true.

The fifth year, he'd figured it out. These graves were newer graves, a small family plot. Must've been some accident or fire or something, because all three tombstones bore the same date: October 15. He had a mother, a father and some young man with a different last name. Maybe a nephew. He wasn't sure. They were nice markers—two-foot-high pink marble on a granite foundation. The top of each stone had a carving of an angel, and that stuff wasn't cheap. The inscriptions reported the name, dates and a generic "May they rest in peace."

Spider decided that they had died in a fire, because fire had always sounded like a big way to go.

But somebody still missed them. Somebody drank fifty-year-old cognac in their honor every year, then left them the bottle. Spider wanted to know who that somebody was.

Last four years, he'd waited up without success. Twice he'd fallen asleep. Once he'd heard a noise and gotten sidetracked chasing it down. When he'd returned, there had been the cognac. The fourth time had been the scariest. He must've fallen asleep, because he could've sworn there was nobody there, then suddenly a shape appeared before him, swathed in black from head to toe. He remembered seeing blazing red eyes, then he'd cried out and passed out cold.

He'd woken up and found the cognac at his feet.

Maybe he should've given up then. The demon trespasser wasn't hurting the graves, and that's what mattered. But he couldn't. Somebody—something—came into his place every year. Somebody treaded on the slow, sweet silence of the only land Spider could call home.

He wanted to know who.

He'd planned it better this year. He'd eaten simple foods for the last few days so nothing would upset his stomach. Then he'd drunk coffee instead of his nightly beer. He was ready. Bring on the demon. Spider could handle him.

The moon rose higher and higher. The crickets grew faint.

Midnight came and went. One o'clock followed suit.

Spider's eyes began to sag, his lashes touching his cheeks.

He jerked himself awake.

And finally heard footsteps.

They were fast but steady. Spider grasped a leering gargoyle with his fingertips and peered out from behind the mayor's grave.

At first he saw nothing. Then his nose began to twitch. He caught the unmistakable odor of perfume.

A woman materialized before him, and he sucked in his breath.

She looked like she'd been cut out of the night. A form-fitting black suit smoothed down a figure Spider had only seen in girlie posters. Black-encased legs that went on for-ever. Dainty feet tucked into spiky black heels. A waist belted so tiny he ought to be able to span it with his hands. And that chest...

She'd swathed her head in black, as well, a veil covering her face. Long, black gloves hid her hands.

She stopped before the graves. She said nothing, she didn't even nod her head. She simply uncorked the cognac, poured the rich, amber liquid into a crystal globe and swirled it three times. She offered a silent toast to the pink marble graves.

Then she raised her veil and tossed back the cognac.

And for one moment, the moon was clear and brilliant on her exposed alabaster face.

Spider shrank back, stunned and terrified. He whimpered without meaning to, and immediately, she stilled.

Was it just his imagination, or for one small moment, did she tremble?

She said softly, without looking at him, "Come out, Spider. I know you're there."

The demon had gotten him after all. He came out of hiding, his head hung between his shoulders.

"I never told anyone," he muttered. "I didn't know it was *you* comin' each year. I thought they'd died in a fire or somethin'...I d-d-didn't know.... P-p-please..."

Her face remained impenetrable behind the veil. Abruptly, she took a small step back as if she'd decided to let him go, after all. His head picked up. His eyes grew hopeful.

"I won't tell, I won't tell," he gushed. "Swear it, swear it, swear it. Miss—"

A gun appeared. His eyes widened. His throat closed up, he couldn't speak, couldn't beg no more.

Her arm was trembling. God almighty, the demon actually shuddered.

"I...I have to."

She pulled the trigger.

He fell bonelessly beside the graves he'd labored to maintain. And the rhythmic singing of the crickets filled the hushed night once more.

The woman in black drove away. She made it two miles before she pulled over beside the deserted road and vomited helplessly. There was still no one to see. Still no one to know. But it had been like that for a long time now. It had been that way for the last ten years.

She climbed back into her car and continued driving.

Chapter 1

"There are two ways of doing this—the easy way or the hard way."

The big man appeared unimpressed. He leaned back in the old wooden chair and crossed arms that were as thick as oak beams over his chest. His eyes carried a dangerous, glassy sheen C.J. knew too well.

He should've never let the big man into his bar. It was obvious the guy and his companions had already had a few too many before ever stepping into the Ancient Mariner. Now C.J. got to clean up some other bartender's mess.

"I don't gotta do nothing," the big man said sullenly. He bent his thick neck toward his burly buddies. "Right?"

Twiddly Dee and Twiddly Dumb both nodded.

C.J. forced himself to stand loose and keep the grin on his face. It was Wednesday night, and on a Wednesday night of all nights, he didn't want a fight in the middle of his joint. But principles were principles, and poor Sheila was still huddled in the corner, terrified, after being pinched by Paul Bunyan here. C.J. didn't stand for disorderly conduct in his place, and he definitely didn't stand for any guy manhandling a woman.

As far as C.J. could tell, there was only one thing to do. "You got two options," he explained again. "The easy way or the hard way."

He rolled his neck and shrugged out his shoulders. At five ten and one hundred and sixty pounds, he hardly intimidated the larger man. The regulars in the bar who knew better were quietly placing bets with the people who didn't know so much. Behind the bar, Gus was unsheathing her knife just to be safe. If these big brutes thought C.J. was harmless, just wait until they saw what Gus could do with a bowie knife.

C.J. wasn't nervous. He'd faced bigger opponents, tougher opponents, more numerous opponents in his life. At this point, he just wanted these drunkards out of his bar with the least amount of damage possible.

"Okay," C.J. said at last. "The hard way it is."

He rolled up his shirtsleeves and assumed a boxer's stance. "Come on, big fella. I got other customers to flatter."

Big Fella lumbered out of his chair enthusiastically. Obviously, he hadn't walked into the Ancient Mariner for the beer.

C.J.'s pulse picked up. He hadn't been in a brawl for months now, and there was something to be said for a good brawl. Once a marine, always a marine. *Semper fi,* baby.

The big guy charged, all force and fury. C.J. shook his head and stood his ground. At the last second, he feinted right. Big Fella went crashing headfirst into C.J.'s freshly polished bar.

C.J. winced. "Hell, that's a hundred dollars' damage right there."

Big Fella reeled back and shook his head like a drunken bull. His buddies rose out of their chairs.

"Man, its gonna be an expensive night."

Behind the bar, Gus snorted and said, "You shoulda bought the tranquilizer gun when you had the chance."

"And miss these Kodak moments? Put some money down on me, Gus. I'm going to need the winnings to cover the damage."

"Bah," Gus muttered. "Bar can handle more than that. You, too."

Twiddly Dee and Twiddly Dumb advanced. C.J. let them crash into the bar once apiece just to be neighborly. After a bit of heavy grunting and fist clenching, the threesome decided for a group rush, costing him two perfectly good tables and one already taped-together chair. The locals groaned then cheered as he took a solid right hook, recovered and danced away on the balls of his feet. He knew how to move, take a blow and bounce back up like a human Weeble Wobble. What growing up poor on the streets of L.A. hadn't taught him, the marines had jammed down his throat in eight weeks of do-or-die boot camp.

C.J. got serious. He blocked out the locals' cheers, Gus's scowl and Sheila's concern. He focused on the men before him, the adrenaline throbbing in his veins, along with the small ore of anger that snaked through him on random occasions. The part of him that never forgot the hunger of L.A., or the agony of his mother dying, or his father leaving him that final time for the skies of Indonesia.

C.J. moved. Jab, jab, followed by two feints and a dozen rapid-fire punches. The three men dropped one, two, three, making loud thuds on his red-tiled floor.

Thirty seconds later, C.J. stood in the middle of the floor, his breathing slightly heavy as the locals swapped cash, shook their heads at the drunken fools and returned their attention to the small TV set up in the corner. C.J. lingered just to be sure, but Paul Bunyan and his friends remained down for the count. He was half satisfied, half saddened by that. His little sister, Maggie, was right—he enjoyed fighting too much.

"All right, all right," Gus grumbled, coming out from behind the bar. "I'll show them to the door."

She shuffled her bulk toward the fallen forms, not in any hurry. A Hopi Indian, she was shorter than C.J., but a great deal more imposing. Her thick black hair was liberally streaked with gray and worn in a tight ponytail at the nape of her neck. She never wore jewelry, just the hideous, twisting scars on her face that hinted of untold stories. C.J. had shared the bar with her for almost six years. He had no idea where she came from, what she'd done, or where she might be going. He figured the first time he asked, she'd simply give him her flat, black stare, then pack her bags and leave.

Now she leaned over the groaning men and smiled in a way that twisted her scarred face even more grotesquely. One man opened his eyes, gave a little yelp and squeezed them shut again.

"Taking out the trash, Gus?" one of the regulars chortled.

"Somebody's gotta."

C.J. left the locals to recap the victory and exaggerate the details. He crossed to Sheila, who stood with her arms wrapped around her middle in a stance that reminded him even more of Maggie.

"How you doing, kid?"

She shrugged weakly. Until recently, her primary occupation had been serving as a punching bag for her alcoholic husband. Then four weeks ago, Mary Campbell from the local church had called C.J., stated Sheila was trying to leave her abusive husband and asked if C.J. would give her a job as a cocktail waitress. He'd agreed instantly, of course. When Sheila had turned out to have no training, he spent Monday walking her through the drill himself. When she'd flinched the first time the bar got too rowdy, he'd harassed his regulars into settling down. When she'd paled at the thought of having to weave in and out of so many men, he'd rearranged the tables so she'd have a wider aisle.

The regulars had been teasing him about it ever since. *"Yep, there goes C.J. again, rescuing another damsel, drying another tear. Think if we were blondes he'd treat us so well?"*

"Nope," C.J. had retorted. *"Because you guys would make damn ugly blondes."*

"Don't let a big bully like that scare you," C.J. drawled lightly now. "You're tougher than he is."

Sheila finally smiled, but it still didn't reach her eyes. He gave her another moment.

"Want to take the rest of the evening off?"

"I need the money."

"It's only one night. Business isn't that great."

"I'm fine. Really."

"Sweetheart, you look like you're going to faint."

Her lips thinned. She looked uncertain, then abruptly she squared her shoulders. "I can do it. I...I *need* to do it."

"All right, it was just a suggestion. Prove me wrong, see if I care."

"I'll do that." She slanted him a narrow look. "You didn't have to fight him. You can't fight everyone who pinches a woman's butt."

"In my bar, yes I can."

"I have to learn to handle men like that sooner or later."

"Fine, next time I'll hold him and you can beat him up. You are becoming more like my sister, Maggie." He said that a bit wistfully. He'd always regarded himself as his little sister's protector, her number one knight in shining armor. Maggie didn't need him anymore, though. She'd found herself a convicted murderer instead, and C.J. had given up ever understanding women. "So you're okay?" he quizzed Sheila again, just to be sure.

"I'm fine."

"Okay, let's get this show back on the road, then."

He strode back to the center of the bar, already picking up the shattered chairs.

"Never met a stray dog or troubled woman he didn't love," Gus muttered from behind the bar to no one in particular. "He sure ain't gonna die of old age."

At 1:00 a.m., C.J. closed up shop, kicking the last four regulars out the door. It being Wednesday night, most of the locals had work the next day. Sedona existed thanks to year-round tourism, a few plush resorts to attract the really rich moths and a solid collection of excellent art galleries. Most of the Ancient Mariner's clientele were the rugged, blue-collar workers fueling the white-collar vacations. The Jeep-tour guides, the hot air balloon guides, the helicopter pilots. The laundry boys and "customer service representatives" from the various resorts. The kind of people who worked hard looking at how the other half lived and knowing they'd never be them. They worked hard, anyway, and at the end of the day, they wanted to kick back, listen to some good, old-fashioned rock 'n' roll and enjoy a cold beer.

C.J. had bought the Ancient Mariner with the money he'd saved while in the marines, and he'd kept it a locals' hangout. The red-tiled floor was scuffed up and boot-friendly. Navajo print rugs added warm colors to beat-up wood walls. The tables and chairs still sported the deeply carved initials of long-since-grown reprobates. It was a place for relaxing, telling stories of the New Yorkers who wore designer wool beneath the Arizona sun or the Texans who considered the Red Rocks to be mere pebbles. Guides could brag about how many people they'd stuffed into a hot air balloon, or how many kids had gotten sick on them that day.

C.J. would shake his head and not believe any of them.

Now he walked to the corner of the room and picked up the TV remote. A news update stated that police still had no leads on the mysterious murder of Spider Wallace, the ignominious cemetery caretaker who'd been gunned down last week in his own graveyard. In other news, Senator George Brennan, Arizona's fine senator, was rumored to be on the verge of announcing his candidacy for president. He was arriving in Sedona—his hometown—next week for a vacation. Insiders predicted he'd declare his intentions then. The old "local boy makes good" angle.

C.J. clicked off the TV. He didn't care for politics. Death and taxes was enough guaranteed suffering for any man. He placed the remote on top of the TV, stacked the rest of the chairs on the wiped-down tables and looked around. Gus had finished cleaning the bar and was now closing out the register. Sheila was sweeping the floor.

Everything was under control as it had been last night and the night before that and the night before that. In addition to running the bar, C.J. did some part-time work as a "bail enforcement officer"—bounty hunter—to keep his reflexes sharp. He hadn't had a case for a while and he could feel it now. He wasn't unhappy, he was just... restless. Dissatisfied.

Lonely.

"Are you going home or you gonna stare at us all night?" Gus grumbled.

"I'm going." He was still standing in his bar, though. He found himself thinking of his father, Max, and that strange year the two of them had whizzed around the globe so Max could conduct his business as "importer-exporter." He saw his mother, pale and ethereal, as she'd lain dying in their shabby studio apartment, still loving a man who was too busy traveling to come home.

"Hey, boss man. Get outta here."

"Yeah, yeah, yeah."

His black convertible Mustang had a five-liter engine

and brand-new tires. He pulled back the top so the clear, warm night wrapped around him. Crickets chirped. The wind carried the spicy, clean scent of creosote.

He hit the back road hard. An experienced SCCA race driver, he took the first corner at seventy-five and the third at ninety. In the straightaway, he came close to triple digits, practicing the speed and control he was learning at the tracks, though his grandmother's voice kept whispering in his ear that this wasn't the place for it. He found the line of the curving road, double-clutched for the next corner and hit it at seventy-five. His tires squealed.

For the first time, headlights appeared behind him—distant, faint beams.

"Cop?" His foot slipped instantly off the gas, but then he frowned.

The lights were growing in his mirror. Belatedly, he realized that could only mean the car was gaining on him and he was still over ninety. His gaze locked on his mirror. The other car was definitely going really damn fast, probably around a hundred and five, and still hadn't put on any sirens. The S curves were about to appear.

C.J. downshifted, taking the set of three corners at fifty-five and hearing his tires squeal. His arms bulged as the car fought him. For an instant, he thought he'd taken the corners too fast and that would be it. He threw his body weight behind his biceps and got his car around the last curve.

"Stupid, stupid, stupid, C.J. What is your problem these days?"

Then he remembered the car behind him. He glanced up. He saw twin headlights dashing wildly. Then he heard the horrible high-pitched whine of burning rubber spinning off the road.

"Sweetheart, are you all right?"

The voice came from far away. She thought that was

odd. She'd been through this drill before, careering off a road in an Arizona night. There weren't other voices, anyone to offer assistance. There had only been her and the sound of the crickets mourning.

"Come on, come back to me. That's it, sweetheart. Draw a nice, deep breath of air."

She opened her eyes. The image took a while to gain substance and form. First the man was hazy; she'd expected that. Maybe he'd have wings and a halo—who knew what angels really wore? He'd be Shawn or her father. Longing welled up in her throat. Reality cut it back down.

This man wasn't Shawn. He was too filled out, with the broad shoulders of a man, not a boy. His fingers brushed her cheek, and they were callused.

Immediately, she stiffened. She was alive. She was conscious. She had better pull herself together.

"Take it easy," the stranger murmured. "I got you."

Arms curled around her, and hands fumbled with the seat belt still fastened at her waist. She tried to shrink back, but she couldn't seem to make her body work. She tried to speak, but no sound came out.

Abruptly, she was cradled against a hard chest and lifted into the night.

"Here we go."

Her head lolled against his shoulder, and the world spun sickeningly. Cool, composed, always professional Tamara Allistair contemplated throwing up on a man she'd never met. Oh, God.

"Honey, we need to get you to a hospital. Lie down right—"

"No." This time her throat cooperated. She repeated the word more sharply. She'd spent two years in and out of hospitals and physical therapy departments. That was enough time in drafty gowns and sterile rooms for anyone.

"Honey—"

"No."

There was a moment of silence. She used it to try to calm her stomach and focus her vision. She hated the feeling of nausea. She hated the way the world refused to snap into focus. She didn't like losing control.

"Drink this." Water dribbled over her lips. She spluttered in shock. Two fingers gently parted her lips, and the cool water slid down her throat.

After a minute, the world righted itself.

She was sitting in the seat of another car. Arms were around her. Against her cheek, she felt the soft, worn fabric of a well-broken-in T-shirt. She could hear a heartbeat. Her gaze drifted up.

Wheat-blond hair. Strong jaw with fine stubble. Incredibly blue eyes that crinkled with natural humor. Firm, full lips meant for grinning. She sat perfectly still, too confused to move. His arms were around her, holding her. That was odd enough—very few men dared to touch Tamara Allistair. Moreover, she didn't feel any pain.

There had been a time when she'd been held a lot, but it had always involved pain. First had been the surgery to insert the metal screws and a rod to anchor her shattered lower leg together. One week later, they'd pinned her pelvis into place with more metal screws and some metal plates. But even after six months of physical therapy, her leg hadn't healed. There had been another surgery for a bone graft. Her leg had improved, her knee had given out and back into the operating room she went. These days, she carried more plastic and metal than bone. And these days, she knew how to separate her mind from her body so she could escape the pain. She even knew how to be hard.

Life didn't favor the weak.

She said hoarsely, "Let me go."

"What?"

"Let me go."

"Honey, did the crash scramble your brains? I'm trying to help you here. Damn, you're bleeding."

His arm uncurled from her shoulders, and she flopped unceremoniously back onto the bench seat.

"I tried to warn you," the man muttered.

Tamara stared at the never-ending night sky and discovered she could now see three of everything. She breathed deep and inhaled slowly, the way Ben had taught her.

Pull yourself together, Tam. Focus, focus, focus.

"Here, hold this against your forehead." A soft cloth was pressed into her hand, chilled with water. It felt cool and soothing against the lump hatching on her forehead. Her ribs felt tender, her stomach bruised. She mentally surveyed her pelvis. Cracked, broken, shattered? Seat belts wreaked such havoc on the human body, pinning it into place so the force of the crash could shove a person's thighs into their pelvis, cracking it like an egg and shattering lower limbs. Toe-box injuries, they called it. She had other words for it, but she didn't use them in polite company.

"How many fingers am I holding up?" The man's hand appeared in front of her eyes.

"You're holding up fingers?" she said weakly.

"Oh, sweetie, we got to get you to a hospital."

"No." She closed her eyes and pressed the cold cloth against her forehead more tightly. "I just need a minute."

"And I thought I was stubborn," the man murmured. She heard him shifting from side to side, but she felt better with her eyes shut, so she remained floating, feeling her stiff shoulders relax, and slowly taking inventory. Her neck was sore. She had a headache. But she could move all her limbs, even her plastic knee.

She lowered the damp cloth and opened her eyes. The man was still standing there, his hands jabbed deeply into the front pockets of his worn jeans, his face wearing a concerned frown. She blinked her eyes twice and he came into better focus. He had a good jawline—strong, square, blunt. He probably was stubborn.

"Time to go to the hospital," he said flatly. "Call me crazy, but I have a policy against women dying in my arms."

"Band-Aids," she said. "In my car..."

"You have a first aid kit?"

"The trunk."

"Huh. At least you pack a helluva lot smarter than you drive."

He stalked toward her Lexus, leaving her alone to test out all her joints. She stretched out each morning religiously, running through the exercises Ben had taught her. Scar tissue grew stiff over time, and she had a lot of it. Now she could get everything to move well enough. Her right wrist twinged, but that was nothing new. Her left ankle—the one that had been fractured, healed badly, then grafted—refused to complete a circle, but she hadn't been able to get it to do much for ten years now, so why should tonight be any different?

Given the speed she'd hit the corner at, the force at which her car had spun off the road, she was doing all right.

"Sweetheart, when you said you had a first aid kit, you weren't kidding," the man declared, jogging back over. "Are you a medic or something?"

"No."

She wrapped her hands on top of the seat and prepared to heft herself up. Immediately, his hands curled around her shoulders. She froze.

"Easy. I'm just trying to help you up."

"Please!" Her voice was sharp, more brittle than she intended. Instantly he backed off, hands in the air.

"Hey, I really am just trying to help."

"I...I know." She managed to sit up, though the world

spun. When it righted, she made out her car fifty feet back, and the man standing in front of her. He no longer looked so gentle or compassionate. His blue eyes had narrowed, and now that gaze was piercing.

Tamara, you are making a mess out of this.

She focused on looking at the red dirt, dimly illuminated by his car's headlights. "I'm...I'm... Could I have the Band-Aid, please?"

"It's your Band-Aid." He handed it over stiffly, then added dryly, "Gonna apply it yourself, as well?"

Her cheeks flushed with shame. "Yes."

"You're from New York, aren't you?"

She stiffened, but he simply shook his head in disgust. "Yeah, your attitude says it all. Big-city car, big-city clothes, and the gratitude of a hound dog acquiring a new flea. I visited my brother in New York once. I still can't believe people would actually *want* to live there."

She nodded weakly, fumbling with the Band-Aid as her fingers began to tremble. He could tell she was from New York? She'd come here knowing that she needed to keep a low profile, and yet a total stranger could deduce she was from New York in a matter of minutes?

How much else could he tell? Why was he out on the roads at this time of night, anyway? And why hadn't her brakes responded when she'd pumped them for the curves?

Her hands shook harder. She couldn't get the backing off the Band-Aid.

"Yeah, you're just fine, sweetheart. No problems here." The man snatched the Band-Aid back impatiently, ripped off the backing with one deft movement and latched it onto her face. "Band-Aid won't do it in the long run. You're going to need stitches."

"I'll be fine."

"Listen, I spent twelve years in the marines and six years owning a bar. Let me tell you, you're going to need stitches."

"I'll be fine."

"I'd believe you a lot more if your forehead didn't look like you'd just had a full frontal lobotomy. Now—" he crossed his arms over his chest "—what would you like me to do?"

"Talk softer." She gingerly pressed her hand against her forehead.

"Oh." He instantly looked contrite. "I'm...I'm sorry. Listen, I'm muddling this a bit. Why don't we start over?" He held out his hand. "C. J. MacNamara. I own a bar, the Ancient Mariner, just a few miles back."

She took his hand, feeling warm, strong fingers curve around her palm. He had a good handshake, firm, but not so squeezing that it cut a woman's rings into her fingers, the way some men were prone to doing. He owned a local bar. It had probably just closed—that's why he'd been on the road. She returned his handshake with more enthusiasm, relaxing a fraction.

"I'm sorry, too," she murmured. "I guess I'm more shaken up than I thought."

"You really should go to a hospital."

"No...I'm..." She didn't know what to say. She didn't like to talk about the first auto accident in the best of situations, and since she'd decided to return to Sedona, she'd realized it was dangerous to bring it up. She settled for shrugging, hoping he would take that at face value.

"Could I have some more water?" she asked. He handed the canteen to her wordlessly, his gaze still sharp and waiting. She *would* be rescued by a man who wasn't easily put off. "Uh... Thank you. I mean...really. Thank you...for stopping."

"Welcome to Sedona. We still help each other out here."

Her lips twisted ironically before she could catch them. Quickly, she smoothed out her expression.

"Lady, what were you doing hitting those corners so fast?"

"I wasn't trying to."

"You hit them going seventy. Only a complete idiot hits S curves going seventy."

"You didn't take them so slow yourself."

"I was doing fifty-five. There's a huge difference between fifty-five and seventy."

"True." She took a step, swayed, and he cupped her elbow. Of course, she flinched; she just couldn't help herself. C.J.'s gaze narrowed again.

"I swear I've had my shots," he said quietly.

She turned away from his scrutiny. Her car was fifty feet back, spun around in a circle of loose rock and red dirt. The good news was that the roadside was pretty flat, so damage to her car was slight. The bad news was, she should never have gone off the road. Mr. MacNamara was right—there *was* a great deal of difference between fifty-five and seventy. Eight years ago, she'd started racing cars so she could learn about all those differences—and so she would never feel terrified or helpless behind the wheel again.

But tonight, she'd panicked. She'd seen the curves looming, pumped her brakes futilely and thought that she'd die. If she hadn't had experience on how to take sharp corners at high speeds, if she hadn't known exactly when to downshift and how to turn into a spin, her car would've hit those curves at almost a hundred, flipped and rolled.

What had happened to her brakes?

"I'm all right now," she said. "Thank you for stopping, but I'll be fine. You can go."

Without a backward glance, she walked over to her car. Her heels sunk down deep into the soft, dusty soil, worsening her limp.

"I'm not just leaving you here."

"Really, it's okay." She dug a flashlight from her trunk, then found her tool kit. "You know us New Yorkers. We like to take care of ourselves."

"Am I being brushed off by a woman with a concussion?"

"I don't have a concussion."

He didn't take her hint. Instead, C. J. MacNamara followed her to her car, invading her desperately needed space with the distinct odor of fresh soap and faint laundry detergent. He stood very close, something she just wasn't used to. She plunged into her tool kit with shaking hands.

"How exactly are you going to get home?" he persisted reasonably. "Civilization is a good five miles back or forty miles ahead. Either way, it's a little late to catch a bus."

"I'm going to fix my car."

"*You're* going to fix your car?"

"Yes." She popped the hood, putting the whole car between them. Shrugging off her silk blazer, she leaned over the hot engine and, with her flashlight, got serious.

"All right, I consider myself to be a modern man. Hell, I was raised by a woman who can make just about any piece of machinery work. But my grandmother runs a hundred-acre dairy farm. She doesn't race around back roads driving a Lexus and wearing designer suits."

Tamara didn't answer. Brakes could stop functioning for a variety of reasons. Problems with the main computer manning the lines. Air in the lines. A slow leak that drained brake fluid. Loose fittings with the master cylinder, leading to drained brake fluid. Baking soda and vinegar or hydrogen peroxide added to brake fluid.

Very few of those options were true accidents.

Get a grip, Tamara. You've been back in Sedona for only a few days. No one knows who you are. No one knows what you're after. You just have to be cautious and careful for a little while longer.

Ten days and you'll have your answers one way or another. You just have to make it through ten days....

The engine was still steaming. She tried to examine the fittings with the master cylinder and nearly singed her finger.

"Here—" C.J. held out the soaked towel she'd once had on her forehead "—at least use this."

She accepted the offer wordlessly, prodding at the fittings. They seemed tight enough. She found a drop of oily brake fluid and lifted it to her nose. It smelled like an engine, no sharp overtones of vinegar. She rolled the heavy, orange-red fluid between her index finger and thumb. It was warm, thick and oily. No grit from baking soda.

Her fingers danced down the rubber brake line, checking for leaks. The bottom brake lines were metal, protecting them from being punctured by jagged potholes or debris. The top brake lines, however...

Two inches down, she found the irregularity. Then another. Then another. Five in all. None very big, but all taking their toll.

A faulty line?

Sabotage.

Immediately, she pushed the thought away. No, not probable. As far as anyone knew, she was just a New York PR executive who'd volunteered her expertise and time to work on Senator Brennan's political campaign. She and Patty had started planning this six months ago and they had been very careful. Their story was simple and straightforward and mixed with just enough truth to have credibility. She'd been back in Sedona for three days and hadn't so much as seen or spoken to Senator Brennan. There was no reason to believe he knew who she really was or what she was really about. No reason at all. Everything was going according to plan.

"Brake lines?" C.J. said abruptly. She startled, having

forgotten that he was there, then startled again when she found him bent over right beside her, his face a mere three inches away. "Looks like you're leaking fluid," he continued matter-of-factly.

For a moment, she simply stared at him, not sure what to do or say.

He had his hands gripping the edge of her car like a man who knew a thing or two. Certainly, his hands were a working man's hands—long, lean fingers, with a trace of Arizona dust around the nails. He wore ridges of yellow calluses and absolutely no rings. White, criss-crossing scars from a lifetime of use webbed his knuckles, while tendons sprang up on the back of his hands. He had broad palms, strong forearms. Those were capable hands. They probably knew a lot about engines, a lot about tools, and a lot about other things a woman like her shouldn't consider.

"Yes," she managed to say after a moment. "The brake lines seem to have suffered some damage."

He frowned. "Punctured?"

"There are holes."

"Kind of hard to puncture an upper brake line, don't you think?"

"Perhaps it was a faulty line. I just had some work done on the car before I drove out here."

"Yeah, maybe." His eyes squinted. "I don't think you should be driving this car any place now. I'll give you a lift to your...?"

"Actually, I have duct tape and brake fluid in the metal tool bin. It'll be fine."

"You travel with brake fluid?"

"It does come in handy." She tried to move away. His hand clamped around her forearm, stopping her. His hand was strong. Those fingers were callused. She was acutely aware of them against her skin—not bruising, but very, very firm.

"Of course, maybe that shouldn't surprise me…seeing how you are also carrying a gun."

Her heartbeat accelerated before she could catch it. Her ankle holster. When she'd bent over, she must have exposed it. Or maybe when he was carrying her. Oh, God…

She said, "Excuse me, I'm trying to get the brake fluid."

"And I'm trying to figure out just who the hell you are."

"I don't remember that being any of your business."

She jostled past him forcefully, grabbing the plastic bottle of brake fluid and the roll of duct tape. C.J. didn't move out of her way. He leaned against the front of her car with his ankles crossed and his arms akimbo. His white T-shirt stretched across his chest, barely tucked into his worn jeans. For the first time, she noticed his boots. Scuffed up, well broken in. A working man's boots. Her father had once owned a pair like them. He'd loved them, said a man couldn't be a man without wearing boots.

"Who are you? You haven't given me your name."

"I'm tired. It's late. I just want to tend to my car and get home."

"Where's home?"

"I don't give out that kind of information to men I don't know." She ripped off a piece of duct tape savagely and wrapped it around the wounded line.

"I've given you my name. I pulled over to help you. How much do you need to know?"

"In this day and age, a girl can't be too careful." She tore another strip. He stood too close. She caught a faint hint of Old Spice. She'd once loved Old Spice. Now it made her eyes sting. She was tired, she was distraught. She was standing on the side of an Arizona highway, too close to another night when her car had gone off the road and she had listened to the people she loved die.

"Here, at least let me put in the brake fluid."

"I don't need your help!" She snatched back the plastic container. "Please, I just want to be left alone."

He didn't say anything. He didn't move. His gaze walked over her face slowly, seeming to peer into each crevice, as if he could find every secret she'd been hiding.

She thinned her lips and met his gaze head-on. Dammit, she didn't cow anymore, she had earned her battle stripes. She snapped, "Doesn't a man like you have virgins to deflower or something like that?"

"That's Friday night. This is Wednesday, and on Wednesdays I only rescue damsels in distress."

"Well, I'm not in distress," she announced crisply, unscrewing the brake-fluid cap and pouring it in. Dammit, she really could take care of herself. But C. J. MacNamara continued to eye her coolly.

"No, you're not," he drawled slowly, "In fact, for someone who was just in a car accident, you don't seem the slightest bit shaken."

"I don't do shaken."

"You don't seem to need help."

"I don't need help." She capped the plastic bottle tightly, tossed it into the metal tool kit and threw in the duct tape and flashlight.

"You show no trace of nerves or hysteria."

"I definitely don't do hysteria."

"What do you do?"

She slammed the tool kit shut with a resounding crash. "I mind my own business."

She stalked past him, too angry to feel her headache or sore limbs. She dropped the kit into the trunk, slammed her trunk door, then climbed into her car. When she tried to fasten her seat belt, however, it hurt her stomach and neck. Damn, damn, damn.

C. J. MacNamara leaned into the driver's side window just as she started the engine. Her heart was suddenly hammering in her chest.

"Who are you?"

"No one. Goodbye."

"What happened to your brake lines?"

"Faulty line. Damn those mechanics. Goodbye."

She eased her car onto the road and took off into the night.

C.J. remained standing there a minute longer, watching the disappearing glow of her taillights.

He said at last, "Liar."

He still didn't get into his car.

The woman was right; it was none of his business. But then his eyes were on the dark spots of brake fluid still staining the ground. A nameless woman with faulty brakes and a .22 semiautomatic handgun. A beautiful woman who froze every time he touched her.

You're sticking your nose where it isn't wanted, C.J., a little voice warned. Probably his grandma's.

Too late, he thought philosophically. His interest was piqued!

Chapter 2

"Miss Thompson. There's a visitor here to see you."

Tamara looked up from her desk blankly, and C.J. knew the minute she spotted him standing behind the receptionist, because her deep brown eyes became instantly wary. He grinned at her charmingly and waved. She scowled.

By day, she was more stunning than he'd remembered. Rich brown hair was pulled sleekly back and tied at the nape of her neck, reminding him of an otter's thick, glossy coat. She wore another one of her fancy New York pantsuits, this one a deep bronze color that picked up flecks of gold in her eyes. A dark brown, green and gold scarf was tied expertly at her neck, adding a splash of color and style. She would have looked one-hundred-percent corporate woman, except for the bulky white bandage plunked over her delicate forehead and the violet purple shadows staining her eyes.

"What are you doing here?" she asked without preamble as the receptionist walked away. They were in the middle of Senator Brennan's "war room," basically a converted ballroom at the El Dorado Hotel & Conference Center. Three chandeliers winked above them, but they were the only signs of elegance left in the room. Otherwise, the huge floor was now covered by wooden tables and metal fold-down chairs. The walls hummed with the throbbing, lively music of people chattering, computers beeping and phones ringing. In the front, a receptionist signed everyone in. After her, three campaign lieutenants directed the throng of volunteers, arranging them into battalions fit for cold-calling voters, stuffing envelopes and canvassing neighborhoods. Senator Brennan's full-color mug shot, blown up to monolithic proportions, beamed benevolently down on the chaos created in his honor. C.J. half expected to see altar candles burning at the man's feet.

"I'm interested in Senator George Brennan," C.J. said casually to Tamara. Ignoring her cool glower and the dozens of people milling around them, he settled his hip on the edge of her desk and got comfortable. She was one of the few people with a computer in her work area. In- and out-baskets overflowed with paper. In front of her, a press release was bleeding to death from her red-ink edits. The pen was still poised in her fingers like a weapon. She looked on the verge of using it.

C.J. picked up one of the papers sitting on the top of the in-basket and began to scan the campaign schedule. Instantly, she snatched it out of his hands and slapped it back onto the pile.

"This is a working campaign headquarters, Mr. MacNamara," she snapped. "I suggest you either state your business, or move on."

"I already told you," he said with complete innocence, "I would like to learn more about the senator. This does seem the place for that."

Her eyes narrowed. "How did you find me here? Did you follow me?"

"A little bit paranoid, aren't you?"

"Just answer the question."

He shrugged. "All right. I looked you up, and lo and behold, here you are."

"You couldn't look me up. I never gave you my name."

"I didn't look up your name. I looked up your fore-head."

She stopped frowning long enough to blink her eyes in genuine bewilderment. "Mr. MacNamara, I have no idea what you're talking about, and I don't have time to play games. I would suggest you start telling me how you got here and what you want, or I'm going to call the security guards."

He leaned over until he could capture her gaze. Her chest was rising and falling a bit with agitation. Her features were pale, shuttered and remote, but he could see her tension in the blue vein pounding right above the line of her scarf. "Your stitches," he said gently. "While you doubted me at the time, I knew you would need stitches. There is only one hospital nearby, so I called the ER. They gave me your name and, with a bit of cajoling on my part, the hotel where you are staying."

She leaned away, clearly not trusting him. He remembered that look on her face from last night. What was it that made her so cautious? He'd honestly never had a woman look at him as warily as she did. He wanted to shake her firmly and cry, "Hey, I'm one of the *good* guys."

"Hospitals don't give out that kind of information," she said firmly.

"I'm a real bail enforcement officer, got a cool plastic badge and everything. You'd be amazed at what kind of information that will earn you."

Her forehead crinkled again. She appeared at once remote and vulnerable, controlled and fearful. But then her expression smoothed over and her chin came up a notch, the seasoned warrior ready for battle. He would've clapped at such a fine display of control, but she probably would've hit him. Given how well she drove and how nicely she was armed, he wasn't sure he wanted to find out how well she could hit.

He tried another charming smile. All his life, women had been telling him they couldn't resist that smile. "So how are you, Tamara Thompson? I worried about you all night."

Charisma didn't appear to work well on her, either. "Huh," she snorted with clear skepticism. "Do you always follow up on the women you save?"

"Only the ones who might be suffering from concussions and are still too stubborn to let me drive them home."

She set down the pen with a sharp rap. "Well, as you can see, I'm perfectly fine. Thank you again for stopping, all's well that ends well, and you can be on your way now."

"You look very tired."

"Car accidents and concussions can have that effect on a woman."

"How are the brake lines? Have you figured out what might have caused one to rupture?"

"I really haven't had the time to look into it."

"I could look at it for you, if you'd like."

She said sharply, "Don't you have a bar to run or something like that?"

C.J. smiled. "My bar seems to take care of itself just fine whether I am around or not—"

"Then your bar and me have something in common!"

He couldn't help it. He chuckled, and for whatever reason, that made her face flush becomingly. "I like talking to you, Tamara. I've never really had a woman so thoroughly put me in my place."

"Obviously." She was trying to sound sharp, but she was clearly flustered. She picked the red pen back up, twirling it between her fingers and no longer meeting his gaze. He had a feeling that it had been a long time since a man had flirted with her. That made no sense to him. She was clearly an intelligent and attractive woman. He figured any self-respecting male would at least try for small talk. Then again, she was from New York. He didn't pretend to understand New Yorkers.

"So you work here?" he prodded.

"I'm trying to."

"What brings a New Yorker all the way to Arizona to work on a senator's campaign?"

"I have family in the area. A...cousin. Patty. Patty Foster. She owns an art gallery in town."

"Yeah, Wild Horses. It's a great gallery."

"I'll tell her you said that."

"You don't look anything like Patty."

Tamara's lips thinned. "All right, Mr. MacNamara. Here's the drill. I live in New York. I work for a big public relations firm called Lombardi's. We like to think we're one of the best firms around, and I like to think I'm one of the sharpest junior partners. As such, I'm entitled to four weeks of vacation a year. Maybe you've heard of vacations?"

"Touché."

"I took two weeks. Monday, I arrived to assist with kicking off the senator's campaign. In another ten days, I'll be returning to New York—"

"Perfect, you know all about the senator. Why don't you show me around? I'm a registered voter. I figure someone has to be president. Tell me why it should be him."

She took a deep breath. He could almost see her mentally counting to ten. Her cheeks had gained more color, and her eyes had taken on a fierce, golden hue. He liked her looking this way—on the verge of chewing him up and spitting him out. He tried another smile.

"You did not come here to ask about Senator Brennan!"

"True, but since I am here—"

"Mr. MacNamara—"

"Please, call me C.J." Her eyes were beginning to burn. Tiger eyes. He was incredibly intrigued. She slapped her pen down on her desk hard enough to make the young girl walking by flinch.

"Stop it! I have no idea why you are here. I have no idea why you insist on following me around. Look, I'm grateful you stopped last night, but I can take care of myself. Now, I want you to leave."

"Tamara, I'm not stalking you—you can call the sheriff for a character reference if you'd like. However, I am very attracted to you—"

"You don't even know me!"

"Exactly. Which I'm trying to remedy, but so far conversations with you are like getting up close and personal with a porcupine—"

"Which you should take as a hint."

"Well, I've always been a little slow that way." He cocked his head to the side, regarding her seriously for the first time. "You seeing anyone?"

Her jaw worked. She was beginning to look a little dazed. He had a feeling there weren't many situations she couldn't control and not many men who gave her a true run for her money. Yep, he liked her.

Abruptly, she shook her head.

"You married?"

She shook her head again, but her gaze was mutinous.

"You're not interested in me at all?" he cajoled. "Not the teeniest bit? Not even one iota of interest?"

"No. Not even one iota. I am completely iota-less."

He beamed smugly. "Liar."

"Oh, you egotistical, insufferable—"

"You're blushing again."

"I am not!" But she *was* blushing, and now her face grew even redder. She was very, very flustered. Her eyes had turned to molten gold; the air around her was beginning to crackle. On her desk, her hands opened and shut in tight movements of frustration. If they hadn't been in the middle of a ballroom filled with people, he would've leaned over and kissed her.

Instead, he stood abruptly, removing himself from the edge of her desk. A volunteer was walking by them. He used the opportunity to say loudly, "Why, Miss Thompson, I had no idea the senator felt so strongly about family values. We sure could use more of those."

The volunteer, an older woman in a bright flowered dress, beamed at them both proudly. C.J. waited until she'd passed to add, "So why does he chase anything with breast implants and a short skirt?"

Tamara closed her eyes. She was definitely counting to ten now. But she was good. Even as he watched, she pulled herself together. "Those are merely rumors," she said crisply. "You know how the press is these days."

"He's not a womanizer?" C.J. quizzed quietly.

"George Brennan has been married for thirty-two years. He's a proud husband and good father. He got both of his kids into Harvard Law. He believes very strongly in family."

"And education?"

"Absolutely."

"What about medicare, social security, the increasing number of homicides being committed by kids under the age of sixteen?"

"George Brennan is tough on crime. As a senator, he backed several key legislative initiatives to try juveniles as adults and build more prisons. He's on record as being pro death penalty."

C.J. nodded, but he was frowning. For a woman who five minutes ago had practically sizzled with frustration, she was totally lacking in emotion now. She recited the senator's political positions like a paid announcer in an infomercial. No passion, no conviction, no religious belief. His instincts resumed nagging—something about this woman wasn't right.

"I always heard that the Senator was an old-school, boys-will-be-boys kind of man. You know, the kind with several ladies on the side, an inflated expense account and enough extravagant presents from the lobbyists to make you really wonder."

"Rumors."

"He's been in politics for twenty years, Tamara. The media nicknamed him The Fox for his ability to consistently evade all hound dog reporters. How much of it really is a lie?"

"I have the senator's position sheet right here, if you'd like," she said coolly.

"Have you ever met the senator?"

"No." She paused for a minute, then added, "He arrives in town one week from Saturday for the big kickoff."

"You must be very excited."

"We're all very excited. This is a very exciting time."

"Tamara, why don't I believe you?"

"I...I don't know." Her gaze had latched on to her computer, her face impenetrable. He wanted to touch her cheek. He wanted to smooth his thumb down the line of her jaw. Then he wanted to brush his thumb over her lips, see if they would gently part, look into her eyes for some kind of sign, some kind of response. For one moment, he'd thought he'd reached her, dug beneath her composure to find a fierce, witty, passionate woman. Now she sat so still, so remote, so contained inside herself.

"Walk me to the door?" he suggested at last, his voice light. He knew how to beat a strategic retreat.

The relief on her face made him smile. "You're leaving?"

"You could at least fake disappointment."

"I would hate to be inconsistent." She rose smoothly, obviously more than willing to show him out if that's what it took to get rid of him. He shook his head, having to smile at the irony. In all of his life, he'd never encountered a female so immune to his charm. If his brother, Brandon, or sister, Maggie, ever heard about this, they'd laugh until their faces turned blue.

Tamara came out from around her desk. She kept a reasonable amount of distance from him and was already turning toward the front doors of the ballroom. Her sharply tailored pantsuit resembled the one she'd worn last night. Between the black, glossy form of her boots and the delicate puff of scarf at her neck, she was basically covered from head to toe. Elegant, striking, a woman who had something to hide.

She took the first step forward and he immediately noticed her limp. "You're hurt."

She shook her head. "Old injury. Nothing to do with last night."

"You're sure?"

"The doctors gave me a clean bill of health. I just need to change the bandage on my forehead. Really, the accident wasn't that serious."

"You handled your car like a professional."

Her lips curved up slightly at his unspoken question. "You know, C.J., you're even more stubborn than I am."

"Just unbelievably curious. You handled a car at high speeds through S curves. You carry more tools in your trunk than even I do, and you fix brake lines as casually as flipping eggs."

"The SCCA," she admitted at last.

He stopped in genuine surprise. "You race cars? I race cars. What class are you in?"

"ITA."

"Really? I'm ITC! I have a 1980 Volkswagen Scirocco,

1.5 liter engine, one hundred horsepower. Just bought it last year. Suspension is a mess, but it's getting there.''

"Mine's a 1983 Toyota Corolla GTS. Bought it five years ago. It needs a new engine, but it's hanging in there. One-hundred-twenty horsepower engine, of course. What can you do with one hundred?''

"You race Limerock, New Hampshire and Pocono?''

"When I can.''

C.J. let out a low whistle. A woman who knew about cars. A woman who liked to spend her weekends *racing* cars. Now he was impressed. More and more women were getting into racing, but they were still grossly outnumbered by the men. In the friendly, low-key world of SCCA racing, the "Leave It to Beaver" family model still applied. Daddy raced the car. Mommy packed the picnic lunch for the day. Little children ran around like hellions amid the stacked tires, piled tools and dismantled engines, while the teenage son attentively went over the engine with dad, checked the tires, adjusted the suspension and waited for the day he would be the one behind the wheel.

This woman belonged to that friendly, easygoing community. This woman with her cool expression and fancy suits knew how to get down and dirty, how to wrestle with mufflers, shocks and pistons to squeeze that last ounce of performance from a car. She could *drive*.

"Wow,'' he said at last. "If you can also handle drywall, tap a keg and burp the ABCs, I'll marry you.''

Her lips curved reluctantly. "I don't burp.''

"Darn. Women have no idea how much that would put men at ease.''

"I'm sorry, but if you'll just keep looking, I'm sure your ideal woman is out there somewhere.''

"What got you into racing?''

She paused, eyeing him up and down. "Last question?'' she negotiated.

"Last question, then I'm on my way. Marine's honor.''

She appeared skeptical but nodded. "All right, I got into racing to learn how to be a better driver. You know how it is back east. December hits, snow starts arriving, and the roads become something out of a nightmare." She shrugged. "I have a demanding job. I have to be able to get around no matter what the conditions. And I don't like being afraid. A race track teaches you what you need to know about handling a car at high speeds, in aggressive traffic and under adverse conditions. I learned. And last night, I was very grateful for those lessons."

For a change, her expression wasn't guarded; her deep, dark eyes were clear.

"Yes," he murmured at last. "I bet you were."

"Here we are, C.J. I answered your questions. Now I have to get back to work."

They arrived at the huge double doors of the ballroom. A steady traffic of bodies flooded around them. C.J. lingered a minute longer. His expression grew serious. After a moment, he gave into the impulse and gently brushed his thumb down her cheek.

She flinched, her gaze dropping to the floor. "Please. I'm really...I'm really not someone you should be interested in."

"You won't consider dinner?" he asked softly.

"No. I'm in town to assist with the senator's campaign. Once things get going, I'll need to return to New York."

"Then we'll make it a short meal."

She shook her head again, refusing to look at him. "I need to work."

"Tamara, are you sure you're all right?"

"Of course."

C.J. crossed his arms over his chest. "Tamara, if you know so much about cars, then you know as well as I do that punctures in a brake line are not common. Especially upper brake lines. I saw your engine, too. There was nothing loose, no sharp edges—"

"The brake lines were new," she interrupted firmly. "I'm sure I just received a bad line. I've called my mechanic about it. It's taken care of."

"Why don't I believe you?"

"It's none of your business."

C.J. took a deep breath, surprised by the spark of anger and frustration that shot through him. It was his business because he wanted it to be his business. And frankly, he was used to getting his own way. Particularly when he grinned.

"My bar," he said abruptly. "It's called the Ancient Mariner. If you ever need anything, ever want to reach me, I'm there."

"Fine," she said, clearly humoring him.

"If you need anything, you will call?"

Her eyes were starting to glow again. "You are so persistent!" Abruptly she threw her hands in the air. "You are insane, C. J. MacNamara, but if it means so much to you, then yes, if a big bad dragon ever shows up at my ivory tower, you'll be the first knight I look up in the yellow pages."

"Good." He pushed away from the door frame. He walked into the throng of arriving volunteers, but at the last moment, he turned back. "Tamara," he said softly. "Take care of yourself, okay? Take care."

"Who the hell is C. J. MacNamara?"

Tamara sat down hard in front of Patty in the sitting room at the back of the Wild Horses gallery. The store had closed an hour ago, and away from prying eyes, Tamara could release the emotions building in her chest. That she had so many emotions was already something of a shock for her. Her life for the last ten years had been a carefully modulated exercise in control and concentration. It had gotten her through physical therapy even on the days when her body had rebelled, and after that, it had turned her into one hell of a public relations executive.

This afternoon, on the other hand, she'd had no focus or concentration to speak of. She'd sat at her desk, trying to edit the senator's announcement speech and thinking about C. J. MacNamara instead. She thought of his blue eyes, his wavy blond hair, the way he leaned against her desk as if he had all the time in the world. The way he smiled as if he was very pleased to see her. The way he gazed at her, as if he wanted to turn her inside out and learn every last nuance of her thoughts. The way his fingers thrummed on the edge of her desk, long, blunt and callused.

Oh, for God's sake! She shook her head hard, trying to erase the images from her mind. She did not get angry. She did not get frustrated. And she did not lose sight of her goals and objectives merely because a nice-looking man with way too much testosterone stopped by for a chat.

"C. J. MacNamara?"

Tamara leaned forward, recognizing the shock stamped on her friend's face. After all these years, Patty was still beautiful. She wore her bright red hair down in a mass of springy curls. Her loose, flowing silk dress in deep purple fit her image as an art gallery proprietor. They had first become friends in grade school. Then, when they were twelve, Patty's mother had died of breast cancer. For a while, her father had been too overwhelmed with his grief to handle his daughter. Patty had adopted Tamara's family instead, becoming the sister Tamara had never had. When Tamara had decided to return to Sedona, Patty had been the first and only person she'd called.

"How did you meet C.J.?" Patty quizzed sharply. Her green eyes appeared anxious.

"He was the one who assisted me last night when I had trouble with my car." Tamara hadn't told Patty all the evening's details; she didn't want to worry her too much. "Then he showed up today at campaign headquarters."

"He's *following* you?"

"Yes…well…" Tamara didn't know quite what to make of it herself. "He…uh, he asked me out."

Patty sat back abruptly, looking even more startled and slightly appraising. In spite of her best intentions, Tamara felt herself blushing. There was nothing to blush about, dammit. He'd expressed interest. She'd said no. He'd persisted. Some men really liked a challenge. Obviously, C. J. MacNamara was one of them.

"He's quite the ladies' man," Patty said softly.

"I got that impression."

"Do you want to go out with him?"

Tamara vehemently shook her head. "I committed myself when I returned to Arizona. I'm here to learn the truth about what happened to my family. For God's sake, Patty, I just saw the list of preliminary donations coming in for the senator's campaign. Several *Fortune 500* companies have given hundreds of thousands for TV commercials, you name it. The senator's announcement won't be half-hearted. He's committed to running for president. If he learns what I'm up to…"

Patty's expression was becoming more anxious. When they had been kids, Patty had been the high-spirited rebel, always getting them into trouble, while Tamara had been the good girl bailing them out. After her mother's death, Patty had really gone off the deep end. She'd started smoking, drinking, breaking curfew. Now, however, the tables had turned, and the adult version of Patty seemed intent on subdued caution.

When Tamara had called about coming to Sedona, Patty had been against it. It was too dangerous, she'd said. Tamara had managed to talk her into it, but it was obvious Patty's doubts remained.

"Go back to New York," Patty said abruptly. "Really,

if you return now, the senator will never suspect a thing
and everything will be all right."

"It'll be okay."

Patty shook her head. "Tammy, please... You live in
Manhattan, you make all this money and drive a fancy car.
You're this incredibly successful public relations person.
You were even dating some big-name doctor—"

"Donald. It...it didn't work out."

"But you'll meet others. The point is, you have this
great life. So what are you doing, Tamara? You're sticking
your nose where it doesn't belong. And if the senator was
the one who hit your family's car, and he does find out
what you're doing..."

"I'm being very careful."

Patty threw up her arms, her red hair crackling.
"Tammy, what about *me?* I live here. I'm trying to run
an art gallery, and frankly, I am *not* driving a Lexus. We're
telling everyone you're my cousin. He starts looking at
you and he's going to find me!" Patty's lips trembled, then
she pressed them into a thin, angry line. "I want to help
you, Tammy. Your family was like my family too. I do
want to know what happened that night. But not if it risks
everything. I've lost enough in my life, and what can either
of us really change?"

Tamara was silent. She wanted to be able to answer that
question; she wasn't sure she knew how. When she'd first
awakened in the hospital and remembered the accident, an
image had hovered at the edge of her mind, the blurred
picture of a man's face leaning over her. She couldn't
make it come into focus. Then, six months later, recover-
ing from the bone graft operation on her lower left leg,
she'd seen Senator George Brennan being interviewed on
the news and she'd realized abruptly, that was the man.
The man who'd leaned over her at the accident site.

She'd followed up with police, but when they pressed
her hard, she'd backed down. No, she wasn't one hundred

percent certain. No, she didn't remember that well. The police weren't going to pursue a state senator without solid evidence, they told her. They were looking for witnesses to the crash. They were trying to find a car matching the red paint they'd taken from her parents' car. The skid marks helped them deduce the tires, suspension, and so forth, to discover the type of car the other person was driving. They'd find that car, they'd find the driver, they would solve the case. She didn't need to worry about it. She needed to work on getting well.

She had. Alone in Manhattan at one of the few hospitals in the nation capable of rebuilding shattered pelvises, she went through enough surgeries and physical therapy to last her a lifetime. Year turned into year. She got a degree. Got a job. Built a career. The police still searched for leads. She learned to live alone. She tried to tell herself she was happy. She used her success to buy the right clothes, the right co-op, the right car. And she woke up on Christmas mornings so weighted down she couldn't get out of bed. She spent Thanksgiving and Easter and her birthdays and their birthdays in a black fog so thick she couldn't cry, she couldn't speak, she couldn't moan.

She won major new PR accounts but never made close friends. She attended all the glitzy PR functions, but rarely with a date. Finally Donald had pursued her, and he'd seemed so patient, so kind, such the right kind of man for a successful PR executive, she'd given it a try. She should get on with her life. She should date. She was strong. She could do this.

It had ended six months ago for reasons she couldn't tell even Patty about. And Tamara had stayed up all night, feeling the dark mood roll over her again, and she'd realized for the first time that she had to go back. She simply had to go back. Maybe if she could determine the truth about her parents' last night, then she would finally be able to go forward.

She'd given herself two weeks. If she couldn't find any new information on a ten-year-old accident in two weeks of focused search, then she probably just wouldn't. Maybe it would be enough to know that she'd tried.

"I have to do this," she said at last, the closest she could come to expressing all the jumbled thoughts and emotions in her mind.

"Tammy—"

"Patty, I'll be careful. I'm hardly running around town accusing anyone of anything. I researched articles on the accident in the library. I learned the senator was receiving an award from the American Legion that night, which would put him on the same road as my parents. I've been asking around campaign headquarters to learn more about him and his habits, just subtle things. Tomorrow, I'm going to talk to a woman who lives by the crash site. Maybe she saw something.

"I won't do anything rash, I promise. I want to know the truth…but you're right…I'm not prepared to sacrifice everything I've built in the last ten years for it."

"What if someone recognizes you?"

"That was ten years ago, Patty. I was just a kid. Most people don't even remember the Allistairs. There's no reason to connect New York PR executive Tamara Thompson with little Tammy Allistair. It'll be all right."

Patty looked away, her face still troubled. The silence grew long.

"That night," Patty said softly, "when my father woke me up to tell me that there had been an accident, that Mr. and Mrs. Allistair were dead, that Shawn was dead, that you were in critical condition and might not live—that was so horrible, Tammy. Like my mother, all over again. I don't want to go through that again. That…that hurt in ways you don't understand."

"I do understand."

"No, Tammy, you don't. You lost your first family. I

lost my second. I went through everything twice. I hate funerals!''

"You and your father are close now. You have family."

"It's taken us a long time."

"I'll be careful," Tamara insisted, her voice curt. She didn't want to discuss it anymore. She just wanted to do it.

After another awkward moment, Tamara gathered her things. "What do you think of C. J. MacNamara? Is it just coincidence?"

Patty rolled her eyes. "Of course it's coincidence!" she snapped, obviously still unhappy. "For God's sake, Tamara, keep your grip on reality. The whole world is not out to get you."

"You're right, you're right." Tamara held up her hands in apology. Suddenly self-conscious again, she said, "Call you in a bit."

Patty nodded but the mood still wasn't right. At the doorway, Tamara paused one last time. She saw her childhood friend sitting on the edge of a funky chocolate leather sofa. She saw the bright coppery hair that filled so many of her childhood memories. She looked at the woman she'd once considered a sister.

And there was a distance between them she didn't know how to bridge. They were the girls they had been and the women they had become, and due to one event out of their control, those women had drifted too far apart. Patty had been the fiery rebel. Tamara the soft hearted girl-next-door. And now?

What did you expect, Tamara? And what is it that you want?

She had no answers. She walked away.

Her hotel suite was large and luxurious. Patty had been right—she was very successful. Alone in Manhattan, she had become more than she probably would've been as Shawn's wife in Sedona.

She didn't bother to turn on any lights. She stripped off her suit in the foyer and let bronze crepe de chine crumple to the floor. Her head was beginning to throb. Her left ankle and right wrist twinged even more than usual. She was in shape, she had a nice form, but she bypassed the mirror on her way to bed. On a night like tonight, she didn't want to see the jagged white scars covering so much of her stomach. The operation to remove her spleen and stop internal bleeding. The surgery to rebuild her pelvis.

She collapsed onto the king-size bed, curled into a ball and hugged a pillow close. She should take a long, hot bath to ease tight muscles and sore joints. She was too tired.

She found herself thinking of C.J., the way his thumb had brushed her cheek, how gentle his touch had been. How it had sent an unexpected shiver down her spine. He was probably at his bar now. The Ancient Mariner, he'd said. She pictured it as a comfortable kind of place with a traditional brass bar and lots of beer on tap. She bet he had a jukebox and it played rock 'n' roll or good country music. She imagined the people there laughed a lot and joked with one another good-naturedly. And C.J. grinned and flirted with the pretty waitresses and made everyone smile.

You've seen too many episodes of "Cheers."

She lay on her bed and replayed every second of his pulling her out of her Lexus.

What if he had been there ten years ago? What if he had arrived and held her and saved her family?

It didn't matter. What had happened, had happened. Her family and boyfriend had died. She had survived.

And soon she would learn the truth. She would get justice for them. And maybe closure for herself?

Her eyes drifted shut. Her fingers relaxed their grip on

the pillow. She let sleep drift over her naked body like a blanket, and, as always, she tried to control the dreams.

Shawn. The feel of his arms around her, the way he always made her feel so safe. The hushed reverence in his voice as he brushed her young cheek and whispered, "I love you, Tamara. More than anything. More than my own life."

Hold me, hold me, hold me. Never let me go.

But then he was gone, and she was alone beneath the Arizona night, twisted and ruined on the roadside. Hearing only crickets, no moaning, no begging, just the crickets.

She was unable to move, unable to speak, trapped in the silence. Waiting and waiting and waiting. For someone to find them. Someone to help them. Someone to hold her and whisper soothing lies, because she could feel the blood seeping from her body and she knew that soon she would join her family in the unknown.

No one came. No noise but the crickets. The sky so vast, the silence so deep. She was lost in it, sinking down deeper and deeper inside herself. While Shawn's hand, still clutched within her own, grew cold and stiff.

Wake up, Tamara. Don't dream these dreams. Go back to the better moments. Remember the family you had. Dream of the life you've built.

But as she tossed and turned on the king-size bed, she couldn't find the better days anymore. Shawn was too distant, a sweetness she'd journeyed too far from, and now she couldn't find her way back. His face was blocked from her, the memory of his touch barricaded away. She'd tried to recapture him, but found herself dreaming of Donald.

His hand on her breast, his surgeon's fingers fine and precise. His voice muffled and hoarse as he peeled down her blouse. "You're beautiful. So beautiful."

She let him touch her. She lay passive and unmoving while his hands brushed over her body. And she waited to

*feel anything. Relax, Tamara. Let yourself live. It's okay,
it's okay. But she still didn't feel anything.*

His body labored over hers. She waited for it to end.
And then he moaned and it was done and they both knew
it wouldn't work out.

Afterward, they lay side by side, not touching. She listened to the sound of his breathing as it returned to normal. She tried to summon any emotion for this man she'd
dated for more than a year. He was intelligent. He was
successful. He was patient. He was kind. Nine years after
the accident, she still couldn't let anyone in. She still
couldn't let herself feel. She was successful. She was
strong. She was frigid.

She said in the hushed darkness of his bedroom, "I'm
sorry."

"Maybe our relationship should take a break for a
while."

"Yes."

"I'll call you...."

"Of course."

And then she knew the silence had won.

Chapter 3

"Mrs. Toketee? I'm Tamara Thompson, we spoke by phone, remember?"

The old woman nodded her head. She looked at least seventy, and her features were weather-beaten and leathery from a lifetime beneath the harsh Arizona sun. An Indian, Mrs. Toketee had spent the last forty years living in this three-bedroom house with a yard filled with rusting automobile parts and a small menagerie of animals winding their ways underfoot. Her thick hair was the color of steel, and her figure had filled out generously. Around her neck, she wore a beautiful silver necklace bearing arrow-shaped pendants and red coral stones. Matching earrings and a bracelet completed the set. The silver was very shiny, giving Tamara the impression that this was nice jewelry brought out only for special occasions.

Now Mrs. Toketee wiped her hands on the flour-covered apron tied around her waist and beckoned Tamara inside. Her house was old, and it wasn't large, but its expanse of bay windows captured the endless Arizona sky and gave the illusion of space. The sun would set in an hour, and the soaring red rocks were just beginning to deepen to a dark ruby. Through these windows, the winding road that had claimed Tamara's family was nearly visible.

Tamara forced her gaze from the view. Carved out of wood and painted with vibrant vegetable dyes, kachina dolls loomed in every corner. Some were ogres, ugly little demons with hideous animal faces and human bodies. As a child, Tamara had been warned that ogre kachinas ate disobedient kids. Certainly, she'd gone to bed every night right on time and never uttered a bad word.

A gray tabby rubbed again Tamara's leg, startling her.

"Don't mind Cecil." Mrs. Toketee clicked her tongue disapprovingly at the cat. "You think you are the best cat, the king of animals." She scratched the tabby's ears with genuine affection. "Don't you, don't you?" she chastised.

"It's okay. I like cats."

"Cats are good. Keep away mice and rats. You want coffee?"

"No, thank you. I'm fine."

"I made bread."

Tamara was about to politely decline, but then she saw the hopeful look on Mrs. Toketee's face. She smiled softly. "Bread would be nice."

Mrs. Toketee's face crinkled into a toothless grin. "Zucchini bread, healthy stuff. My daughter sends me recipes. She worries about my health. I don't get visitors often."

"You have a beautiful home."

"Too cluttered. Too many things. You never realize how old you are until you look around and see so many things. I keep meaning to clear it out."

"The dolls are gorgeous."

"Kachina dolls are good."

Mrs. Toketee disappeared into the kitchen, reemerging a few minutes later with a large tray piled high with slices of bread, a dish of butter and, despite Tamara's refusal, two cups of coffee. Tamara tried to assist with the heavy tray, but Mrs. Toketee would have none of it. In the end, Tamara took her seat on an old wooden chair across from the woman and was promptly joined by the purring gray tabby.

"As I mentioned, I'm doing a piece for the *Sedona Sun*, a 'Where are they now?' sort of thing."

"Uh-huh." Mrs. Toketee worked on pouring the coffee. Her movements were very slow but capable, like sap pouring from a tree. Tamara clutched her pen and notebook more tightly, wanting to help but understanding that it would insult her hostess.

"Do you remember October 15, 1987, Mrs. Toketee? Do you remember the car accident?"

Mrs. Toketee finished pouring the first cup of coffee. She shuffled it toward Tamara's side of the table. "Bad night."

"Yes." Tamara's fingers were starting to tremble slightly. She forced herself to be calm. She was supposed to be a reporter, talking to a potential witness; the Toketee residence was the closest house to the crash site. It had all happened to strangers.

"A family died, yes?" Mrs. Toketee murmured.

"Three people. A mother, father and the boyfriend of the daughter. The daughter survived."

"Happened down there. There's a cross in the road at the site. You like the coffee?"

"The coffee is great." Belatedly, Tamara took a sip. It was good but very strong, and she hadn't eaten all day. It settled hard in her stomach. She set the cup back down.

"Bread?"

"Uh...well...yes, please. Mrs. Toketee—"

"The accident happened late, yes? The family was there all night. I remember now."

"What do you remember, Mrs. Toketee?" Tamara

leaned forward. The sticky slice of zucchini bread was forgotten in her hand.

"The road curves there. It is a very dangerous road. At night, people go too fast."

"This family's car wasn't speeding."

"But the other car was. Hit-and-run, the newspapers said."

"Did...did you see anything, Mrs. Toketee? Did you *hear* anything?"

Mrs. Toketee set down her coffee cup. Her weathered face creased into a deep frown. "That was a long time ago."

"Yes. I understand that. Please..."

"I think there was a moon that night."

A full moon, like a globe up in the sky, casting the canyons into dark shadows, slashing across the man's face as he leaned over her. Illuminating his figure as he ran back to his car and sped away.

"I heard something. Something loud. At first, I think it is something in my yard."

"Yes?"

"I wake my husband. I tell him to go look. He grumbles, he doesn't like getting up in the middle of the night. I make him go, anyway."

"Your husband?"

"He's dead now. Buried in the cemetery in town. The one where the caretaker was shot. It is no longer such a good place."

"I'm sorry."

"He comes back to bed, tells me there is nothing. We both fall asleep."

Tamara nodded. Her eyes were wide, her breathing shallow. She felt at the verge of a precipice, and the tension inside her was almost unbearable. The woman was going to say more. She was so sure the woman was going to say more.

"And then?"

Mrs. Toketee sat back. "It's morning. We hear ambulances. We see the accident. My husband feels bad. If he would've searched harder, maybe gone down to the road. It bothered him for a long time. You don't like the bread?"

Tamara looked down. She'd squeezed the heavy bread flat with her fingers. Belatedly, she released her grip. "Sorry," she murmured. "The bread is fine, I was just...caught up in the story." She set the bread down and spent several long minutes arranging it on the napkin. She concentrated on breathing deeply, then exhaling.

"Did you go to the accident scene?"

"My husband did."

"Did he tell you anything about it? Did he see the car, maybe, or skid marks, or anything?"

Mrs. Toketee shrugged. "I don't remember."

"They never caught the man who drove the other vehicle."

"The man?"

"The...the person. The other driver."

"That could be. The police, they questioned my husband, but he didn't have much to say. We didn't go down until it was too late. There was nothing to see anymore."

Staring at the zucchini bread, Tamara nodded. By morning, her family had been dead and the other driver long gone. She'd gotten to read the police reports. Traces of red paint had been found on her parents' car. The force of impact indicated that the other vehicle should have been seriously damaged and the other driver probably hurt. But twelve hours later, when the search began, a damaged red car and hurt driver were never found. The police checked with auto body shops, car rental agencies and tow truck companies. They checked with taxicab businesses for anyone looking for a ride. They checked the local junkyards for the car and the local hospital for the driver. Nothing.

Whoever had done it seemed to have simply disappeared.

Or had the resources for a solid cover-up.

"I'm not much help," Mrs. Toketee said. She was nodding almost in a rocking motion. "You're disappointed?"

"A little," Tamara admitted, then summoned a smile. "But it was very kind of you to take the time to speak with me."

"I don't get many visitors."

"The coffee and bread were excellent."

"Maybe if I think of something, you'll come again?"

"Of course." Tamara gathered up her notepad and pen. She drained the coffee cup, though the strong brew made her stomach roll queasily. She needed to be better about eating. She needed to be better about sleeping.

"Here, you take this." Mrs. Toketee was holding out one of the dolls. This one was a richly clad figure of a wolf dancing on a wooden block. It had been intricately painted with deep turquoise, yellow, red and blue. The detailing was incredible and had probably taken Mrs. Toketee a very long time.

"I couldn't. It's too much." Tamara waved the doll away as gently as possible.

"You know the kachina dolls?"

"Not much. They're good luck charms, or something like that."

"In the pueblo, we believe the kachinas are real beings. In the past, when our people needed them, they assumed human form and visited us. They brought gifts, taught us arts and crafts, how to hunt. But our people took them for granted, lost respect for their caring. Struggles broke out and the kachina stopped visiting. Their love, however, is better than ours. And though we mistreated them, they care for us still. When a person is sad or lonely, the kachina will come and dance for her. Make her understand that she is not alone. You take the kachina. The kachina will be good for you.''

Mrs. Toketee placed the doll in Tamara's hand. It felt warm and smooth. The wooden figure was so richly colored. It vibrated with the grace of the dance.

''Thank you. You are very generous.''

Mrs. Toketee bobbed her head. ''It fits you. Very nice.''

''Here...'' Tamara jotted down the number of her hotel. ''If you think of anything, please give me a call.''

A minute later, Tamara eased her car—with its new brake line—down the steep driveway. There would be no magical follow-up call; she understood that. After ten years, an eyewitness account was just too unlikely. Patty had been right—she was silly to pursue this. She should go back to Manhattan, return to the job she did so well.

Buy another car. Take another trip to Europe. Get on with her life.

She turned onto the highway and did her best not to look at the wooden cross protruding from the roadside as she drove by.

By the time she pulled into her hotel parking lot, she was lost in thought once more. She needed to know more about the mysterious red car. When the senator came into town, how did he get a car? Did he always sign up for a limo or driver? Or did he sometimes rent a car? Say a red car? Who would he rent from?

And how could she ask such questions without arousing suspicion?

Her head hurt. She pulled into a parking space, killed the engine and rested her bandaged forehead against the steering wheel for just one moment. When she looked up again, she groaned.

C. J. MacNamara stood in the parking lot. He was leaning against the convertible black Mustang she recognized from two nights ago. His booted feet were crossed at the ankles, his trim body resting quite comfortably against the door. His fingers threaded through the belt loops of his faded blue jeans, his arms akimbo and nicely sculpted beneath the short sleeves of his white T-shirt. Wheat blond hair rippled back from his face, looking freshly finger-combed. Of course, he was smiling, and that smile grew as he spotted her looking at him. That smile became smug.

Damn, egotistical, overly persistent, misguided fool. She took a deep breath and climbed out of her car ready for battle.

"No," she said firmly before he uttered a word. "It's Friday night. You should definitely be taking care of your bar."

"It's only six-thirty. Even on Fridays, the bar doesn't get hopping for another few hours." He flashed a mischievous grin. "But thanks for being so concerned about my business."

"I'm not going out with you."

"You haven't heard my offer."

"It doesn't matter. I've had a long week. My head hurts. I want a long bath and then bed."

"Wow, and here I thought I'd have to at least buy you dinner first."

She scowled, but he winked at her so playfully it was hard to maintain her ire. The man had obviously taken lessons from a puppy dog.

"You look very nice," he said softly, and his blue eyes took on a warm, appreciative hue that let her know he meant it. For a moment, she thought she was going to blush. Flustered, she smoothed her hand down her suit. Today's ensemble was an olive green, safari-style pantsuit. The jacket buttoned all the way to her neck and ballooned out with four big pockets. A wide, dark brown leather belt clipped the jacket sharply at her waist. She'd bought the suit because it concealed well, as all her clothes did, but also because it emphasized her figure, which very few of her clothes did. A moment of weak vanity, particularly for a woman who knew better.

"I had to work today."

"Ah, that senator's a real slave driver."

"Presidencies aren't built overnight."

"No, I'm sure they're not." He cocked his head to the side. His hands were still resting comfortably on his lean hips. In contrast to her, he looked casual, relaxed and comfortable. His face and arms held a golden hue. When he looked at her, his eyes were bracketed by laugh lines, signs of a man who grinned easily and often. She found herself settling against her own car. Not stepping closer, but not turning and walking away when she really should.

"Here," he said abruptly. "I figured you had had a long week. So I brought just the thing for you."

He reached into the back seat and produced a big wicker picnic basket. He lifted the flap, letting the tempting odor of fried chicken waft across the parking lot.

She went weak in the knees. Her mouth salivated. She groaned. "You do not fight fair."

"Fried chicken, coleslaw and apple pie. Put the color back into your cheeks."

"And the cholesterol into my heart."

"Uh...this is cholesterol-free fried chicken? Come on, Tamara. It's just a meal, and I promise to be on my best behavior. The evening can end whenever you'd like."

She wanted to say no. She knew the smart thing was definitely to say no. Her gaze locked onto the wicker basket. She hadn't had real food in twenty-four hours, and Mrs. Toketee's coffee was settling badly in her stomach. The thought of chicken, slaw and apple pie sounded so tempting.

And dammit, some small, treacherous part of her was happy to see C. J. MacNamara. Some silly, naive part of her responded to his smiles. She had this ridiculous image of him running a warm, comfortable bar where everyone knew your name. She swore that after this she was never going to watch "Cheers" again.

"It's only because I like fried chicken," she warned.

"Of course."

"And I haven't eaten all day."

"Of course."

"All right, dinner. But only for an hour."

"Your gratitude warms my heart," he assured her. She rolled her eyes. But she still wasn't as immune as she should have been. Shaking her head and muttering at her own weakness, she climbed into his car.

She had forgotten how beautiful Sedona was. As C.J. turned onto Highway 179, the sun set behind the red rocks and the landscape fired to life. For eighteen years, Tamara had grown up amid this incredible landscape, never appreciating the stark beauty, never wondering why the rest of the world didn't have anything so lovely. Now, quiet and alone in the passenger's seat, she could drink her fill of towering red rocks and a vast amber sky. Hundreds of years of eroded sandstone and petrified sand dunes combined in swirling streaks of pale gold and bloodred. Forest trees added a lush carpet of deep green.

She had been living amid glass skyscrapers and bustling traffic. She'd forgotten what it was like to stand in the middle of land and feel at once part of something so big and something so small. The rock monuments had formed more than several thousand years ago. They would still be here in another several thousand. Only Tamara would be forgotten.

C.J. pulled over on the side of the road, the way people did in Sedona. "Why don't we walk up here? The view from the top is amazing."

"All right." She bit her lip before she suggested a different stopping point. She was a vacationing New Yorker—she wasn't supposed to know Sedona that well.

"Will you be all right with your leg? It's not that far up. We can take it slow."

"I'll be fine. Exercise is good for it. Keeps it loose."

"Hmm, let me grab a blanket. Arizona can be hot as hell during the day, but once the sun goes down, it cools off in a hurry."

He lifted out the picnic basket, unburied a blanket from the trunk and led her to the trail cut in the sandy red ground by other hikers. They climbed without a word, weaving among the pine trees, creosote bushes and agave plants that dotted the lower grounds. Slowly, they worked their way up, the smooth sandstone rising in a series of undulating swells that started off easy and grew progressively steeper. Tamara, unfortunately, was wearing boots meant for form, not function. A third of the way up, she pulled them and her stockings off, and went at it barefoot. C.J. slowed his pace to match hers. Having donned a sweatshirt and hiking boots, he was perfectly attired for the climb. His strides were long and steady, revealing nicely muscled thighs. As he moved in front of her, she had a clear view of his firm butt caressed by worn denim. Fool that she was, she spent more time with her eyes on him than on the scenery. He was a very good-looking man.

In New York, she was surrounded by the ultra successful *GQ* sort of guy. Pierre Cardin suits, Armani wire-rimmed glasses. Donald, in particular, had been a very snappy dresser. When he'd smiled, however, laugh lines had not bracketed his eyes. His face was too smooth for that, having spent a great deal of quality time with expensive men's facial care products. Certainly one of the best things to come out of her year-long relationship with Donald had been a host of new conditioners that left her hair silky, shiny and full-bodied.

C.J. didn't look like a deep-conditioning sort of guy. She figured him as wash-and-wear. He probably didn't use a loofah or exfoliate. His hands were formed like the sandstones from years of exposure, erosion and use. Strong, enduring, commanding. The kind of hands a woman couldn't ignore as they brushed through her hair or lazily outlined the curve of her breast.

"Okay. Here." C.J. stopped abruptly.

She looked at him blankly, requiring several moments to pull herself together. Her mouth was dry. "What?"

"We'll eat here. We don't have the gear to climb higher."

Belatedly, Tamara looked past C.J. to the towering red rocks. It soared almost straight up now, for several hundred feet.

"Oh. Of course."

C.J. came to stand beside her, smelling of soap and shampoo and, darn it, Old Spice again.

"Look," he said, and twisted her slightly. "Look there."

She caught her breath. The sun was captured like a sinking doubloon between two canyons. It retaliated fiercely, showering the cliffs with dazzling gold rays. The colors were so bright, they hurt her eyes. She watched, anyway, transfixed by the beauty.

"This is my favorite spot," C.J. murmured by her ear. "I like to come here and just look."

"It's…it's something." It was more than something. It was beautiful, it was primordial. And it was odd and strange and powerful to see it and feel C.J. standing next to her. She heard the soft rhythm of his breathing. Her stomach tightened again. Strange, exotic sensations danced in her blood. When she looked down, her hands were shaking slightly.

She fisted her fingers and ordered the trembles to stop.

"Umm…maybe we can eat now. The chicken?"

"Sure." C.J. opened the picnic basket and briskly set out everything. She helped arrange things on the blanket, needing something to do with her hands. He sat down, not

across from her as she would've liked, but right beside
her. When he leaned forward to pick up the chicken, his
cheek brushed her hair. When he turned to offer her a
piece, she felt his breath whisper across her lips.

His eyes were clear, blue, gentle. Blond hair waved
across his brow. It looked like it would be soft to the touch.

She turned away, feeling absurdly self-conscious.

"Chicken?" C.J. asked quietly.

"All…all right." She edged back a few inches, needing
the space. Unconcerned, C.J. fell to eating, ripping into a
piece of breast meat with sharp white teeth as if he hadn't
a care in the world. After a moment, she followed his lead.

"How's your ankle?" C.J. asked.

"Fine."

"Surgery?"

She stiffened, then realized that her ankle was now exposed since she'd taken off her boots and socks. She had
three very distinct scars. Two round holes, almost like bullet wounds, where the screws had been for the external
fixation. Then a thin, snaking line from the surgery that
had happened later, when the fracture still hadn't healed.

"Bone graft," she said.

"Ouch."

She shrugged. "At least the bone graft healed the fracture once and for all."

They ate in companionable silence. C.J. finished off one
piece and reached for a second. Then he uncovered the
coleslaw and apple pie. Tamara finished her first drum-
stick, then grabbed a second.

Behind the cover of his chicken, C.J. watched her with
genuine appreciation. Her shoulders had come down, her
posture easing. Her long sable hair swept down her back
like a beautiful scarf. She tossed her head a little when
strands threatened to interfere with eating her chicken. By
the end of her second piece, she had a grease stain on her
cheek and a gleam in her eye.

He had a feeling she wasn't eating or sleeping enough. At least now she was beginning to relax. He liked that. He liked that a lot.

"So what do you think?" he asked at last, tossing aside a second bone and digging into the coleslaw. "Is Arizona beautiful or what?"

"Stunning." She perked up at the sight of coleslaw.

"I spent the first half of my youth in L.A.," C.J. volunteered. "Certainly Sunset Boulevard and Sedona cannot be compared. Then I lived with my grandma for a while in Tillamook, Oregon. That's a small dairy community nestled on the coast. You ever been out west?"

She shook her head, her gaze clear and curious for a change.

"It's beautiful, Tamara. Green mountains and rolling fog. Nothing at all like Sedona, and yet, I really think Tillamook and Sedona are two of the most beautiful places in the world."

"That's why you moved here?"

"Absolutely. Besides, real estate's cheap and there's enough stuff to keep a guy like me happy."

"Women?" she quizzed dryly. "I thought they were everywhere."

He chuckled and offered her a bit of coleslaw on his spoon. After a brief hesitation, she accepted it. "Hmm. Good slaw."

"Thank you, I bought it myself. Oh, yes, the subject of 'stuff.' Not women—though of course I checked that out— but outdoor activities. Some of the best hiking, rock climbing and white-water rafting in the world is right here in Arizona. Oh, and golf."

"Of course."

He held out another spoonful of coleslaw. This time she took it without hesitation. She was definitely beginning to catch her second wind. When he'd first spotted her pulling up into the parking lot of her hotel, he'd thought she looked like a woman with the weight of the world on her shoulders. And almost immediately—hell, instinctively—he'd wanted to do something about that.

Once, one of the barn cats on his grandmother's farm had given birth to six kittens and hidden them under the flooring of the hayloft. He and Maggie had discovered them, and C.J. had promptly picked one up—at which point the tiny, trembling creature had split open C.J.'s hand from the base of his finger to his wrist. He'd dropped it with a howl, Maggie had leapt back ten feet, and they'd run out of the loft as if they had the very devil on their heels. His grandmother, Lydia, had shaken her head the whole time she'd cleaned up his hand.

"They're wild cats, C.J., not meant to be coddled. Leave them alone."

He'd nodded, but both he and Maggie had ended up there again the next afternoon. Maggie simply adored kittens and wanted to see them. C.J...C.J. couldn't let them go. They looked so tiny, so helpless. He wanted to touch them, to hold them. And yet the one orange kitten had hurt him fiercely, and he hated it for that. He wanted to walk away, he wanted to hate the kitten. He glowered a lot. Blamed it all on Maggie and her obsession with "dumb animals." But he couldn't keep away. He made it one week, then simply had to try again. The orange kitten had grown, and so had its claws. He came racing back to the house with Maggie hot on his heels, both of them convinced he was going to bleed to death. They'd slapped a whole box of Band-Aids onto his hand, then waited in fear for Lydia to find out.

"You tried to pick up the kitten again."

"Did not."

"Don't lie to me, C.J. You're not on the streets anymore. You're part of a family. You don't lie to family."

He'd scowled. His father had lied a lot, especially to his

mother. In the end, *he'd* lied to his mother a lot, too. *No, I didn't steal the sandwiches. Of course I went to school.*

Hey, your temperature is coming down. You're getting better. Everything is going to be all right.

"It's just a damn kitten," he'd muttered to Lydia at last.

Lydia had handed him a bar of soap to wash out his mouth for swearing. When that was over, she'd sat him down. "You're going to try again, aren't you?"

"Maybe." He was trying to sound tough. He kicked at the ground a few times for good measure. Lydia was patient, but he was never sure how patient. He'd gone through a mother and a father. At this point, he was pretty sure this grandma was just passing through, as well.

"All right, C.J., this is what you do. Go every afternoon. Sit there with Maggie. Move a little closer each time. Let the kittens get used to you, your presence, your smell. Just be, and after a while, they'll know you. And soon, they'll be so curious, they'll approach you. Then you be very gentle and very patient. And someday, you'll get to hold that kitten again, and it won't hurt you."

"I don't care."

"Of course."

But he and Maggie had done exactly what Lydia had recommended, and Lydia knew the day they finally achieved contact because they carried their newfound friends back to the house for inspection. C.J. had named his orange kitten Speedy, and she'd been his cat until he'd turned eighteen and joined the marines.

He'd loved that cat. And over the years, he'd come to love his grandmother for everything she'd taught the wild, destructive, angry boy he'd been.

"Your family in New York?" he asked Tamara at last.

For the first time, Tamara hesitated over her chicken. "No. My...my parents died when I was younger."

"That's hard."

She shrugged, clearly not wanting to talk about it. "That was a long time ago."

"My parents died when I was younger, too. That's why I was raised by my grandmother in Tillamook."

She looked at him silently, and he realized she'd never ask the questions on her own. If he wanted to volunteer information, she was leaving it up to him.

"My parents never married," he said easily. "My father, Max, apparently only married women with money. So he married my half brother's mother, who had a decent-size inheritance from England, and he married my half sister's mother for her inheritance. My mother, he liked to say, he was with out of love."

"And she didn't mind?"

C.J. shrugged. "I think she did. But I think she also thought it was romantic. My mother...she was sweet. Gentle. Sometimes she didn't have the best judgment. Max said he would take care of her and me, so she trusted him to do that and she was always happy when he came to visit."

"I see."

"She became very ill when I was eleven. We didn't have much money. The doctors put her on antibiotics, but they didn't seem to help. I tried to find Max, but he traveled all the time. I couldn't reach him. Eventually, her condition deteriorated. By the time Max arrived, it was all over."

"Oh."

C.J. offered her a reassuring smile. "It's okay. I don't expect you to murmur any magical words that make it better. Life goes on, you know?"

Mutely, she nodded.

"I lived with my father for a year, traveling all over the world, but then his plane went down in Indonesia and that was that. I stayed with my grandmother, Lydia, and met my other half siblings, Maggie and Brandon."

"What did your father do?"

C.J. grinned, he couldn't help it. "That's subject to some debate," he said dryly.

"Debate?"

"Honestly, I think he was a crook." That got her full attention. He winked. "Think about it. The man called himself an 'importer-exporter.' He was always traveling around the globe, he seemed to have unbelievable sums of cash, yet none of us ever saw him actually conduct any business. My grandma, his mother, to this day doesn't know what his job really was. None of his wives ever understood it. As a kid, I was very impressed with the whole nine yards—the travel, the plane, the presents. As an adult, I look back at him and I think he had to have been a smuggler. It's the only thing that makes sense."

"I...I suppose."

"Now, my sister, Maggie, is a romantic. I think she's decided he was a secret agent because that sounds like a great dad thing to be."

"That would be romantic," Tamara agreed. She hesitated a moment, leaning forward ever so slightly. He held his breath. He didn't think she was aware of it, but her eyes were large and clear, her expression earnest. In spite of herself, she'd gotten caught up in the conversation. Perhaps she was even enjoying his company. "You're very close to your half siblings."

"Yeah. My grandma brought us together because she wanted us to learn how to be a family. My grandma is a very smart woman."

"I never had any brothers or sisters."

"Yeah? I have to say, I like mine more than I thought I would when I was a streetwise only child hell-bent on taking care of himself. When my grandma introduced me to Brandon, my first words to him were 'Go to hell.' Luckily, his English reserve allows him to blow off such things."

"You told your brother to go to hell?"

"I was a bit of a head case," he admitted. He grinned. "Not at all the charming young man you see before you now. These days I would never dream of doing the slightest misdeed. I am an angel. Ask anyone."

"Uh-huh," she said with just the right note of skepticism.

"Are you besmirching my reputation?"

"Uh-huh."

"After I just fed you chicken?"

"Uh-huh."

"Well." He crossed his arms in mock indignation and gave her his most affronted gaze. Slowly, but surely, her lips curved into a smile. It brightened her whole face, brought a luminescent sheen to her eyes. He liked it very much when she smiled. He intended to make sure she smiled again and then again after that.

"You're very beautiful, you know?"

Her smile vanished. She looked startled, then uncomfortable. She drew back, and he could tell she was suddenly awkward. It puzzled him.

"Surely you've heard that before."

"I'm...I work a lot. In fact, I have work to do tonight. I really should get back to the hotel." Her fingers fumbled with her napkin. She began to pick up chicken bones.

He covered her hand with his, stilling her motions. He watched her chest rise and fall too rapidly in the silence. "Tamara, I'm not trying to make you uncomfortable."

Her gaze remained locked on the blue-checked picnic blanket. "I'm...I'm not very good at this."

"What is 'good at this'?" he quizzed gently. "You either enjoy being with someone or you don't. You're either comfortable with someone or you're not. I don't expect anything from you. I'm happy we had dinner together. I enjoyed talking with you. I do think you're beautiful. Especially when you smile."

Her head turned slightly. For a moment, she studied him as if she was trying to figure out whether he was lying or not. Then she removed her hand from his grip, and in a gesture that was curiously vulnerable, she pressed it against her stomach.

"Thank you for dinner," she said quietly. "I did enjoy the conversation. Your family...they sound very special. Now I need to go, C.J. I have work to do. And in one week or so, I will be returning to New York."

"Understood," he said softly, though he was disappointed. Acutely disappointed. More disappointed than he had been in a long time. He worked on shrugging it away. "That's still at least a week away, you know. And a girl's gotta eat...."

"Maybe, C.J. Maybe."

After pulling up in the parking lot, he waited while she retrieved the items she'd left in her car. He complimented the kachina doll, but she didn't seem to have much to say about it.

They walked through the lush garden and swimming pool of the resort until they came to her hotel room. C.J. could tell she was becoming nervous again, tense. Her face had shuttered over. Her shoulders were square. She was retreating somewhere deep inside herself, marshaling her energies, cutting herself off.

He waited until she put her key in the lock, then gently turned her around.

He was aware of the softness of the night, the way the dry, dusty shadows swirled around them. He could hear crickets, the whir of gilla woodpeckers, the rhythmic lap of pool water against the patio. He let the sounds settle and linger, his arms still around her.

And he waited for the moment of awareness to hit her, too. That sharp, electric moment when her breath would suddenly slow, her eyes widen and her lips part. That moment when her gaze would meet his again and finally bloom with warm wonder. That moment when her body would subtly and unconsciously lean toward his.

It didn't happen. Nothing changed. Her body remained as rigid and tense as the very first time he'd met her. She was frozen.

Puzzled, he bent and slowly brushed her lips with his own. Then he brushed them again, testing the full softness, feeling them part. He dipped his tongue in and tasted her. Warm, he thought. Sweet. And totally unresponsive.

He pulled back. She'd already averted her face.

"Is it me?" he asked quietly.

Her mouth opened, her throat working. It looked like she was saying yes. Maybe she wanted to say yes.

Instead, she stated abruptly, "No. It's not you. It's just...it's just the way I am."

"Tamara—"

She pushed out of his arms, already shaking her head. "It's been a long night. I need to go." She yanked open the door and disappeared inside her room without preamble.

His hand was still reaching out for her when the door slammed shut.

Damn. Damn, damn, damn. He stood there feeling like an absolute idiot and having no idea what to do about it. He raked his fingers through his hair once, twice, then three times.

Finally, still shaking his head, he turned to walk away.

Just as he stepped forward, however, the silence of the night was broken. Behind him, Tamara screamed.

Chapter 4

"Tamara!" He pounded on the door. "Tamara!"

Her screams grew louder, then broke off in a strangled cry. C.J. gave up on civility. He took six steps back, then barreled into the door with the full force of his body. It burst open.

Tamara stood in the middle of the luxurious room beating at the floor with her kachina doll. Her dark hair flew around her face. Her pale cheeks were covered in beads of sweat. She pounded at the floor harder and harder, lost in a frenzy.

Beneath her rage, a good-size scorpion was being pulverized to bits.

"Tamara! Tamara, it's dead."

She slammed the kachina doll more furiously, her hair crackling. C.J. made a grab for her arm but couldn't catch it. "It's okay, sweetheart. It's okay."

She finally looked at him, and the fear in her face caught him off guard. Then so did the rage. She hammered the wooden doll hard.

C.J. moved forward forcefully, catching her full-shoulder and spinning her around. She raised the wooden statue unconsciously, and he blocked the blow, grabbed the doll and tossed it onto the bed.

"Stop it, stop it. Sh. It's okay. It's okay."

She remained, struggling. "I don't need you!" she cried fiercely.

"Tamara—"

"Get out! Get out!"

"Tamara—"

"I don't need you! I don't need your smiles or your chicken. You have to be able to stand alone, don't you get it?" Her fists suddenly beat his chest. "You want to learn how to walk, you take the first step yourself, that's what Ben always said. No one's going to do it for you. There's only yourself. Only yourself!"

C.J. finally caught her flailing fists and pinned them between their bodies. He gripped her shoulders hard, his fingers welting her skin. "Tamara, calm down! What the hell are you talking about?"

Her head fell back. Her eyes killed him, and he didn't even know why. She looked unbelievably angry. She looked unbelievably scared. She looked like she might shatter into a million pieces and never be put back together again.

He didn't understand what she was saying or thinking. He followed instinct, cradling her body against him, her cheek against his shoulder. She went rigid, like a rod of steel, and then the spell broke and she sagged against him.

"Sh," he whispered against the top of her hair. "Sh. It's all right now. It's all right."

He rocked her, rubbing her back, stroking her long, silken hair, then her arm, her waist. He waited for tears. He waited for her to wrap her arms around him and hold him as if he were the last anchor in the storm. She did neither. She just stood there, slumped against him like a puppet whose strings had been cut. He could feel the delicate structure of her ribs, the slender curve of her waist, the gentle swell of her hips. She hardly made a dent against him, her build was so slight. She must have lost weight recently—a fair amount of it.

"It's okay," he murmured again, wishing he knew what she needed—or what she was so afraid of. He rested his cheek against the top of her hair, still rocking her back and forth. Her body was warm and fragrant. He smelled Arizona sandstone and windswept creosote tangled in her hair and dusting her skin. Just as he was beginning to relax, she pushed away.

She stepped back too quickly, her bad ankle not ready and almost sending her to the floor. He caught her arm, and when he was sure she wouldn't fall, withdrew on his own.

Her chest rose and fell rapidly in the silence, her breath labored. Abruptly, she raised one hand and scrubbed her pale cheeks.

"Tamara," he asked quietly, "are you all right?"

A shiver snaked through her body. "I don't know what came over me...."

"You had quite a shock." He waited a moment and, when she still didn't speak, asked, "Did you just find the scorpion on the floor?"

"No. The bed. In the middle. I went to sit down to take off my boots and..."

"And that probably scared the living daylights out of you."

"Yes. It did." She rubbed her arms, her head finally rising to look out her window. The emotion had left her face. Now her skin was the color of bone, her smooth cheeks and chiseled jaw like the face of a marble sculpture.

"Tamara, who is Ben?"

"Ben? He was my physical therapist."

"I see," C.J. said, but he didn't. He didn't understand

why she had become so angry, and he was beginning to wonder if *she* knew. She was a study of contrasts, a strong, composed, professional woman who said she didn't respond to kisses. An enraged, angry female who could pulverize a scorpion better than any marine.

He took a step toward her. Instantly she raised a hand, halting him.

"Please," she whispered. "I just…I need some time to myself." She looked at him finally. The shadows seemed to have darkened around her eyes. She appeared at once vulnerable and wary.

"You don't have to be alone, Tamara. No, no…" he said when she opened her mouth to immediately argue. "I'm not hitting on you this time, that's not what I meant. But you've been through a big shock, you've had a long day. If you'd like, I'll stay here on the sofa. Sometimes it's nice to have someone around."

She hesitated, her gaze going from him to the sofa to him. He could tell the idea appealed to her at least a little bit. But then she drew herself up, the fierce, independent, stubborn woman winning out.

"I appreciate your offer, but I'm fine. Honest. It was just a scorpion. I'll call hotel management and have them take care of it."

"Like you called your mechanic to take care of your car."

"What…what do you mean?"

"I don't know, Tamara, you tell me. First you have a problem with your brake lines in a car that shouldn't have problems with a brake line, then you find a live scorpion in a room that shouldn't have problems with scorpions."

"I guess I'm having an unlucky week."

"Sounds like a rather dangerous one to me."

"C.J., please. It's just coincidence. Don't be making more out of this than is necessary."

"Tamara, if something was going on, would you tell me?"

"You don't even know me. We're just two strangers—"

"Thank you," he interrupted quietly, "that answers my question." Abruptly, he was angry with her. No, frustrated. Tired of being knocked down when he was honestly trying to be helpful. The distance between them grew tense and unhappy. A rift had appeared in their very tenuous relationship, and he didn't feel like mending it.

He wanted her to make some effort. Instead, as minute turned into minute, she brought her chin up stubbornly and squared her shoulders.

That did it. He headed for the door. There was a certain point where a man went from being a romantic to being a fool. Of course, after opening the door, he hesitated just long enough to give her a second chance at reaching out.

She didn't take it.

He exited stage right, and Tamara was left standing all alone with only her pride to protect her.

Finally, she closed the door, fastened the bolt lock and retrieved her gun from her purse. Long after housekeeping came and removed the dead scorpion, she remained sitting in a dark corner, eyes peeled, gun ready, for a danger she couldn't name.

She thought of the anger that had possessed her when she'd started to beat the scorpion, the white-hot rage that this thing would try to hurt her. She'd been so angry, she hadn't recognized her own self. It was as if some dark, gnashing beast had taken over. Something ugly and hurting and feral. Then C.J. was trying to tell her it would be all right and the beast had turned on him. It would not be all right. Other people did not make things all right. Other people died and left you alone.

She rested her forehead on her knees and squeezed her eyes shut.

She didn't know where any of the emotions had come

from. She didn't know what had possessed her, or why she had lashed out at C.J. like a madwoman. She was the cool, composed businesswoman. She was the determined person who'd taught herself how to walk even when her body had hated her. She had put tragedy behind her and built a successful career.

There was nothing to be angry about anymore.

Five days in Sedona, and she was unraveling like a cheaply woven sweater.

Get a grip, Tamara. Get a grip.

She tried to sleep, but the nightmares snatched it away. She was at the Chapel of the Holy Cross, the cross-shaped church carved in rock that had helped make Sedona famous. She was looking for her family. She was supposed to meet them here for services. She was supposed to find Shawn.

She stood at the arching, cross-shaped window, looking out at Sedona's soaring red rocks and pressing her cheek against the cold glass. The church was so unbearably silent.

She walked across the tiny chapel, hunting beneath the pews for her family, gazing up at the vaulted ceiling as if they were hiding from her there. But she couldn't find her parents. She couldn't find Shawn.

She stood alone in the middle of the cold, empty church.

Why did you take them from me? And why did you let me live?

How could you have been so cruel?

But she couldn't find her parents, she couldn't find Shawn, and even in the church of her childhood, she could no longer find God.

She woke up with a start. The clock glowed 3:00 a.m. The exhaustion pressed against her and made her limbs heavy. She crawled out of bed, anyway, pulled herself together and formulated a new plan.

After tossing out two drunks and breaking up one brawl, C.J. finally closed up the Ancient Mariner and made it home. His mood hadn't improved since leaving Tamara, and he was definitely looking forward to a long night's sleep. In the morning, he told himself grumpily, he'd figure out the rest. In the morning.

He'd just dozed off when the phone rang.

"No," he moaned from beneath the covers.

The phone rang again.

"Absolutely not. It's three in the morning."

The phone rang a third time.

"Dammit!" He snatched the receiver off the phone and dragged it beneath the covers. "What?" he demanded to know, still refusing to open his eyes for the occasion.

"Temper, temper," a distinctly male voice drawled. "Am I interrupting something? Please tell her I said hi."

"Brandon!" C.J. scowled, gave up on getting any sleep in the near future and sat up in bed, raking his hand through his hair. Since his wife's death three years ago, Brandon had been traveling the globe in a rambling, restless fashion eerily similar to their father, Max. The last time C.J. had seen his brother was a year ago when Brandon had returned to Oregon to help rescue their sister, Maggie, who had been taken hostage by an escaped murderer, Cain Cannon. A former investment banker, Brandon had supplied a six-digit reward and his razor-sharp intellect. C.J. had brought guns and considerable other skills.

Maggie had stunned them both by saving herself and then turning around and marrying the man. Go figure.

"Brandon, where the hell are you, and why can't you remember the time zone the rest of us are in?"

"It's 3:00 a.m. where you are."

"Thanks."

"And tomorrow here in Iceland."

"What?"

"Iceland. You're right. The country is beautiful."

For a moment, C.J. was too stunned to speak. He knew Iceland. After his mother had died, Max had taken him to Europe ostensibly on business. A few months later, Max had announced that they deserved a vacation, and they'd gone to Iceland. For two weeks, they'd stayed up all night to enjoy twenty-three hours of sunlight. They'd hung out in bars with the grinning, happy locals, who could toss back beer like nobody's business. Twelve-year-old C.J. had gotten his first taste of vodka and his first hangover. His father had taken him horseback riding across the breathtaking green landscape.

And for one moment, C.J. had forgotten the dirt and graffiti of Sunset Boulevard. He forgot cracked sidewalks filled with too many people who'd given up on their dreams. He forgot the nights he'd gone to bed hungry because he'd given all the food he could scrounge to his coughing, feverish mother. He forgot the hot, angry tears that had dribbled down his cheeks as he'd held her hand and watched her die, still calling for the man she insisted was the love of her life—Max Ferringer.

C.J. forgot some of his hatred. He saw Max as the strong, laughing, exotic hero his mother had claimed him to be. And for two weeks, he'd been proud to be Maximillian's son.

Two months later, C.J. was on a farm in Tillamook, Oregon, while a grandma he'd never met quietly told him his father wouldn't be picking him up. His plane had gone down in Indonesia. A search party was still trying to find his body.

"Why are you in Iceland?" C.J.'s voice was sharper than he wanted it to be.

"I've never been."

"Dammit!" C.J. no longer tried to hide his anger. "This

is me you're talking to, Brandon. Don't play your slick,
Ivy League double-speak games with me. You think Maggie and I don't know what you're up to? Do you think
we're not worried sick about the way you're treating yourself? When I saw you last year, you looked liked you'd
dropped a good thirty pounds. Maggie complains that
you've forgotten how to smile. For God's sake, if you
don't care about yourself, at least think of Maggie and
Lydia. They deserve a helluva lot better than—''

"Another Max?"

"You said it, Brandon, not me."

There was a long silence filled with the crackling static
of under-the-ocean phone cables. "Did you know that Iceland is one of the most volcanic regions on earth?" Brandon asked abruptly.

C.J. scowled, hating the way Brandon could so easily
change topics. The man was scary bright, and his stint as
a Wall Street investment banker had given him a hard edge
that C.J. at once respected and abhorred. "Gee, Brandon,
sitting in Arizona at 3:00 a.m., no, I had not contemplated
that Iceland was one of the most volcanic regions on the
planet. But thanks for the geography lesson."

"So is Indonesia."

"So?"

"So don't you think there could be some connection
here?" Brandon asked.

C.J. blinked his eyes a few times, then he shook his
head. "No. No way. There is no connection between
Max's vacation with me in Iceland and his plane going
down in Indonesia. For God's sake, Brandon, the man hit
about every country there was. It was what he did. Given
your itinerary for the last few years, you ought to know
that better than anyone."

"Haven't you ever wondered what Max actually did for
a living?"

"He was an importer-exporter," C.J. said blithely.

"Didn't you ever wonder where all his money came from?"

"Maggie's and your mothers." C.J. zinged, then bit his own tongue. "Sorry," he said after a moment. "That was unfair."

"Yes," Brandon said quietly, "but I understand."

For a moment, neither of them spoke. There was nothing Brandon, C.J. and Maggie wouldn't do for one another, and in that sense, Lydia's plan had worked. But Max still hung between them. They had shared different experiences with him and had come to terms with him in their own ways. C.J. tried hard not to resent the fact that Max had married his half siblings' mothers when he'd refused to marry C.J.'s. Brandon and Maggie tried not to resent that for one year, C.J. had gotten to live with Max. More than any of them, he'd spent time with their enigmatic, unreachable father.

"Brandon, why are you doing this? Maggie, Lydia and I are beginning to really worry about you. For God's sake, let Max go. Let Julia go."

"I can't."

"You need to get a job again."

"And make more money?" Brandon's laughter was harsh. "No thanks."

"Brandon," C.J. sighed, but his older brother wouldn't let him finish.

"I think there's a connection," he announced suddenly. "C.J., I think Max had something to do with Julia's death."

"*What?* Brandon, your wife was killed by a mugger in Central Park. And it was horrible and it was tragic and God, Brandon, I would do anything I could to help you, but this is insane—"

"Listen to me. Julia was working on a surprise birthday present for me when she died—a complete family history. To do that, she'd been researching Max. I found files, C.J., with articles she'd clipped, notes about his business partners. Julia was an academic, a research fiend. Once she got started... I think she may have asked too many questions. I think...I think she may have rocked the boat."

"What boat?"

"I don't know." Brandon clipped the words out. "But don't try to pretend our father was normal. He was *not* normal. Our mothers knew nothing about him. *We* don't know anything about him. Not even Lydia understands the man he became. Why don't we know more about him?"

"Why do we care?" C.J. was yelling. So was the normally reserved Brandon. The subject of Max was never without emotion.

"Because he was our father! And I want to know. I want to know exactly what kind of man—"

"Abandons his wives? Abandons his children?"

"Exactly!"

"Brandon," C.J. groaned, "You're obsessing. You've been obsessing since the day Julia died. Come on, *get over it!* Move on with your life. And leave Max alone. He was always best from a distance."

"I can't."

"Brandon—"

"I'm going to continue this, C.J. I have to."

The line went dead. C.J. was left sitting in bed, clutching the phone and swearing into the darkness. Damn, damn, damn. After all these years, Max was still messing with their minds. Dammit, he was still messing with their minds.

Tamara didn't know what she was doing. She did it, anyway. At 4:00 a.m., she entered the El Dorado Hotel and Conference Center in black jeans and a dark gray cashmere turtleneck. The outfit would have screamed "Stop, Thief!" if not for the deep green raincoat she had belted over it. Her gun was tucked into the small of her back.

She had a flashlight, notepad and pen tucked in her coat's deep pockets. And she was working very hard at not hunching her shoulders and skulking through the hotel.

There was hardly anyone in the lobby at this time of night. The front desk was manned only by a dutiful night clerk and droopy-looking bellboy. She walked by them as if she had every reason to be there and headed down the vast main hall leading to the ballrooms. Chandeliers winked overhead. Marble tables with elaborate, wrought-iron pedestals boasted huge arrangements of larger-than-life cacti. Silk flowers in rich pink, burnt orange and deep red gave the illusion of blooms even in October. Elaborate mirrors reflected her image back to her a dozen times over.

She discovered quickly that the ballroom doors of the Brennan campaign headquarters were solidly locked. She tugged on them once, then twice, as if that would help.

She glanced down the huge hallway and waited to see if the bellboy was running after her. In the distance, he was flipping through a magazine and rubbing his temple. She looked back at the door. She was a public relations executive, for God's sake. She knew how to package the most mundane lock as a complete home security system, but she had no idea how to force one open. She chewed on her lower lip.

Go home, Tamara. Get some sleep. You're exhausted. You're losing your grip. How many hours have you even slept since arriving in Sedona? Ten? Eight? Six?

She couldn't go back to her hotel room. She couldn't bear the thought of crawling into bed and trying to sleep. She just couldn't.

She moved down the end of the hallway, found a door marked Employees Only and ducked into the bowels of the hotel. Gray concrete floors and exposed pipes haunted her passage. She encountered doorway after doorway, peering through each tiny window into an inky blackness her eyes couldn't penetrate. One by one, she tried the doorknobs. Some were locked. Some were open. Obviously, the hotel staff was lax about such things. How lucky could she get?

The fifth door led her into an antechamber she recognized. From it, she walked into the gaping black hole that was the campaign war room. She stood in the middle with her flashlight, feeling the silence throb around her like a drum. The cold air curled around her cheek. The empty metal chairs and abandoned tables made her feel hollow.

She was shivering.

Find Mrs. Winslow's desk, Tamara. Just find Mrs. Winslow's desk.

Mary Winslow had been an active member of Senator Brennan's various campaigns for the last fifteen years. She'd served as his head lieutenant in Sedona on the last three. There was nothing done on Senator Brennan's behalf in Sedona that Mrs. Winslow did not know about and approve. Hopefully, that included car rentals.

Why would she keep car rental agreements that were ten years old? What do you really think you'll find, Tamara?

She cut off her own doubts and sat down at Mrs. Winslow's desk. Placing her flashlight upright on the desk like a lantern, she booted up Mrs. Winslow's PC.

An arm swept around her neck and clamped over her mouth. One instant she was sitting nervously on the edge of a metal chair, the next she was dragged up and flattened against a wall. She cried out, but a callused palm muffled the scream. She lashed out with her foot, and muscled thighs clamped her legs. She began to struggle in earnest. The man pressed his full body against her, his arm trapping her arms, her breasts flattened by his torso.

Oh, God, think Tamara, think. Do something!

The rough rasp of a twenty-four-hour beard scraped her cheek. And the strong, well-toned man buried his lips in her hair and whispered in her ear, "What the hell do you think you're doing?"

She sagged against the wall, the relief so piercing it stung her eyes. C.J. would have none of it. He pressed his body against her more tightly, his eyes cutting through her like lasers.

She said against his palm, "Are you following me?"

"Dammit, Tamara, you don't want to mess with me after the night I've had. If I were you, I would start talking now. And I'd say the truth, the whole truth and nothing but the truth. Got it?"

His forearm pressed against her throat with just enough pressure to let her know he meant business. For some reason, it made her more stubborn. She leaned back against the wall as much as she could and dug in her heels.

"How is it you manage to show up every place I am?" she whispered fiercely. "What the hell are *you* doing, C.J.?" She glared at him right back, and the air between them heated up another few degrees.

"I am here," C.J. growled, "because I followed you."

"You are stalking me!"

"You stubborn, ungrateful fool. I'm not stalking you. I'm worried about you! I drove to your hotel at three-thirty in the morning because I couldn't sleep and I kept thinking about your punctured brake lines and scorpion-decorated bed. So I went back to your room, Tamara, and lo and behold, I found *you* sneaking across the parking lot in a trench coat. A dark trench coat. Have you seen too many movies or what?"

"Maybe." Her voice had lost some of its fierceness. He had been worried about her? Or maybe he was lying. How would she know? Her lips were dry. She kept licking them, but they were dry, anyway.

"So there you have it. I followed because I was *worried* about you. And then I discover you breaking and entering the good old senator's campaign headquarters. So you'd better start talking, Tamara, because I may have been worried once, but I only play the fool so many times.''

She stared at him in the darkness, feeling the intensity of his gaze, the way it seemed to bore into her, turn her inside out and reveal all her weaknesses like dirty laundry. His body was still pressed against hers. His legs clamped her thighs. His torso flattened hers, but the pressure was merely firm, not bruising. And in a crazy way, it was reassuring.

When was the last time anyone had worried about her? When was the last time anyone had held her and stroked her hair and whispered, "Sh. I have you. I have you."

The exhaustion, the raw, aching need, hit her suddenly. She wanted to lean into him. She had the teeniest desire to wrap her arms around his waist, press her cheek against his shoulder and rest her head. Maybe for a moment, he would make her feel safe. He would make her feel less alone.

She pulled herself up tightly. She squeezed her fists so hard her fingernails welted her palms and caused her pain.

She stated firmly, "I do not need you to worry about me."

"Good, because I'm not anymore. I just caught you breaking and entering. Now I'm worried about the senator. Are you working for his opponent?"

"No."

"Are you a thief?"

"Hardly."

"Well what in the name of God are you doing skulking around campaign headquarters at four-thirty in the damn morning?"

She gazed at him haughtily. "Would you honestly believe me if I told you?"

"Tamara..." His voice rose with warning. She had the distinct memory of her father saying her name just that way. Generally when she'd stayed out too late with Patty.

"All right," she said abruptly. The silence between them grew taut. "I'm a reporter."

"A reporter?"

"A reporter. I have reason to believe the senator was responsible for a hit-and-run automobile accident ten years ago that killed three people."

C.J.'s breath inhaled sharply, his body easing back a little and giving her more room to breathe. "Keep talking."

"The hit-and-run vehicle was a red sports car. The police could never find the car or driver, even though there should have been serious damage to both. I think the senator took himself and his car someplace out of town and paid to conceal his own injuries and destroy the automobile. However, I have no proof of that. I was hoping to find some here."

"Huh." His tone was neither believing nor disbelieving.

"Are you going to let me go?"

"I haven't decided yet. First you're an eager-beaver PR specialist. Then I find you skulking around like a thief. Now you claim to be hot on the trail of the next Chappaquidick. One thing is for sure, you tell a good story."

"Well, we can't stay like this all night. People are going to start arriving soon."

"That would make it int—" His sentence was cut off by a small beeping. Belatedly, Tamara looked down and realized it was coming from C.J.'s waist.

"Damn," he swore. "Now what?"

He held up the small beeper until the digital display glowed in front of his eyes. He was frowning. "That's the number for my bar. Oh, dammit. Sheila. I have to go!"

He was already clipping the beeper to his waist and stepping back. Tamara began to breathe again. Saved by the bell.

"We'll talk later," she said, edging toward the door.

"Oh, no, you don't." C.J.'s hand snapped around her

wrist. His grip was tight and his gaze was hard. "I still don't trust you, Tamara, and until I do, you're coming with me."

"I am not—"

But it was already too late. C.J. simply dragged her with him.

Chapter 5

C.J. drove like a true racer. It wasn't that he drove fast—
any fool could do that. It was that he drove with such
incredible control and concentration. He pushed his car the
way a jockey might push his horse, urging it toward its
limit but never losing grip on the reins. He climbed upward
of a hundred and ten on the straightaways, his eyes narrow,
his face grim. Tamara gripped the armrest on the door, still
uncomfortable being the passenger after all these years.
She liked to drive. Drivers were the ones in control. Pas-
sengers…passengers couldn't do a thing when it all went
wrong.

She kept her eyes on C.J., and she discovered as long
as she did that, the fear remained a dull shadow, whispering in her subconscious but unable to gain substance. She
understood the look on C.J.'s face. He was paying attention. He was in the zone, listening to his engine, eyeballing
the road surface, determining the best line and computing
the absolute breaking point. His jaw was tight with concentration, his eyes squinted. His hand rested on his gear-

shift, and his lean, muscled thighs rippled as he accelerated, shifted and braked. He knew this car. He knew this road. He owned the experience.

A sharp corner loomed. The fear crept up Tamara's throat. She kept her gaze on C.J. She trusted him to know what to do. She *needed* him to know what to do.

He didn't hug the inside of the turn as amateurs did. Instead, he treated the looping corner like a pivot point, downshifting and heading in a straight line for the apex of the turn. At almost the far left corner of the road, with red dust dunes looming beside them like Arizona's version of a tire wall, he cranked the wheel, stepped on the gas and accelerated like an arrow shot to the track-out point. They zipped back toward the far right, already set up for the next curve.

He was good, very, very good.

And suddenly Tamara heard her mother's voice clearly in her mind. *"Slow down, Robert. It's not like we're in a hurry to get home. Besides, who knows what kind of idiots are out driving at this time of night?"*

Tamara shook her head and her mother's voice was gone. She sat alone in the passenger's seat, confused and feeling slightly nauseated. Goose bumps had broken out on her arms.

They hadn't crashed because her father was speeding, they had crashed because of Senator Brennan. He'd hit them. He'd sped away. He'd cost Tamara her family. She knew this.

She eased her grip on the door. Sweat beaded C.J.'s upper lip and brow. At the second corner, a slow trickle began down the side of his face. He didn't seem to notice. He glanced once at his mirrors, confirmed there was still no traffic behind them, then returned to the road. He didn't waste time with his gauges. The sound of his engine as it accelerated, decelerated and labored told him when to shift, when to brake and when to accelerate. His arm and shoulder flexed as he worked the clutch.

People thought racing was easy, just sit and steer, but Tamara knew from firsthand experience that it was physically and mentally grueling. Dressed in a thick, flame-retardant Nomex jumpsuit with flame-retardant socks, shoes and face mask, a driver quickly overheated and began to sweat. Five crisscrossing seat belts bolted the person to the roll cage, placing incredible pressure across the hips, stomach and chest. The constant movement of shifting, braking and steering slowly took its toll on arms, while the heavy weight of the helmet strained the neck and shoulders. Even with earplugs, the sound of twenty raw, unmuffled racing engines was like standing in front of a screaming jet, the noise hammering against temples and pounding against eardrums. A driver couldn't afford to notice any of this—the heat, the discomfort, the fatigue, the sound. Drive at more than a hundred miles per hour on a track filled with twenty other speeding objects, passing, breaking, swerving, crashing, a driver had to concentrate on driving and only driving. The first five minutes weren't bad; neither were the next. By halfway through the race, however, the elements took their toll. Reflexes slowed, minds grew tired. Mistakes happened.

And then the physically and mentally fit emerged from the pack, focused, capable and strong till the bitter end.

C.J. would be one of those. She could tell from the fierce, composed look on his face. He wouldn't tire. He wouldn't lose concentration. He could go the distance, for himself and for the people he cared about.

He wouldn't make a stupid mistake and get anyone killed.

She returned her gaze to the window.

C.J. braked hard, let the back end sweep around and suddenly gunned the car into a parking lot. Belatedly, Tamara saw a midsize, two-story wooden structure identified as the Ancient Mariner.

"Wait here for a moment." C.J. reached across the seat, unlocked the glove compartment with a tiny key and immediately palmed a handgun. He did it so fast, Tamara was still cataloging the moves as he popped open his door and bolted across the parking lot.

Of course, she followed. She had her own gun in her purse. She had very little experience with how to use it, but she had her gun.

She crept through the front door that C.J. had left swinging open. The bar was dark and shadowed. At 5:00 a.m., the sun was just beginning to rise, and the whole world had the hushed, reverent calm of a newly dawning day. She saw a red-tiled floor and old wooden tables with the chairs stacked on top. Brass bar trim gleamed dully in the shadows.

Overhead, she heard sudden footsteps. She stiffened, spotted the stairs in the corner and headed toward them.

"It's okay, it's okay," she heard C.J. saying. "You did the right thing to call me." And then she heard the sound of a woman's muffled sobs.

Her foot raised for the first step, she froze. Suddenly she felt like an intruder. He was up there with another woman. A woman who had paged him. A woman he had driven like a maniac to help.

She should go back to the car. She should call a cab and return to her hotel before C.J. had a chance to think about her. Hell, she should get on a plane and return to Manhattan, because she was accomplishing nothing here and the whole thing had been a horrible mistake. She was trembling, shaking and overwhelmed with exhaustion. She couldn't sleep and she was snappy and temperamental. She didn't know herself anymore. She never should have come to Sedona.

She never should have met C. J. MacNamara.

She found herself heading up the stairs.

The hallway was narrow and poorly lit. Thick floor-boards creaked beneath her feet. She followed the faint ray of daylight spilling out of an opened doorway, and the sound of sobbing grew louder.

She found C.J. sitting on the edge of a narrow bed, holding a young brunette and rocking her back and forth as she cried. The girl had her arms wrapped around his neck. She was sobbing hysterically despite C.J.'s efforts. Then Tamara saw the man sprawled facedown on the floor. He wasn't moving. A shattered lamp decorated the floor beside him.

Tamara didn't require any other explanation. Keeping her gaze averted from the sight of C.J. holding the weeping girl, she asked, "Have you checked for a pulse?"

"No. Could you?"

She bent down and felt the man's neck. This close, she could see the blood trickling from his forehead and matting his hair. He'd taken quite a blow from such a small girl. She found a faint but steady heartbeat.

"I'll call 911."

"Thank you," C.J. said as the girl's sobs began to subside. "That's Sheila's husband," C.J. murmured. "Or, her soon to be ex-husband, Al."

Tamara nodded. She couldn't bear to watch C.J. He held the girl so tightly, comforted her so naturally. And the girl clung to him. She collapsed, and he put her back together. Because that's the kind of man C. J. MacNamara was— the kind you might dream of someday saving you.

Tamara crossed to the window and stood alone until the ambulances arrived.

The rest happened in a blur. The EMTs arrived in a cacophony of sirens, pounding footsteps and demanding yells. Al was immobilized, placed on the stretcher and whisked away. Sheila sat the edge of the bed, pale and cried-out.

The police pulled in next. While C.J. stood beside her, his hand steadying on her shoulder, Sheila related how she'd been down the hall in the bathroom. She'd just returned to her room when she'd heard a noise behind her. She grabbed the lamp as Al had stepped out from behind her door and hit with all the strength she could muster. Al had collapsed like a rag doll. Honest, she hadn't meant to kill her husband, not even send him to the hospital.

Sheriff Brody jotted it all down, occasionally nodding. The sheriff was a large man, with a big barrel chest and a comfortable girth. In his late forties, he had thinning hair that was cut so short none of it appeared beneath the wide brim of his dark brown cowboy hat. In contrast, his mustache was still thick and luxuriant, and he stroked the graying brown strands from time to time as he listened. Beneath the wide brim of his hat, he possessed a pair of keen brown eyes that reminded Tamara of her father.

The sheriff seemed to know both Sheila and C.J. quite well. Apparently, this wasn't the first time he'd had to deal with Al, either. The biggest difference was that this time, Al was the one going to the hospital.

"She's got a restraining order against him," C.J. supplied.

"Yup." Sheriff Brody made a note of it in his little spiral pad.

"I found a broken window in the back, that must have been how he got in."

"B & E." The sheriff wrote that down, too. "Wanna take us to it?"

"Be glad to." The words were casually spoken, but Tamara had a sense there was a great deal more subtext. Obviously, C.J. and Sheriff Brody were worried about Sheila. No doubt they'd have quite the discussion downstairs—out of Sheila's hearing—on just how to protect her.

Of course, from what Tamara had seen of Al's forehead, Sheila was doing just fine.

The men bustled out, their faces serious and intent. They would go secure the perimeter. Fix broken windows. Protect pretty women from evil ogres. Talk about sports.

Tamara remained in the room with Sheila, staring at the hardwood floor, the old rocking chair, the red-and-brown Navajo rug adorning the wall. Sheila was still sitting on the edge of the twin-size bed, her arms wrapped around her middle, her blue eyes dim and shell-shocked. Tamara felt the silence stretch awkwardly.

She'd never been good at this kind of thing. Other women had nurturing, mothering impulses. Tamara snapped at her assistants to get back to work and kept slugging away right beside them. *"You have to learn to walk for yourself. Ain't no one that's going to walk for you."*

"How…how are you?" Tamara asked at last. Bad question. The woman had knocked out her abusive husband. Obviously, she was not doing well. Tamara was ready to go home now.

Sheila shrugged. "I'm tired," she whispered. Her hands rubbed her arms. She was covered with goose bumps and shivering. Tamara found a blanket and gingerly wrapped it around Sheila's arms. The girl didn't seem to notice.

"Come on," Tamara said brusquely. She sat on the edge of her bed and began to rub Sheila's hand rapidly. "Everything's all right now. Al's been taken to the hospital. C.J. and the sheriff are downstairs. You took care of yourself, Sheila. You knocked the man out. That was quick thinking."

Sheila still seemed dazed. Tamara tucked the first hand beneath the covers and picked up the second.

"I didn't mean to hit him," Sheila said abruptly.

"I know." Was that the right thing to say? Tamara tried to remember how her mother would've comforted her. It was so long ago, she couldn't bring the pictures into focus. "I'm sure you did the best you knew how," she said, trying again. It still sounded weak.

"He surprised me. I was scared."

"I know."

"I just...I just reacted." Sheila finally moved. She looked at Tamara with miserable blue eyes. "I could've killed him. I...I kinda wanted to."

Now Tamara definitely didn't know what to say. When she had been hurt, when she had needed comfort, none of her family had been left alive to give it. She had turned inward and that had gotten her through. She didn't know what worked for other people.

She patted Sheila's hand again. "You...you probably have a lot of anger."

"Sometimes I hate him."

"It's understandable."

"He's my husband."

"It sounds like he wasn't a very good one. Listen... You have the right to protect yourself. You have the right to take care of yourself. I don't know much about your situation, but it doesn't sound like Al was a very nice man, and I doubt he broke into the bar just to talk. You did the right thing, Sheila. You thought fast, you protected yourself. See, you're learning how to stand on your own."

Sheila's face brightened. She sat up straighter. Her chin rose up a notch. "You're right. I took care of myself."

Tamara nodded more enthusiastically, encouraged by the color returning to Sheila's cheeks. She hadn't done so bad, after all. She'd said the right thing. Sheila appeared to feel better, and for a moment, so did Tamara. She felt...connected.

They sat together in silence, no longer needing words, and everything was all right.

Tamara finally glanced at the doorway. C.J. was lounging against the doorjamb, and it appeared he'd been there for a bit. He smiled when he caught her gaze, and there was a tender, proud gleam in his eye.

"So do you believe me or not?" Tamara asked at last. They were back in C.J.'s black Mustang. Sheila had been tucked into bed to rest, and Gus had been called to stand guard. Now it was almost seven and Tamara was due at campaign headquarters in only an hour, even if it was Saturday. The senator was arriving in a week. At this point, efforts were entering high gear.

"That you're a reporter?" C.J. was driving with only one hand on the wheel. His left arm was propped up on the edge of his door, his fingers raking through his hair. He looked tired, but in good spirits.

"Yes." She needed to know how well her lies were working. She had a busy few days ahead of her.

"I haven't decided."

"You haven't *decided?* What does that mean?"

C.J. merely shrugged, apparently not that concerned with the situation. "It means I want to look into it."

"My word isn't good enough?"

He grinned lazily. "Nope."

She scowled, feeling ridiculously injured even though she knew he was right. If she were him, she wouldn't believe herself, either. After all, she was lying. "What are you going to do, then?"

"I'm going to get some sleep. Frankly, rescuing damsels in distress is a lot more taxing than you women seem to realize."

"My heart goes out to you," she muttered. He didn't believe her. Most people believed her. She was an intelligent, sophisticated, well-paid executive, what wasn't there to believe? For a moment, she fantasized about having C.J. in a boardroom just so she'd have the upper hand.

"On the one hand," C.J. continued blithely, "I'm pretty sure you're lying. On the other hand, how bad can it be?

You had plenty of opportunity to 'flee the scene,' so to speak, back at the bar, and yet you stayed, helped out with the situation and comforted Sheila. Those don't seem the actions of a master criminal.''

"Maybe I'm a bad master criminal.''

C.J. glanced over at her. His bemused smile told her he didn't believe her. Then abruptly, he reached across and brushed his hand down her cheek. She froze. She didn't pull away or flinch, she just froze. For a second, she was even struck by the sensation of his rough, thick thumb rasping gently down her smooth, tender skin.

"That was a very nice thing you did," he said softly. "You told Sheila exactly the right things."

"I didn't know what I was doing."

"No one ever does. Well, all right, Ann Landers probably does, but the rest of us figure it out as we go along. You stayed with her. You were simply there. After a big trauma, a lot of times we just need someone to be there."

Tamara nodded. She'd wanted someone to be there. She'd wanted her parents to be there. She'd wanted Patty or Patty's father to come so she could see a familiar face while she lay in a foreign hospital room, watching other families visit other patients, talk to other patients, laugh with other patients. No one had ever said that life was fair.

"You...you care for Sheila very much."

"Sheila's like a sister to me," he said bluntly. "Don't worry about that."

"I'm not worried about that." She pulled herself up with haughty indifference. "Who you date is your business. Why should I care?"

"Uh-huh."

"I don't care."

"Uh-huh."

Her gaze narrowed dangerously. "You say that like you don't really believe me."

"I don't. I think I'm starting to get to you. I think maybe

a little bitty bit of you might actually like me. Maybe even be attracted to me. And on a really good day, might even miss me.''

"I...I..." She knit her fingers together quickly on her lap. Her heart was beating too hard in her chest.

"It's still just an itty, bitty bit," he continued casually. "You know, a tiny portion."

"An iota?"

"Yeah, an iota."

"I don't know," she said at last, which wasn't the same as no and they both knew it. C.J. pulled into the parking lot of her hotel. He parked next to her Lexus.

"Any more problems with the brakes?"

"No."

"And your room?"

"Housekeeping removed the scorpion. They think it crawled in while they had the door propped open to clean."

"Uh-huh."

"They are just coincidences, C.J."

He cocked his head to the side, his blue eyes frank and piercing. "Who knows you're here, Tamara?"

"What...what do you mean?"

"Who knows that you're trying to determine if a soon-to-be presidential contender was involved in a fatal accident?"

"Not many people," she said honestly.

"At this point, I would say one is too many."

"They are just coincidences," she insisted, but his fears were getting to her. She popped open the door and crawled out quickly, needing the space. Her ankle had stiffened in the car, and she had to cling to the door for a bit to get her balance.

"Tamara," C.J. said quietly, "was there anyone there for you? You know, after the car accident. Was there anyone there to hold your hand?"

"I don't know what you're talking about," she said faintly. She gripped the door harder until her knuckles went white.

"The car accident you spoke of earlier. You were in it, weren't you, Tamara? That's why you limp. That's why you're back in Sedona. That's why you're investigating the senator. It was your family, wasn't it?"

"I don't know what you're talking about."

"Yes, you do. I know, Tamara. I can see the fear in your eyes."

She stiffened her spine immediately but knew it was too late. C.J. saw too much. She'd never met a man who could penetrate her shields so easily.

"The senator is a powerful man, sweetheart. Do you know what you're doing?"

"No," she said abruptly. "I don't. But I'll figure it out. I'm doing all right."

C.J. got out of the car. Before she was ready, he was standing in front of her. "Let me do this," he whispered. "For once, just let me do this."

His hand enfolded her shoulders. His fingers were warm and strong. He pulled her against him slowly, as if he knew that at any second she would bolt. His left arm curled around her waist, his hand flattening on the delicate curve of the small of her back. He pressed her against him and cradled her cheek against his shoulder.

She stood rigid and wide-eyed. She felt the soft comfort of his worn T-shirt. She heard the steady rhythm of his heartbeat. She felt his hand burning into her back. She felt his long, workingman's fingers lift and thread through her hair. He massaged her scalp until little tingles swept down her neck. He smoothed her hair back until she found herself leaning against him. She didn't want to lean against him. She didn't want to lean against anyone.

He shifted and bore her weight effortlessly.

His fingers moved down, found her shoulders and dug

in. She almost moaned. She'd felt like she was carrying the weight of the world on her shoulders for years now, and the tight, knotted muscles testified to each moment of doubt and fear. Now his strong, callused, wonderful fingers squeezed and kneaded and pressed until her muscles gave up, turned into Silly Putty and begged for him to mold them.

Her arms had become wrapped around his waist. Her eyes had drifted shut. He smelled of soap and Old Spice. She loved Old Spice.

Oh, God.

She was going to cry. She was going to weep. The traitorous emotions were welling up again. She didn't know where they came from, but now they were a tidal wave sweeping up her gut, rolling into her throat and about to gush from her eyes. She knotted her hands. She squeezed her eyes shut. She held her breath.

She would not lose control. She would not lose control.

"Sh. It's okay, Tamara. It's okay. Relax."

And then she was angry again. Unbelievably angry. An intelligent, rational human being like herself should never be so angry.

But she was furious. It would not be okay. Why did people say it would be okay? People told you they would take care of you. People told you it would be all right. People let you love them, trust them, need them. And then they were gone and you had only the memory of their lies. No one could take care of you. No one could comfort you. No one could protect you.

You had only yourself and the red Arizona desert and the sound of crickets as your family gave up one by one, and left you.

She planted her hands on C.J.'s chest and pushed hard. Immediately, his hands snapped around her wrists.

"No, dammit! Enough of this advance and retreat. I've

never been good at dancing. Tell me what's going on, Tamara. Tell me what's going through your mind.''

She stared at him, her eyes blazing, her throat thickening traitorously. She was so sick and overwhelmed by all these emotions she didn't understand and never felt. She acted on instinct. She acted with rage. She grabbed his cheeks, yanked down his head and kissed him hard.

Suddenly his arms were around her. If she'd thought he was only tenderness, she'd underestimated him. He met her inch for inch, his mouth opening, his tongue plunging. He devoured her, he consumed her. He buried his hands in her thick sable hair, angled back her head and showed her what it was like to be kissed by a man who knew how.

Her breasts flattened against his chest. Her hips were molded against his thighs. He grabbed her lower lip with his teeth, suckling it fiercely. Then he was kissing the corner of her mouth, nibbling on her jawline and rasping his twenty-four-hour beard against her soft cheeks. She felt hot. She felt achy. Need and desire swirled and swarmed, and she at once pulled him closer and tried to step away.

His teeth fastened on her earlobe, his tongue teased the edge, and the shivers ripped through her. Her knees were weak. Her leg muscles trembled.

She'd lost her mind. She'd lost control.

It was too much.

She pushed him away vehemently, dancing back as fast as she could. Their chests were heaving, their breaths loud and labored in the silence. They looked at each other without words, and the distance between them heated up another few degrees. C.J.'s gaze was not tender or gentle. It was a bright, fierce blue, and it told her in no uncertain terms just how much he wanted her.

She stared back at him just as intensely and hated herself for succumbing so easily.

"I do not want this!" she hissed.

"Wrong. You're afraid of it."

"Don't tell me how I feel!"

"Then, stop telling me lies and admit to it yourself."

"My life is none of your business!"

"Too late."

"I am not one of your damsels in distress!" she practically cried. "Stick to your waitresses!"

"Too late," he growled.

She threw her hands in the air. She wanted to strangle him. She wanted to hold him. She wanted to hate him. She wanted to run back into his arms. The ice had finally broken. She'd found a man whose touch and taste drove her crazy. Lucky her, lucky her.

She gave up on composure, and fled.

C.J. watched her go with dark eyes. He stood in the parking lot long after she'd disappeared into the courtyard, still too wired to move. His body was rock hard, the desire in his groin painful. His jeans were not cut out for this kind of pressure. Hell, his body was not cut out for this kind of raging need.

Holy mother of... He took a deep breath, then another, then another. When he finally trusted himself to move, he crawled gingerly back into his car and stared at the dash.

Bloody hell, he thought in perfect imitation of his brother Brandon. How did a man get through to that woman, anyway? And why couldn't he just let her go?

Bloody hell. He slammed his car into gear and roared away as if driving fast would help. Of course, it didn't.

Tamara was shaking so hard, it took her four attempts to fasten the chain lock on her door. She stood in the entryway of the suite, still breathing too hard. Then in a flurry of movement, she ripped at her clothes as if getting them off quickly would finally rid her of C. J. MacNamara's touch, taste and smell.

The clothes pooled at her feet. Naked, covered with snaking scars she hated to see, she made a beeline for the

bathroom and its whirlpool tub. She cranked the water to
the hottest setting she could find. She dumped in half a
bottle of hotel shampoo for suds. She climbed at last into
the steaming, whirling, floral-scented water, closing her
eyes and willing it to soak the last of the emotions from
her pores.

She didn't want to be angry. She didn't even want to
be passionate. At this point, she wanted her composure
back so she could return to New York as intact as possible.

She heard her mother's gentle reprimand. *"Slow
down..."*

She heard her father's hoarse cry. *"Oh, God!"*

She heard Shawn's pain-weakened voice. *"It'll be okay,
Tammy. They'll...come. Some...one...will...come. The...
Lord...is...my shepherd. I shall...not...want..."*

She pressed her hands against her forehead. She
squeezed the horrible, conflicting pictures back into their
special place.

She didn't want to know. She just wanted justice.

The steam rose around her. It curled her hair. She kept
her face buried in her hands for a long, long time. When
she finally looked up again, the memories were pushed
back. The emotions were gone. She let the hot water soak
into her limbs, and suddenly, she was unbearably exhausted.

It was okay. She could handle tired.

She climbed out of the tub, toweled off and got ready
to go to campaign headquarters. She didn't need C. J.
MacNamara or his piercing eyes, or his strong embrace.
She just needed to find traces of the red car. And she would
do that on her own.

Chapter 6

"Where are the bumper stickers? What is this? I thought we had a full five thousand coming in. Come on, come on, where are they?"

"Printer had a slight problem," Celia called out from across the bustling, churning, phone-ringing chaos. "Delivered them this morning with Brennan spelled with only one *n*."

"What?"

"They'll have them here by Monday morning, they swore."

"Jerry!" Mrs. Winslow barked, "Get me the phone and the number for the printers. I will handle this personally. Celia, find the pins, instead. If there is a man, woman or child in this county, I want them wearing a Senator Brennan for Our Future pin. Hannah, get me four focus groups, heavy on women and minorities. We just got the new campaign commercials in and we need to test them. Scott, did the newest version of the senator's announcement speech come in?"

"Yes," Scott said glumly.

Mrs. Winslow practically grabbed him by the shoulders and shook him. One week before the senator's arrival, the campaign war room was living up to its name. "Spit it out! What's wrong?"

"I ran it by a dozen test groups in the last three days," Scott said, the words rushing out. "It rates high with middle-aged men, both white, Indian and Hispanic, but women didn't respond to it at all, while voters under thirty-five complained it was too old school. At this point, he's hitting only forty percent of the voters. We ran the numbers, Mary. That won't do it, not with a young, well-respected outsider like Matthew Phillips throwing his hat in the ring. Women love him, young voters adore him. Basically, he's a really sexy version of Ross Perot."

"Scott, repeat after me— There is no such thing as a sexy Ross Perot."

"Mary," Scott said just as testily, "I'm telling you now, with speeches like this, the senator's not going to carry his home state. How can he not carry his own state? Demographics have changed around here, and somebody had better explain that to the senator and his head speechwriter."

Mary scowled, chewing on her lower lip. Then her gaze latched on to Tamara, who was sitting in front of her computer, trying to look like she was working while she blatantly eavesdropped on the senator's woes. She'd dressed for the day's chaos in a slimming black pantsuit. Generally, it made her look sharp and chic. Today, it merely accentuated the pallor of her skin and the shadows beneath her eyes. Apparently, Mary Winslow thought the same.

"My God, you look like hell. Are you feeling all right?" What the question lacked in genuine concern, it made up for in razor-sharp demand.

"I'm fine. I just had a late night."

Mrs. Winslow's hands settled on her trim hips, garbed

in a sensible navy blue schoolmarm's skirt. "I know you are just a volunteer, Tamara, but it's two days before the senator's arrival and I can't have my staff up late drinking and performing poorly—"

"I know—"

"Don't you understand how important this is? Don't you realize how much the senator is trusting us to do this right? This isn't some high school most-likely-to-succeed contest. Here in this room, we are working on molding the future. We are setting our sights on determining the next leader of the free world."

"I drove here all the way from New York," Tamara fired back, a little bit on edge herself. "It occurred to me it might be important."

Mary Winslow's eyes narrowed to laser-blue pinpricks. "They told me you were a good writer."

"I've written a few press releases in my time."

Mrs. Winslow abruptly picked up a file and slapped it on Tamara's desk. "These are the voter surveys we've conducted for the last six months. They report what issues are most important to women, to white males, to Indians, to the elderly, to Gen-X. Read them, get to know them. Then I want you to take the senator's speech and see if you can fine-tune it—and I mean *fine-tune,* nothing huge, nothing drastic—to better reflect wider demographics. Then we'll fax it back to the senator's head speechwriter and see if we can get it to fly."

"Wouldn't it be easier to have the speechwriter do it?"

"Alex is a little busy these days, as I'm sure you can imagine. Besides, we don't need anything major. Just enough to show that the senator is a broad-thinking man. He cares about the Navajo. He cares about the Hispanics. He understands the plight of the working mother. He feels the pinch of the middle-class family struggling to send their first child to college. He's a family man."

"That's what all the young, pretty blond aides on Capitol Hill think, too," Tamara murmured, picking up the file.

"I don't need your sarcasm right now."

Beneath the desk, Tamara's hands curled into fists. Funny how composure used to be as second nature to her as breathing. Now she might as well sign up for a one-way ticket to Bellevue. Lovely. "Sorry. I'm a little tense."

"Welcome to the club." Mrs. Winslow stabbed her index finger toward the file again. "I'll need this by end of day. Don't get too wedded to anything, either. The senator likes to edit edits. Hopefully, however, we'll end up with a version more appealing than this."

"All right."

Mrs. Winslow was already turning away, her finger pointed at the next victim.

"Mary—" Tamara said abruptly, seeing an unexpected opportunity. "What if we looked at more than just the senator's speech?"

"Such as?"

"Well, the fundamental issue here is how do we repackage an older, old-school conservative politician to appeal to a younger, more diversified audience. Sure, we can tweak his speech, but it's also the man himself. I don't know why his publicist hasn't gone over this with him, but those navy blue single-breasted suits and red striped ties he likes to wear? For crying out loud, he should just stamp Twenty Years Past Freshness Date on his forehead."

Around them, a few eavesdropping volunteers giggled. Tamara warmed up for the kill. Her exhaustion was gone. She felt nervous, almost euphoric. She had an opening she hadn't realized she would get, an opportunity to pry into the senator's life. Her voice deepened to a rich, husky baritone that knew how to hold an audience. "We get the senator into a charcoal gray, double-breasted suit with a silk, maroon and navy blue abstract tie. Then we let him make an entrance." She paused. Mrs. Winslow leaned forward.

"How does the senator normally come into town?" Tamara pressed innocently. "Limo? Lincoln Towncar with dark-tinted windows and his own driver?"

"He prefers a Towncar, yes, with his own driver. We always take care of the arrangements for him through one of the executive driving services in Phoenix."

"Entourage?"

"Of course! He has his publicist, his secretary, his aide. This time his family will be joining him, of course, plus he has a few bodyguards. A man like him can't be too careful."

"It's old school. Don't you see? It reeks of everything the voters are rejecting. Matthew Phillips isn't traveling with a funeral train of black sedans and private drivers. He drives his own car. His aides drive their own cars—or actually, cars he probably bought for them. What if we put the senator in something younger, hipper? We could get... We could get one of the senator's cars. He must own a few."

"I'm sure he does."

"Isn't his house on the outskirts of Sedona?"

"Of course, it's a lovely home. I believe...I think he may have a Cadillac, maybe a Buick, something like that. I really don't see the difference between that and the car service we've already arranged for him."

"What about something younger? Something, say...sportier. Does the senator have a sports car, you know, a...a red sports car?"

"What in the world would a man the senator's age be doing with a red sports car?"

Tamara met Mrs. Winslow's gaze blandly. "I don't know. I thought men of all ages liked sports cars."

"Not the senator," Mrs. Winslow said firmly. "He's a very image-conscious man, and for as long as I've known him, he's driven fine, reliable American-made sedans. Really, to put him in a red convertible? That may appeal to the young voters, but that would destroy his image with his established fans. A man of his age in a red convertible. It just…it just wouldn't do!''

Mary Winslow dismissed the notion once and for all with a negative shake of her finger.

"No," Tamara said faintly after a bit, "I suppose it wouldn't.''

Mrs. Winslow bustled away, leaving Tamara alone with her computer, press releases and a speech she was now to target toward women and minorities. The adrenaline had left her, killed by Mrs. Winslow's simple but firm assertion that the senator had never owned a red sports car. He was an American sedan man. And most of his driving needs were taken care of by a professional service.

So if the senator had been at the American Legion to accept an award, how would he have ever left in a red sports car? Mostly likely the same driving service that took him to the ceremony took him home. No red car. No senator driving a sports car.

The phones around her were still ringing off the hook. Mrs. Winslows voice rose again as she lit into a new campaign soldier not performing up to par. Tamara sat there, rubbing her temples.

What if she was wrong? She'd glimpsed the man's face so briefly and such a long time ago. Maybe it was just some guy, some totally random guy, and all these years, she'd doubted the wrong man, hated the wrong man, condemned the wrong man.

She didn't know anymore. She just didn't know, and the phones kept ringing and the people kept shouting and it was too loud to think. She picked up the speech. She couldn't get herself to make a single edit.

I know it's him, I know it's him, I know it's him.

Do you, Tamara? Or are you just that desperate for someone else to blame?

The memory came out of nowhere. She wasn't prepared for it.

It was her own voice in the back seat of the car, ten years ago. *"Look, Dad. Through the right-hand window. Isn't that the most beautiful moon?"*

"Oh, my God, Robert! Look out! Look out!"

Her fingers snapped the pencil she was holding. Her fingers were trembling again. She got up, holding herself together very carefully. She went to the women's rest room and splashed cold water on her face.

She still couldn't get her own voice out of her mind.

At eleven o'clock that night, Tamara finally left the campaign war room. Others remained behind. With one week to go, the sheer volume of work was overwhelming. In New York, Tamara routinely worked until one or two in the morning. The machine, they called her. The woman who could always get it done.

In Sedona, she was the volunteer with the bloodshot eyes and the drooping expression. Mrs. Winslow hadn't been able to stand looking at her anymore.

"Go home," she'd barked. "Get some sleep. Take tomorrow off if you have to. I need you one hundred percent on Monday."

Now Tamara stood in the darkened parking lot, inhaling the dry, spicy air and listening to the soft whir of late night birds. The Arizona sky spread above her like a lush expanse of midnight blue velvet. In the distance, dark cutouts indicated the looming Rock Monuments. Stars dusted their forms like sequined trim. Desert nights were so unbelievably soft. She'd never really considered it before. In contrast, Manhattan nights were harsh and meant only for the hard at heart.

She walked to her car, her gaze scanning the parking

lot. Then she realized she was looking for signs of C.J. and forced her gaze back to her car. Did she really expect him to be out here waiting for her? It was late on a Saturday night. The man had a bar to run. And a good thing, too; she was tired of him always appearing. She was tired of dealing with him.

Her hand paused on the door of her Lexus. Her gaze was still scanning the darkness for his familiar form. Dammit. She scowled. She missed him. She did. Somehow, she'd gotten accustomed to him showing up at the darndest places, with his quick grin, probing gaze and strong shoulder.

You will not need C. J. MacNamara. I forbid you to need C. J. MacNamara.

"I forbid you to need anyone," she muttered out loud, then, realizing she was talking to herself in the middle of an empty parking lot, she crawled into her car before she made a total spectacle of herself.

She headed straight back to her hotel. She needed a good night's sleep. Maybe a swim to loosen up tensed muscles. A late, hearty breakfast to regain some of the weight she was losing. She knew better than to let herself run down like this. She should take better care of herself. Health mattered.

She found herself pulling into the parking lot of the Ancient Mariner without knowing how she got there. By night, it was everything it hadn't been by day.

The parking lot was jammed full of cars. Bright outside lights lit up the wooden structure with gay welcome. A spotlight rested on a three-foot-high carved statue of an old sea captain leaning on a cane, while painted white letters announced The Ancient Mariner.

Music spilled out of the wood. Tamara could hear the pounding pulse of a deep base and the high, trilling crescendo of an electric guitar. Rock 'n' roll. Good, old-fashioned, foot-tapping, finger-snapping music. The kind that made you smile while you listened. The kind that made people laugh and talk louder and clank beer mugs. The walls were practically shaking with it.

And she could picture C.J. standing in the middle of it all, like a captain at the helm of his ship, guiding it effortlessly through the storm. It was his kind of place. Vital, wild and fun.

She sat in her car, her hands flexing and unflexing on the wheel.

She should just go in. She could say she wanted to see how Sheila was doing. She could find a bar stool, she could order a beer. She didn't remember the last time she'd had a beer. She didn't remember the last time she'd been in a working-class bar. She could sit and listen to the music and watch the people and see if she sat there long enough, would that fun seep into her? Would she finally relax? Would she finally wear herself out to such a point she could sleep without dreams? She was so tired of the pictures creeping into her mind.

She wanted to see C.J. She just did.

I don't need him.

You miss him.

I don't miss anyone. It's stupid to miss people. They are either there or not.

He's a handsome man. He smiles. He makes you smile—when you let him. There's nothing wrong with that.

There is everything wrong with that. I'm not his type. We have nothing in common. He likes me only for the challenge.

He cares. He understands you better than you realize. And he's gotten to you—just an itty, bitty bit.

She scowled. Again. She hated it when she lost arguments with herself. She stared at the lit-up, pulsing bar with open yearning—like the little girl on the fringe of the party. She hungered to go inside. To belong. To feel at home.

She didn't move. She was afraid. She was isolated, and she didn't know how to crack the ice. She felt like Sleeping Beauty, lying in the crystal with her eyes open, wanting to move, to sit up, to walk away, but only able to lie there and hope the prince would get smart and kiss her.

No, I will not be passive. Ben taught me better than to be passive. You want to get to the end of the parallel bars, you take a step. So take the step, Tamara. Stop thinking of the damn consequences and just take the step.

She shoved open her car door. And one of New York's most accomplished public relations executives bolted across the parking lot so she could get into the bar before she changed her mind.

"Uh-oh," Gus drawled. "Look at the door. That's gotta be trouble."

C.J.'s head popped up instantly from behind the bar where he was loading beer mugs in the tiny dishwasher. Who was trouble? Then he spotted Tamara in the open doorway, light spilling around her. She was easy to recognize. In her trim black pantsuit, discreet pearl earrings and upswept hair, she stood out amid the Ancient Mariner's casually dressed clientele like a princess visiting the peasants.

"Wow," C.J. said, unable to tear his gaze away. He was supposed to be angry with her. He'd told himself he'd had enough—he wasn't going to look her up today, he wasn't going to keep chasing her. She'd made her opinion clear, and he had better things to do with his time than pursue a woman who changed her story every five minutes. Now she was here, in his bar, and like an alcoholic confronted by an icy, cold beer, his good intentions went out the window. God, it was good to see her.

"New York," Gus said as if it were a curse.

"Yeah, Gus, but I know her. That's Tamara. The one Sheila's been talking about. She's nice. And she races cars."

Gus screwed her scarred face into a look that screamed skepticism. C.J. didn't care; his gaze was still on Tamara. From across the room, still standing uncertain in the doorway, she finally spotted him. Her lips curved slightly. Hesitant, tremulous, she smiled. And because he knew her, because he'd spent days memorizing her, he understood exactly what that kind of welcoming smile cost a proud woman like herself. He wanted to bolt across his wooden bar, sweep her into his arms and dance her around the floor until her hair fell out of its fancy twist, her face grew flushed and her eyes glowed gold.

Instead, he stood like a statue as she carefully wove her way across the crowded red floor. People were standing and jostling, screaming to one another to be heard over the jukebox. Even then, Tamara managed to keep a wide berth of empty space around her. In her fancy black suit, she emoted the kind of presence that made others step back.

"Hi," she said at last, arriving at the bar. The word was whispery, not at all certain.

"You don't know why you're here," he filled in for her frankly.

"I wanted to see how Sheila was doing."

"You told yourself you shouldn't come. You told yourself you didn't really miss me. But then you found yourself here, anyway."

"Is Sheila around?"

"I'm happy you came, Tamara. I've thought about you a lot. I'm really, really happy that you're here."

"Oh." Her eyes were no longer distant, her face no longer so pale. She was leaning forward slightly, and he caught the unmistakable longing. It froze the breath in his throat. He wanted to know exactly what she longed for.

At this moment, he would give it to her. He would give her the earth, the moon, the stars if he could.

"Could I...um..." She licked her lips nervously. "Could I have a beer?"

"Okay." His gaze remained on her freshly moistened mouth. Her lips were devoid of lipstick, a natural, deep, kissable red. He remembered kissing those lips, too. He remembered the first, unsatisfactory kiss when she'd stood so stoically. And he remembered last night, when she'd practically sucked his mouth off his face.

Gus reached across him and yanked the tap down so that beer flowed into the mug he was holding beneath the spout. "Got customers," she said.

"Oh, oh yeah." He belatedly handed the beer to Tamara, introducing her to Gus. The women exchanged wary glances, but seemed to decide that each other would do. "You'll stay for a bit, right? Here, here, come here." C.J. motioned Tamara down to the end of the bar, starting to feel a little giddy. She was in *his* bar, and it reminded him of the first time he'd invited a girl to sit in *his* car. He was possessive, nervous and excited all at once. He loved his bar. He was damn proud of his bar. He found he wanted her to love it, too, to see it the way he did. Of course, it was just a bar.

"Sit right here, it's the waitress section. Sheila will be by a lot with orders, and I'll have to stand here to fill them and...and we can talk a bit. Between the madness."

"Gus won't mind?"

"Gus will give me hell," he assured her, then grinned. "But hey, I'm the boss." He winked, and her lips slowly curved into a smile. God, she had such a smile. He clutched his chest dramatically and her cheeks flushed red.

"I'm really happy you're here," he said softly once more. He whirled away before she had a chance to reply and resumed pouring beers.

"Chest puffs out anymore," Gus said, "you're gonna crow."

"Isn't she something?"

"New York," Gus said again.

"Nice New York, Gus. Nice New York. Even Manhattan has good people."

"Bah."

Tamara seemed to be having a good time. He glanced at her all he could, sneaking little comments when he dared, but the Ancient Mariner's owner was a popular man on a Saturday night, and all his money-spending patrons wanted fresh beers. The third time by, he pulled up short and realized she hadn't touched her mug.

"Don't like it?" he asked immediately. For some reason, the thought left him stricken.

"The idea of beer was better than the taste," Tamara admitted. She shrugged helplessly. "Actually, I'm kind of a wine person."

"I have wine! Chardonnay, white zin, Riesling. What would you like?"

"Chardonnay would be perfect."

"Coming right up." A pair of cute blondes flashed a ten-spot so he'd take their order. He ignored them and filled a glass for Tamara. Then he waited while she tasted it.

"Oh." Her face lit up. "Nice."

That crisis momentarily diverted, C.J. returned to the other customers. When he looked over again, Sheila had stopped by and both women were deep in conversation. As soon as the hospital had doctored Al's head, the sheriff had thrown him in jail, providing Sheila with at least momentary peace of mind.

The volume of the bar grew steadily. The jukebox never stopped pumping. The people never stopped talking. He poured beer. He mixed cocktails. He popped popcorn. He loaded dishwashers and started the process all over again. And he refilled Tamara's wineglass again, watching her eyes melt to a liquid gold while her cheeks filled with a slow burn. But one o'clock, she was standing in front of the jukebox with good old Walter, arguing whether Elvis or Eric Clapton was the greatest musician who had ever lived. In the end, the conversation was a draw and the bar got a song from each of the rock 'n' roll masters.

Tamara's jacket somehow became unbuttoned. She wore a solid black satin camisole beneath it, covering enough and shifting enough to drive a man crazy. More tendrils of hair broke loose, and more men seemed to find a way to pass by her corner. C.J. had never realized before just how many men came into his bar, and by God, he was beginning to resent each and every one of them. He wanted to hang a sign on her chair— Taken. No, nothing territorial or possessive about him. No way.

A little after one, Tamara was on her third glass of wine and the crowds began to thin out. Before long, C.J. was announcing last call and kicking out his customers with more haste than necessary. He wanted the evening to end. He wanted this flushed, smiling, subtly glowing woman all to himself.

"I should go," Tamara said at last, but she was leaning over the bar, her feet propped up on the rim of the stool, and making no effort to leave.

"Absolutely not. I just need a half an hour to close things up, secure the place."

"I sleep here tonight," Gus said from behind the bar. She was stacking more glasses into the dishwasher.

"You don't have to," Sheila said automatically, wiping off the last of the table tops.

"Don't want to drive home," Gus said shortly.

"You're sweet, Gus. You really are." Sheila began piling chairs on top of the table.

"Should I help?" Tamara asked from her corner, earning a surprised glance from Gus. Her face was still flushed. She looked more relaxed than C.J. had ever seen her. He suspected she was just a little bit blotto.

"No, you're fine," he assured her, drifting down her way. He needed to close out the register. He leaned against the bar, instead, and gave her his most charming grin. Her lips twitched. Her smile grew. And kept growing. It became a big, goofy smile.

"Yep, you're blitzed."

"Am not."

"Are, too." He tweaked her nose. "But you're a cute drunk."

"I never get drunk." She was trying to pull herself up with indignation, but that made her sway slightly. Her eyes widened. "Oh," she said after a moment, clearly surprised.

"Oh," C.J. agreed. "And how many bottles did you drink?"

"Three glasses. That's it. I'm a three-glasses-of-wine woman."

"And how much dinner did you eat?"

"Ooooh. Dinner. I knew I forgot something."

"Yeah, that probably did it. Here, I'll pour you a cup of coffee. Nurse that, and we'll get this show on the road."

C.J. worked fast. Not that it was hard to close up the bar. After all these years together, he and Gus moved like a well-oiled machine, and Sheila blended with them nicely. By 3:00 a.m., everything was shipshape and ready for noon opening on Sunday. Gus and Sheila said their good-nights and disappeared upstairs with the usual complaints of tired feet and aching backs.

C.J. turned off the main lights. Now the shut-up room glowed with just the track lighting. It illuminated Tamara's face gently, casting the rest of her into shadows. He walked over quietly. He leaned against the bar beside her, so close he could catch the musky scent of her shampoo. It reminded him of sandalwood, of being outdoors. He stood there, letting the silence envelope them, content to gaze at her profile as she twirled her empty coffee cup absently.

"I don't generally get drunk," she said after a moment, the words carefully enunciated, as if she had to concentrate on forming each syllable.

"You're not that drunk. Just tipsy."

"I don't get tipsy."

"It's not so bad, Tamara. I don't recommend anyone make a habit out of it, but take it from a marine, everyone has their days."

"Yeah," she said at last. "Yeah." Her gaze was focused on the wall behind his bar. By the dim glow of the track light, she looked unbelievably delicate. She also looked vulnerable.

"Did you have one of those days, Tamara? Is that why you came here?"

"No. Yes." She twirled the coffee cup again, her expression pensive. "I don't know."

He leaned closer. He brushed back a loose strand of hair, letting it slide like heavy silk between his fingertips. She didn't flinch, she didn't pull away. This time she looked at him, and he saw her gaze drop to his lips and linger. Her mouth parted slightly. He was keenly aware of the change in her breathing, how it went from normal to shallow, how her gaze remained on his lips.

"Tell me what you want," he whispered.

"I don't know."

"Yes, you do. You came here for a reason."

Slowly, her eyes came up to his. They were no longer golden. They'd gone dark, filled with shadows he didn't understand. "I don't know myself anymore," she said abruptly. "I get so angry.... I never used to get angry."

"Maybe you should have." He took her hand. "I loved my mother very much," he said quietly, stroking her slender fingers, watching them tremble on his palm. "But when she died, I hated her for a while. And when Max died, I hated him for a while, too. I spent a few years as a very angry kid.''

"I can't imagine you angry."

He smiled. "Ah, sweetheart, you should've known me then. I thought there was no one in the world tougher than me. I swore. I swaggered. I disrespected my elders and I disrespected myself. I was hell on wheels. There wasn't a fight I wouldn't pick or a loved one I wouldn't reject. Ask my grandma sometime. She'd love to tell you about the brat she inherited. The things that woman put up with qualify her for sainthood."

"You're not so angry now."

"No, I'm not. I got over it." He shrugged. "Some things you can't fight, Tamara. Some things you *can't* control. You just have to experience them. You probably need to experience them to get them out of your system. You don't hate your family now because you never liked them. You hate your family now because you loved them so much."

Her eyes grew luminescent. He could see her conflict, the need to understand mixed with the need to shut it away, the need to grieve mixed with the desire to be strong, invincible. He wanted to pull her into his arms and tell her it would be all right. But he couldn't protect her from her loss. That was something everyone had to work through on their own.

Her gaze fell. She focused on the coffee mug, turning it around and around in her hands, as if her world counted on turning that coffee mug. After another moment, she pushed it away. "I'm drunk," she said softly. "That's all."

"Sure, sweetheart. Sure. Come on, I'll drive you home."

She didn't protest and she didn't say much. She was lost in the tumultuous world of her own thoughts—he respected that. They drove in silence, not speaking again until he pulled into her hotel parking lot.

"If you'd like, I'll pick you up again around eleven and you can fetch your car."

"All right."

"Good night, Tamara. Sweet dreams."

She remained sitting in the passenger's side. "You don't...you don't want to...come in?"

He closed his eyes, searching for willpower. "No."

"No?"

"No."

"I don't understand. You don't..." Her voice broke off. She abruptly bit her lower lip and grappled with the door handle. He caught her wrist before she could go any farther.

"Tamara, if you only knew how much I want you."

"You don't have to lie." She was still trying to open the door.

He took both her hands, the only way he knew how to keep her from bolting. Then he gave in with a groan and claimed her lips. It was earnest, it was eager, and he pulled away even though it killed him. "I want you," he said again, his voice ragged. "But not like this, Tamara. Not on a night like tonight. You and I are going to make love. And when we do, it will be slow, it will be perfect, and you will be so aware of each and every second that years from now when you replay it in your mind, you'll want me all over again."

Her breathing slowed. Her eyes lingered on his face. In that heartbeat, he felt the connection with her. He felt her tentative desire, her hesitant need, her fragile hunger. Then her eyes closed, the moment passed, and just as clearly, he felt her retreat.

She pulled her hands from his grasp. "No," she said quietly. "It won't be like that. I'll never want anyone that much. I don't want to."

"We'll see."

"I'm serious."

"So am I. Good night, Tamara. Dream of me."

"No," she said, and climbed out of his car. "I don't do that anymore, either."

She slammed his car door shut. Then she walked away proudly, and the night swallowed her whole.

Chapter 7

"I'm returning to Manhattan. It's time to go home."

It was seven in the morning. Patty stood in the doorway of her four-bedroom house, looking at Tamara with shocked eyes while she tightened the belt of her simple navy blue terry-cloth robe. That robe wasn't right. Patty should be wearing the silk, bloodred dragon kimono she'd bought when they were fifteen. That robe had been wild, fierce, a bold statement of budding sexuality and rebellion. Tamara had looked at it with awe. This robe Tamara resented, even if it was stupid to resent a bathrobe. In this robe, she saw the yawning gap between her and Patty, between the innocent girls they were in her mind and the reserved, world-weary women they'd become. She wished Patty still wore bloodred silk. How silly.

"Why don't you come in?" Patty said at last. "I'll get us both cups of coffee."

Tamara nodded. She was shivering unconsciously on the doorstep, clutching her trench coat for warmth. The cab that had delivered her had already come and gone.

This early, the sun was just beginning to burn the haze from the sky, and dew still glistened on leaves of mesquite trees and the fine needles of saguaro cacti. Patty lived outside of Sedona on a large tract of land. Despite what she'd stated earlier, she seemed to be making a very nice living. Her house was surrounded by a luxurious oasis of emerald green grass, expensive to maintain. Sturdy yucca soap trees and bundles of barrel cacti fringed the perimeter, helping conceal the black wrought-iron fence guarding the backyard. Her stucco walls had been freshly whitewashed and her red-tiled roof, recently cleaned and well maintained, gleamed darkly beneath the rising sun.

The inside looked the same, tastefully upper class. Huge vaulted ceilings and a rising expanse of windows revealed the kidney-shaped pool and lush garden in her backyard. Ceiling fans stirred the air. Jade green marble framed a decorative fireplace and glossed over the kitchen floor. Cream-colored leather sofas sat on plush white Berber rugs, while tasteful landscape paintings of Arizona sunsets hung neatly on the walls.

The room was elegant, without reproach, and lacked a single spark of life. It depressed Tamara even more.

"How would you like your coffee?" Patty asked politely, filling the void.

"Cream. A little sugar." Generally she drank it black, but the thought of straight caffeine already made her stomach roll. When had she eaten last? Twelve, sixteen, twenty-four hours ago? She had no insides left.

Patty crossed to the adjoining kitchen, which was separated from the living room only by a green-tiled bar. "Tamara, are you all right?"

"I'm not sleeping well, that's all." That was an understatement. She was exhausted and overwrought. She'd tossed and turned since C.J. had dropped her off at three, dozing off to sleep twice and suffering horrible nightmares on each occasion. Right around six, she'd given up on

sleep and she'd given up on peace. She'd made her decision and called Patty.

"I think I was wrong about the senator," Tamara said
abruptly.

Patty froze, her hand suspended over the coffeepot.
Then after a moment, she resumed spooning in the freshly
ground beans and turning on the pot to brew. "Orange
juice?" she asked. "Bagels? You look like you need to
eat more."

"I know. I..." Tamara didn't know how to explain it.
She leaned against the green-tiled bar, and for a long time,
she just looked at her best friend. At this time of the morning, Patty wasn't wearing any makeup. Her pale, redhead's
complexion was as fresh and unmarred as a young girl's.
Her luxurious, flame-colored hair tumbled thickly down
her back. Tamara remembered the nights they'd stayed up
late, giggling and braiding each other's hair and talking
about boys. And Tamara would ooh and aah over Shawn
until Patty would push her off the bed. Funny how far
away those days seemed. So simple, so easy. So much
laughter, so much ease.

Now Patty shifted from side to side, clearly uncomfortable beneath Tamara's scrutiny. Her gaze was guarded, her
face uncertain. And Tamara understood. She felt the same
way.

"I made a mistake," Tamara said softly.

"I don't understand."

"You were right, Patty. You were. I came here thinking
I could change things. I don't know...I guess I expected
us to be the same. And Sedona would feel the same and...
I was naive. Hopeful, I suppose." *Desperate, lost, lonely.
Realizing how empty my life in Manhattan was and not
knowing how to fill it.* "I don't belong here anymore. I
should go back to New York."

Patty frowned. Her shoulders were hunched up, tense.
"But what about the senator?"

"What about the senator? I've checked around all I can, and there's absolutely no evidence that the senator was involved with the accident. He's never owned a red car, he's generally driven around by a car service. I've been grasping at straws, obsessing over nothing, looking for someone to blame. And it's just prolonging the inevitable. My family is dead. No one knows who killed them, but hopefully what comes around goes around. As for me…" *As for me, I have to learn how to sleep at night. How to eat again. How to forget, because maybe then I can at least have my cold, sterile peace back.* "I need to go home."

Patty, however, appeared uncertain. Maybe she was just confused, given how vehemently Tamara had defended her decision to return to Sedona. "You're sure?"

"Yes."

"So what are you going to do? Pack up and drive away this afternoon? Disappear, just like that?"

"Tuesday, probably. I'm committed to helping prepare the senator's announcement. I should see that through."

"Why? If you're ready to leave, then you should go. Face it, Tamara, you don't even like Senator Brennan. You're not planning on voting for him. Working at campaign headquarters at this point would be hypocritical."

Tamara shrugged. "Leaving them in the lurch seems unfair."

"Who cares?" Patty said bluntly. "If you really don't think it's him, if you really want to get on with things, then if I were you, I'd just hit the road, drive straight through to Manhattan. You don't owe them anything, Tamara. They don't even know your real name."

The vehemence of Patty's words startled Tamara. For just a minute, her friend sounded the way Tamara remembered her—the strong, rebellious girl who thought more of herself than others. Tamara didn't know whether to smile or shake her head. "Midweek," she said. "That will give them a few days' notice."

"It gives you time to give a few other people notice, too. You know, like C. J. MacNamara?"

Tammy sucked her lips against her teeth. "How...how did you know?"

"In a town as small as Sedona? With a man as sexy as C.J.? It's all I've heard from the locals when they come into the gallery. 'C.J.'s found himself a city woman.' 'C.J.'s chasing some executive skirt.' Tammy, he's not your type."

"I know," Tamara said immediately, but her voice wasn't firm. How would Patty know what her type was? a little part of her cried. She quashed the voice ruthlessly.

"He just likes the chase."

"I know."

"The minute he thinks you're interested, that will be the end of it. Ask around, Tamara. There isn't a red-blooded woman in a fifty-mile radius who hasn't had her sights set on C. J. MacNamara at one time or another. He's a nice man. He's a sexy man. But he has the attention span of a two-year-old."

"I know."

"I just don't want to see you hurt, Tammy."

"Then stop bringing up his name!" Tamara snapped. Immediately she caught her lower lip with her teeth, as if she could bite back the harsh words. Too late. Patty had recoiled a step. Now her face was clearly masked. "I'm...I'm sorry," Tamara said weakly. "I'm not sleeping well. I'm on edge."

The silence still felt tense. After a moment, Patty pushed a coffee cup in Tamara's direction. Then the cream. Then the sugar. Now Tamara could see that her friend's hands were shaking. And for the first time, she took notice of the shadows staining Patty's green eyes, the gaunt lines of her cheek. The past week had taken its toll on her as well, and Tamara had never appreciated that. She was ashamed.

"You know, Tamara," Patty said stiffly, clutching her white porcelain coffee cup, "it's never been easy being your friend. You were like this little princess with two perfect parents who doted on you, and Shawn, who adored you. Even before my mom got sick, my parents were always going at each other. And boys...well, what boys wanted from me *wasn't* a relationship. I was the popular one, the fun one, but you, Tamara, you were the one everyone *loved*."

"That's not true—"

Patty held up her hand. "And you deserved it," she said quietly. "You really were sweet, kind, sugar and spice. When my mom died, you were the one who was there for me. When I was angry, you hugged me. When I yelled at you, you forgave me. I was the rebel, and you were the choirgirl."

"You were going through a rough time."

"You shared your family with me, and you never complained."

"You were my best friend!"

"But Tamara, after the accident, you were gone. My father said you'd been taken to some special hospital in New York, and that was that. I didn't see or hear from you again until six months ago. Suddenly you have this idea to pursue the senator. You need me to check on this, you need me to pretend that. Suddenly, you're putting my life on the line and I can't say no to you, Tamara, because you once gave me your whole family. How can I refuse anything to you now? But it's not the same. You're not the same. You've changed, Tamara. You're...you're much more brittle now. Driven. Self-centered. You've become hard."

Tamara was too stunned to reply. Patty abruptly opened the refrigerator door. "Orange juice?"

"No," Tamara said weakly. She was having a hard time hearing herself above the ringing in her ears. She couldn't argue with what Patty said. It was all true. And it hurt her a great deal more than she would've expected to hear it put into words. *You're much more brittle now. You've become hard.*

She hadn't meant for it to happen. She hadn't meant to become this cold, frigid creature, more at home in a boardroom than with her childhood friend. But after the accident, there didn't seem to be anything to believe in anymore. Her parents had died on her, Shawn had died on her. Even God had abandoned her. Suddenly there was just herself and a horrible pain she had to learn to overcome on her own. No one to lean on, no one to help her. No one to believe in.

And all of a sudden, she felt a burst of raw anger. She wanted to grab Patty, shake her and cry, *"If I was so sweet, so wonderful, why didn't you ever come to the hospital? Why didn't you ever realize how much I needed to see you, any familiar face? I took you into my family when you needed support. But where were you when I needed support?"*

She recoiled, taking a step back from the counter. She wasn't prepared for such a thought or its intensity. Now she looked at Patty and she saw the red haze hanging between them like a gauzy curtain. Patty's anger, because Tamara had been in a car accident when Patty had needed Tamara and her family to be immortal. Tamara's anger, because Patty hadn't been there when Tamara had needed someone to hold her hand and make her feel less alone. Had the haze always been there? Patty always resenting Tamara's "princess" life and Tamara just too naive to see it?

No, there was a friendship there once. I know we were friends!

But she wasn't so sure. She wasn't sure of anything anymore.

"I should go," Tamara announced. Her voice sounded shaky. "You're right. It was selfish of me to call you. So much has changed. I should've considered that. I shouldn't have been so presumptuous."

Patty's chin was up mutinously, her pale face like hard sculpture, but her sapphire eyes glistened.

"I'll call you before I leave for New York," Tamara whispered.

"Fine."

"Patty...thank you for being my friend when we were younger. I didn't mind sharing my family with you. I thought of you as becoming my sister. I'd always wanted a sister."

Patty's face crumpled. A tear spilled over and ran slowly down her cheek. Then another. Then another.

"I'm so sorry," she whispered abruptly. "For what I've said. For what I've done. Oh, Tamara, I feel so awful. All the time, this huge knot in my chest... You have no idea." She turned away. The tears had become a small flood.

"I should go now," Tamara repeated. She didn't know what to do or say. She felt wooden.

"That would be best."

"I'll call you before I leave."

"Sure."

"Goodbye."

Tamara made it back out to the street. She should've called a taxi from Patty's place. There wasn't another house for a mile. She didn't go back to the house. She couldn't bear to return. She started walking, feeling the cool tendrils of morning against her cheek.

The end of friendship was like breaking up with a long-time lover. She had to concentrate on putting one foot in front of the other, and though she was too exhausted to cry, she felt a huge hole in her chest. She kept walking.

"Ain't no one who's going to walk for you. Ain't no one who's going to walk for you."

I know, Ben. I learned, I learned. I learned too much.

C.J. woke up early and ready to go. For a moment, he just knew he was happy and excited about the day, though he couldn't remember why. Then it came to him—Tamara's visit to his bar, his promise to pick her up this morning and bring her to her car. He'd get to see Tamara. Probably, he would even kiss her again. His body was already hard and hot with anticipation. He rolled over with a groan and stared at the exposed beams of his cabin's ceiling.

"Oh, man," he muttered, "I got it bad."

But the thought didn't keep him from whistling merrily as he crawled out of bed and into the shower. He'd pack another picnic lunch. That seemed to work well the first time, and it would give him a good excuse to spend the afternoon with Tamara. Plus, it was obvious she wasn't eating enough. A hearty turkey sandwich, potato salad and fresh fruit would be just what the doctor ordered. He knew the perfect deli where he could pick it all up.

He finished sluicing the moisture from his body with his hands, grabbed a towel and attacked his hair. Five minutes later, the towel precariously perched around his lean hips, he lathered up his face and prepared to shave.

Of course, the phone rang. He eyed his white-frosted cheeks in the mirror.

"Let the machine get it? Hmm, what if it's her?" He shook his head and informed his reflection quite seriously, "You're getting just a little bit punch-drunk over this woman, don't you think? Whatever happened to Love 'em and leave 'em MacNamara?"

Love 'em and leave 'em MacNamara was too worried she would be on the phone and he'd miss her call. He gave up on dignity, swiped up the receiver and implanted it in his shaving-cream-covered cheek.

"C.J.'s Taxidermy. You snuff 'em, we stuff 'em."

At the other end of the line there was a long silence. C.J. sighed. "MacNamara's," he said more formally.

The silence grew. He could hear the distant sound of static, as if the person was calling from a long way away. Then a voice came over the line, slow and distorted.

"C. J. MacNamara?" The voice was dragged out in eerie, metallic tones.

C.J. stiffened. He could feel goose bumps on his back now. Automatically, his gaze moved to his front door. It was still locked. He saw no one through his windows. He moved toward his gun, senses alert.

"Yes," he said finally. "Who is this?"

"C. J. MacNamara?"

"Yes, this is C.J. Who the hell are you?"

"That's…not…important." The voice rose. The chilly sound of tinny laughter swept over the line. "Ferringer's son. The one who went to Iceland."

C.J. grabbed for his Baretta. He couldn't breathe. A tightness gripped his chest, like a vice squeezing his ribs. His knuckles had gone white on the phone. "Who is this?"

"Stay away from Tamara Allistair."

"Who the hell is this?"

"You're interfering in things you don't understand."

"Who the hell is this?"

"Your father's body was never found. Haven't you ever wondered why it was never found?"

"If you don't tell me who the hell this is, I'll… I'll…"

"Hang up the phone." The laughter was ghostly. "C. J. MacNamara, the marine, the bounty-hunter son. We've been watching you for a long time. We've been interested. You're almost as good as your father. You're just a little too straight."

C.J. was hunched over now. His ears were ringing, his stomach tensed. He felt like he was going to faint. Worse, vomit. Be violently ill. He hated the voice speaking about his father, about him, and yet he couldn't make it go away. The voice was the first connection to his father he'd had in over twenty years and the voice knew it.

"What do you want?"

"Leave Tamara Allistair alone."

"I don't even know who that is." But then, of course, he did. Tamara Thompson. Tamara Allistair. She'd lied about so many other things, why not her name?

"Stay away from her," the voice intoned. "She's not your concern."

The rebel in him rose instantly. "Damn you," he barked.

"You are like your father."

"I'm nothing like Max!"

The voice was still amused. "Do this for us and maybe someday we'll help you."

"What can you help me with? I don't even know who you are."

"We know about Max," the voice whispered. "Maybe someday we'll even tell you."

C.J. was going to be sick. He pressed his hand against his stomach, but it didn't help. Some little part of him fought to say yes, struggled to push out his throat and yell, "Yes, yes, I'll do anything if you'll just tell me about my father." It was the little boy in him who could never believe that his larger-than-life father had just gone. The little boy in him who clutched the memory of Iceland after all these years because it was the only good memory he had.

He whispered into the phone, "Go to hell."

The voice replied just as firmly, "Stay away from Tamara Allistair."

The line went dead, and in a final burst of emotion, C.J. hurled the phone on the floor. It shattered, the bits and pieces spraying his ankles. He remained hunched over, his elbows pressed against his thighs as he hung his head between his knees and struggled for air. Finally, the white spots gone before his eyes, he straightened. He took another deep breath. He crossed back to the sink and picked up his razor.

The face in the mirror wasn't smiling anymore. The blue eyes didn't crinkle with secret humor. They were hard, they were fierce. They were angry.

He shaved cleanly, the movements precise and efficient. Five minutes later, he stormed out the door, his Baretta tucked in his waistband. He stilled for a minute in his front yard. His Scirocco was still up on blocks, but the racing tires, neatly stacked in the corner, had all been slashed.

"Dammit. Dammit, dammit."

He found his Mustang and gave it a thorough checkup while the muscle twitched in his jaw. His Mustang was untouched. No, the voice was still playing games and delivering warnings. The racing tires were only worth about eight hundred dollars, but the fact that someone could get that close to his house without his knowledge—that was costly.

And it wouldn't be happening again. He'd teach that damn voice to play with C. J. MacNamara.

He climbed into his car and peeled out without preamble. He was going to find Tamara Allistair. And this time, she would be doing a helluva lot of talking.

"Who the hell are you?"

Tamara had just cracked open her hotel door when C.J. exploded through the two-inch space. Now he backed her up all the way, like a lion cornering prey. His face was dark, his blue eyes narrow. His shoulders filled the space, muscles bunching dangerously and stretching the thin fabric of his T-shirt. He advanced farther, his attention honed in on her like a laser, his features screwed into a horrible glower.

"Who the hell are you?"

"What...what?" The backs of her legs hit the king-size bed. She couldn't retreat any farther. She bent backward, but it was no use. He leaned over her, his breath expelling onto her cheek, his nostrils flaring. Abruptly, his gaze latched on to the open suitcase behind her.

"Packing up? So eager to leave?" In one smooth move, he ripped her suitcase onto the floor, sending the clothes flying. She flinched, still pinned by his body against the bed.

"Tuesday," she barely whispered, wetting her lips to get the words out.

"Why are you packing now?"

"I...I wanted to. It made it seem more final."

"When were you going to start telling me the truth...Ms. Allistair."

She froze. His angry words hung between them, and she couldn't summon a reply. His hard, muscled chest was pushing against her. She could feel the heat of his skin and smell the fresh fragrance of aftershave. His tanned jawline was smooth, his lean cheeks damp. This close, she could see a faint sheen of moisture up by his earlobe. Lower on his neck, she spotted a ruby red pinprick of blood. His hair was water-darkened to a honey wheat and rolled back from his square face in waves. Normally, a wayward lock dangled over his forehead, breaking up the harsh lines of his stubborn features, giving him a reckless charm. Today, even his hair was obedient, and his eyes burned into her with incredible force of will.

Her gaze fell to his hands, those strong, capable, firm hands that had captured her attention from the very beginning. They were knotted into fists, the tension so tight, sinew sprang up like roping veins on his forearms. His arms were slightly bent, ready for action. His biceps rippled, cleanly defined. He was clearly on edge.

She licked her lips again. Her mouth was still dry. Her gaze came to rest on his lips.

"Don't," he growled.

"What?" she whispered.

"Don't think you can buy me off with your *charms*." He practically spat the word.

"I don't think that," she said honestly. But she was acutely aware of the soft, worn fabric of his jeans barely containing the tensed muscles of his thighs. She felt his hip nestled against hers. And slowly, as she stood there feeling her breath grow shallow and listening to his own harsh breathing suddenly still, she knew the awareness was washing over him, too. The moment suspended, lengthened, and then with almost an audible pop, the air between them seemed to burst into flame.

Suddenly the worn fabric of his T-shirt was rough and uncomfortable against her. She resented it fiercely, wanted it gone, pictured it on the floor and his naked torso bared for her touch. She hated his jeans, his belt buckle, his boots.

Her hands were twitching at her sides, her lips parting, her brow growing shiny with a light sheen of moisture. She wore a fine linen shirt in creamy yellow and expensive linen slacks in chocolate brown. She wanted the fragile, overpriced fabric ripped from her frame and tossed on the ground. She wanted his mouth on hers again, without gentleness, without coaxing.

She wanted him to lose control. She wanted C. J. MacNamara ravishing her, devouring her, consuming her.

Maybe if he lost his control, she would be able to lose hers. Maybe the darkness would leave her, the growing heaviness of too many sleepless nights and too many emotions would finally depart. She could throw herself at this man with all the vengeance and fury and hurt and pain she had. He would meet her halfway. He would take it and demand more. She knew it. He would take her outside herself, strip the unbearable sense of isolation from her once and for all.

They remained standing there, bodies touching but not hands. Pulse rates joining and soaring, but minds still battling. She felt him grow hard against her hip, his flesh become a ridged line that dug into her softest spot, making her want to shift a little closer. Making her want to whimper. Making her damp.

"Who are you?" he growled low, the words whispering across her lips.

"Tamara Allistair," she murmured, no defenses left.

"Why did you lie?"

"I just wanted to be safe."

"You think the senator killed your family in a hit-and-run accident? That's why you came back? That's why you broke into the campaign war room?"

"I thought so, but I was wrong."

His eyes narrowed, squeezing her down even as his body shifted closer, his arousal pressing into her. Her eyes drifted shut helplessly. She couldn't think anymore. She wanted to dig her fingers into his strong shoulders. Her hands remained fisted on her side, resisting that last capitulation.

"How do you know, Tamara?"

"No red car," she murmured. "The senator doesn't even drive when he's in town. A car service does it for him."

"So who did it?"

"I don't know. I have no idea. It was ten years ago, and I can't find any leads. Honestly. Please..." Her hips shifted against him helplessly. She wanted, she needed. She couldn't stand her own skin anymore.

Her eyes opened. She gazed at him without guile. *Take me. Strip the control from me. I am so unbelievably tired.*

His eyes darkened. A muscle flinched in his jaw, and his breathing became loud and ragged in the silence. "Why should I believe you now?" he said, grinding the words out. "Why the hell should I trust anything you say?"

"Because I need you to," she whispered simply. "Because...I want you."

He succumbed, his groan angry and furious and as needy as hers. Finally his hands moved. He gripped her shoulders, he held her back one last minute, giving her time to pull away, and when she simply remained in his arms, he yanked her against him and devoured her mouth.

Her hands fisted his shirt. She angled her head back and gave her mouth to him completely, welcoming his tongue as he raked it across her teeth. Opening to him so he could plunge into her mouth. Her hands moved on his shoulders, rubbing, squeezing, yanking him even closer. His clothes enraged her. She wanted him naked, wanted everything gone, hot, slick skin pressed against hot, slick skin. She wanted desperately to feel all the things she'd never thought she could feel.

Abruptly, he pushed her back onto the bed. She dragged him down with her, finding the hem of his shirt and pulling it off his body. She sucked her breath in. He was poised above her, his strong thighs clamping her hips, his torso bent over hers. He had such smooth, golden skin, as if it had spent a lifetime being kissed by the sun. On his chest, a delicate mat of honey blond hair swirled in patterns. She ran her fingers through it, marveling at the fine, silky touch.

His eyes were still dark, his jaw clenched in his effort at control. But she saw something else in him now. With the passion, with the fury, was tenderness. He would not hurt her. He would not force her. He would not use her.

Her eyes began to sting. She was horribly afraid she was going to cry.

"The light," she whispered.

"What?" His voice was hoarse. His hand had settled on the full, delicate curve of her breast. She arched her back helplessly, feeling his fingers like fire through the fine fabric.

"The light. Please." She needed the darkness to hide the myriad scars that kept her body from being as fine and beautiful as his.

He snapped off the bedside lamp. Her shades were still pulled from the night, blocking the sun and forming total darkness. In this murky abyss, she could finally open her eyes and let the first tear squeeze out.

She ran her hands across his shoulders, drawing a line with her thumbs along his collarbone. She squeezed his muscled shoulders, working her hands down his arms, finding the curve of his triceps, the muscled swell of his biceps. His skin reminded her of hot satin, stretched by his bones and muscle, giving him the sleek lines of a jungle cat. She memorized him by touch, finding the tender indent of his elbow and the rough, raspy pads of his palms. Her hands flattened on his stomach, and she heard him inhale sharply.

Abruptly, his fingers were on her shirt. Nimble and quick, he felled the buttons one by one and wrestled the fabric from her body. Her bra, a sensible white lace, was whisked aside and suddenly his bare torso pressed against her bare torso and the hot, electric feel made them both gasp in the silence.

"I want you," he muttered thickly, fiercely. "God, Tamara, I want you!"

She wrapped her arms around his neck and kissed him hard. It was no longer slow or tender. They rolled and wrestled on the bed, their tongues dueling, their hands tearing. Belts and pants and socks and shoes and underwear flew in panting, gasping flight. His legs were long and lean and dusted with fine hair that prickled her skin and made her rub her legs against him helplessly. His hands were plunging into her thick hair, sweeping it back from her face so his lips could nuzzle her earlobes, her throat, her breast. His mouth closed over her nipple and sucked so hard it was almost painful. Her hips arched up, her leg wrapping around his lean hips and positioning him against her intimately. She could feel him, hard and hot. He was big and swollen. She had no idea how he would ever fit in her slender frame, but the feel of him rubbing against her, teasing her folds, was making her crazy.

His mouth switched to her other breast. She dug her fingers into his scalp, urging him closer.

"Please..."

"Not yet." In a quick move, he rose up, snapped his hands around her wrists and pinned her hands above her head. She writhed helplessly, wanting to hold him against her, wanting his body deep within hers. "I want to know you, Tamara. I want to know everything."

He ducked his head down. He nuzzled her throat again, rubbing his smooth cheek against her like a purring cat and making her smile. Then he was licking her throat, and the delicious tingles made her giggle and squirm, then giggle some more because it had been so long since she'd last giggled. He mouthed her shoulder like a toothless old man, then switched back to a hot, searing kiss that made her moan, breathless and fierce as her hips arched against him once more.

He drifted lower. Even in the dark, his lips found her scars, the long, smooth lines of snaking tissue that divided and separated the soft flesh of her belly. She felt him pause. She turned her face into the mattress, understanding that she wasn't pretty, she wasn't beautiful. She was a woman with too many scars, too many reminders of a night she could never quite leave behind her. And even now, in the shadowed darkness of this room, in the protective embrace of this man, she mourned.

He whispered his lips over the first scar, then the second. He kissed them softly. He kissed them reverently, as if he would heal them for her if he could. If she would ever let him.

He rose up. She parted her legs wordlessly and immediately. She wanted him. For one moment, she wanted something beautiful.

Her legs wrapped around his flanks. He planted his hands on each side of her head. He positioned himself against her, and she sucked in her breath.

Slowly, he eased into her, her damp, silky skin stretching, easing, folding around him tightly and drawing him in. Then he was sheathed fully inside her and she arched her hips helplessly, striving for some respite from the tingling, hungry restlessness shooting through her belly.

She was acutely aware of him inside her. The feel of his flesh, stretching hers. The unique sensation of being conquered, of being taken. The power of him. The size of him. The pleasure.

He moved. Her eyes opened wide. Sweat bloomed across her skin. Desire flooded her veins. Her limbs grew heavy, her thoughts spun away. Her universe narrowed down to his body impaled in hers, his body moving inside her, his voice whispering her name.

She needed... Oh, God, she needed.

She could feel the hunger building. Foreign and mysterious and exotic. She gasped, her hips writhing. She struggled against him, seeking something she couldn't name and feeling his strong body shudder.

She was so close, so unbelievably close.

"Take it, Tamara. Take it."

And then suddenly she couldn't. She was afraid. Terrified. The need was bigger than her, out of her control. She couldn't lose that much control. She couldn't give that much of herself away.

The fear washed through her like a cold wave, dousing the passion, leaving her still.

"Tamara..." C.J. growled.

She turned her head against the mattress and squeezed her eyes shut with her shame. She dug her fingers into his flanks. She arched her hips.

"It's okay," she whispered. "It's okay."

"Dammit," he muttered. "Dammit." But then it was too much for him. His body vowed, his neck arched. He groaned again, his body suspended above hers as if in agony. But when she looked at his face, she saw only a pleasure she'd never known.

He collapsed on top of her, his body still shuddering with the aftermath. She stroked his shoulders and did her best to hold back her tears.

Chapter 8

Tamara. C.J. felt her breathing finally ease. Wordlessly, he rolled to the side, then cradled her slender body against him, her head pillowed on his arm, her naked back curved against his torso. She didn't say anything.

"Are you all right?" he asked at last. He felt awkward. He didn't remember the last time he'd felt awkward in bed with a woman. Of course, he didn't remember the last time he hadn't satisfied his partner.

"I'm tired," she whispered. Her voice was hoarse.

He stroked her hair for a moment, trying to figure out what to do. Finally, he simply held her. And as minute turned into minute, he felt the last bit of tension drain from her body. A few minutes more and he could tell that she'd drifted to sleep.

Tamara. He stroked the thick silk of her hair, he stroked the long, slender line of her arm. He'd fantasized about her since the first night he'd met her. He'd hungered for her, imagined making love to her. Certainly, he'd imagined it ending a little differently than it had. When she was rested, he had every intention of discussing it, too.

Odd how life worked. This morning, after receiving the phone call, sex had been the farthest thing from his mind. He'd been prepared to hate her. Prepared to fight with her. Hell, prepared to tie her up and wrest every last bit of knowledge from her.

Instead, he'd fallen faster and louder than a three-hundred-year-old oak. He'd wound up taking her to bed and... And realizing once more that she was an incredibly complex woman. A woman who'd been through a lot. A woman who was still making the journey from that dark place where you lived after losing the people you loved.

He should've been slower with her. He should've taken more time, helped her relax more.

The air-conditioning became too cold. He found the edges of the comforter and wrapped it around them, spooning his body against hers. Beneath the covers, he splayed his fingers over her belly and found her scars.

There were so many scars, varying in size and length. This one along the side of her hip. This one cutting across. This one small and slender, almost like a delicate web. They bore mute testimony to her story and convinced him once and for all that she had finally told him the truth.

What had it been like for her, driving along with her family one minute, waking up in a hospital the next and hearing that her family was gone? Had there been anyone to hold her? Friends or distant family? A kind nurse?

If something ever happened to Maggie, he, Brandon and Lydia would move heaven and earth to be at her side. No one should have to go through that kind of trauma alone. Just...no one.

Suddenly, he was angry. Deeply, darkly, intensely angry. Tamara had been robbed of something precious. Worse, she'd been forced to deal with it alone. It wasn't right. She should've had a Lydia. She should've had Maggie and Brandon. God knows, Maggie would offer comfort to a granite statue—and probably get the marble to finally break down and cry.

C.J. pressed Tamara more tightly against him, as if on this late date it would make a difference. Of course it didn't. She had suffered the accident alone and survived alone. And judging by the car she drove and the clothes she wore, she'd built a very successful life. She'd just had to repress most of her anger and grief to do it.

Had anyone ever spoken to her about post-traumatic stress disorder? He was hardly an expert, but she'd certainly gone through a major trauma, and her insomnia, flashes of rage, even her drinking at his bar, could all be symptoms. Had she undergone any counseling? Would she ever admit she needed that kind of help?

His lips thinned in the dark. If there was one thing he knew about Tamara, it was that she made his stubborn streak look mild. She would probably admit she needed help with about the same graciousness Brandon would. Which meant not at all.

God, he was crazy about her.

How do I get you to trust me, Tamara?

And what does your car accident have to do with my father?

Frustrated and slightly fearful, C.J. gave up on finding immediate answers. He closed his eyes and drifted to sleep.

Tamara woke up groggy and disoriented. It had been so long since she'd slept, truly and deeply slept, that a part of her fought waking. She wanted to remain in the black abyss, where the world was peaceful and a strong, comforting form held her in a cradling embrace. She'd dreamt of being held. In her dreams, she stopped fighting the pain of her shattered pelvis and her shattered leg. In her dreams, her broken body floated away and Shawn was with her again, young and earnest. This time, he didn't let her go. This time, nobody left her alone.

Tamara woke up. And she stilled.

"Don't," C. J. MacNamara whispered against the top of her head.

"What?" she murmured weakly. The words were shrill with uncertainty and panic.

He rolled her onto her back and regarded her steadily. "Don't run. Don't pretend we didn't make love."

She couldn't produce a reply. She wanted to tell him he didn't know her that well, but that would've proved her a fool. He did know her that well. There was no one on earth who knew her better. And yes, at this precise moment, she wanted to run.

She shut her eyes. She wasn't a child. She refused to act like one. She was a scared adult and, well, adulthood was scary.

She finally released her breath. C.J. still wasn't wearing any clothes. She could feel the crisp hair on his legs brushing the backs of her thighs. His groin nestled her hip. She could feel him against her, soft but beginning to grow and lengthen with that first swell of desire. For a moment, she wanted to push against him, throw her leg over his flanks and nestle him more tightly into her.

And then what?

And then what?

She turned away, shamed by her own inadequacy.

"We should talk about it," C.J. said quietly.

"There's nothing to talk about. It wasn't your fault. It's just…it's just the way I am. How long did I sleep?"

"Only forty-five minutes. You look like you could still use some sleep."

"I'm fine. I feel much better."

"Mule-headed idiot." He caught her chin and turned her toward him until she had no choice but to meet his gaze. His blond hair was rumpled, waving over his forehead the way it should. His blue eyes were serious, but the corners crinkled. He had pillow creases on his cheek.

He looked unbelievably sexy, and that made her feel worse.

"Tamara, I want to help you—"

"I'm not one of your special little projects."

"Of course not. They're all a lot more gracious than you. Sweetheart, I care about you. And so help me God, I've wanted to make love to you since the first time I saw you driving. And I wanted you to enjoy it as much as I did. I wanted it to be about us."

"It's not your fault—"

"Has anyone ever spoken to you about post-traumatic stress disorder?"

"What?"

"Look at you, sweetheart. You have shadows under your eyes thicker than a black velvet Elvis painting, and it's obvious you've lost weight."

Her hand curled over her protruding pelvis bone automatically. C.J. drew it back.

"I think you're very beautiful, Tamara. It's obvious I'm attracted to you. And not just your body. I like your intelligence, I like your strength. Hell, I even like the fact that you're stubborn, though that probably makes me insane. But I'm also very worried about you."

"Don't. I don't need you to be—"

"Tell me about it, Tamara. Tell me all about what happened ten years ago. I need to hear it, and, honey, you need to talk about it. You really do."

"I don't like to talk about it."

"I know. Do it, anyway."

Tamara appeared troubled. When they'd been making love, her eyes had burned gold, like a tiger's. Now they were a deep, luminescent brown, the fire burnt out and leaving them dull. He pulled her closer against him. He tucked the covers around her to make her feel warm and safe. And he willed her to speak to him because he hadn't been lying. He needed to know, and she needed to tell.

Finally, she said, "We were coming back from dinner. My parents, my boyfriend, Shawn, and myself. It was my parents' nineteenth wedding anniversary, so we'd gone to Guardo's to celebrate. My mother was wearing a new silk dress in deep bronze. She looked so beautiful...." Her voice trailed off. She swallowed. "My father was driving, of course—he always drove. Shawn and I sat in the back."

"Had your father been drinking?"

"A glass of wine with dinner. He and my mother weren't big drinkers. He liked to have cognac on special occasions or at the end of a long day, that was it."

"Had the other driver been drinking?"

"Possibly. The other car swerved into our lane. I don't remember seeing it. There was a full moon out that night and the sky was clear. I remember being very happy, and holding Shawn's hand, and thinking that someday we'd have a nineteenth wedding anniversary, too. And then I heard my mother cry out."

C.J. held her closer. She felt fragile, but her voice was strong.

"I don't remember much after that. I heard my mother shout at my father, and the next thing I knew, I was on the side of the road and the moon was straight above me. I was very cold, which was strange, because the evening had been in the seventies. Shawn's hand was still in mine, but I couldn't see him. I could turn my head only a little, and I couldn't move my legs. My hips felt like they were on fire. I was so cold."

"It's okay," C.J. murmured. "It's okay." She didn't seem to realize it, but goose bumps had broken out all over her body. He rubbed her arms as the chill swept through her.

"Someone leaned over me. I just saw his face—heavy-set, crinkled, short-cropped hair graying at the temples. He looked horrified. I kept waiting for him to do something, to help. Then all of sudden, he turned and ran away. I heard a car start up and peel out. Then I could only hear my mother crying.

"He didn't come back. No one came. Shawn spoke for a bit. He kept saying someone would come, but his voice was weakening. I listened to him pray."

Her voice broke off. Her gaze was fastened far away, as if peering off into other times. The desolation was finely etched into her composed, still features.

"I think my father died on impact. My mom cried for a bit, but then she was silent. I listened to Shawn's voice fade, waiting for someone to come. He died before the sun came up. And then I was alone, hearing just the crickets, waiting for my turn."

"Oh, sweetheart—"

"Don't. I don't want you to be horrified, even if it's horrifying. I don't want you staring at me with pity even if you think I deserve it. And I don't want you looking at me and seeing only the accident, because, dammit, when I look in the mirror, that's all I see, and it's not enough. It was one horrible, horrible night and it has to end. I just... It has to end!"

"I know, I know. Sh." He wrapped her in his arms. She felt delicate, and he knew he was doing exactly what she'd told him not to do—he was treating her as if she were made out of glass. Dammit, he didn't care. He wanted to comfort her. He *needed* to comfort her. And if he ever met the person who hurt her family, he figured he'd need to break every bone in his body, starting with the toes and moving up from there.

That was it. A man had needs.

Suddenly, Tamara moved. She buried her face against his shoulder and wrapped her arms around him. Her whole body began to shake. She trembled, not speaking, not sobbing, but trembling, trembling, trembling, like a shipwreck survivor. His hands splayed across her naked back. He swung his heavy leg over her hip, pulling her tightly against him. He wrapped his whole, lean body around hers and rocked her back and forth until finally she was sobbing.

He held her. He would hold her into the new millennium if that's what it took. Because, dammit, someone should've held her long before this. Someone should've let her fall apart, just so she would know that it was okay. Everyone fell apart sometime. And everyone learned how to put themselves back together.

Her body grew soft and damp against his, her muscles exhausted and pliant. He rubbed her back for a bit, letting the last of the emotion drain out of her as her sobs quieted. Then he slid his knuckles beneath her chin and slowly tipped back her head.

Her eyes were large, moist and tear-stained. Her long, thick lashes were spiky, her cheeks pale and framed by a thick matting of dark, lush hair. Her lips parted soundlessly.

"How long has it been since you've let yourself cry?" he whispered.

"I cried too much in the beginning. It didn't change anything."

"And so you bottled it all up, didn't you."

"What was I supposed to do? Sob and feel sorry for myself? Lie in the hospital bed and mourn? They were gone. Nothing, no one, could bring them back. And I had doctors all around me, talking about fractures and breaks and internal ruptures. Debating how long it would take for my bones to heal, what were my chances of walking again. How many surgeries would it take?

"You don't understand, C.J. I *had* to get on with things. Healing for me wasn't lying in a bed. I had to learn how to sit up on a shattered pelvis, how to pull myself onto a wheelchair, how to pull myself from the wheelchair onto a toilet. When my fractured leg and pelvis had healed enough, I had to learn how to stand. I had to learn how to balance again, how to walk again. Dammit, I had to put together puzzles!''

"Puzzles?"

"Puzzles! That's what they do so you have something to distract yourself with while you try to get your legs to relearn something as pedantic as standing. You stand up and you put together puzzles for as long as you can handle it.''

"You mean like those one-thousand-piece jigsaw puzzles?"

She scowled, her temper returning, her eyes beginning to glow gold. He didn't try to allay her anger, because it allowed her to discard the last of her grief and fall back on her natural strength. She was very strong.

"One thousand-piece puzzles?" she cried. "Are you kidding? My first puzzle was some six-piece thing meant for two-year-olds, and I was out of breath and in unbelievable pain just to slap those six pieces together. I'd just finally got to the puzzles for children ages eight to twelve when they decided my fractured leg was never going to set on its own and sent me back for a bone graft. Then I started all over again. Puzzles for children ages two to four. Made it up to ages ten to twelve, and my knee gave out once and for all. Back to surgery I went. This time I get a whole new knee.'' She rapped her left leg. "Made from the finest metal with a plastic liner, and good for twenty-five years or 150,000, miles whatever comes first.''

"You have a fake knee?"

"Yes, I do, as well as enough pins and plates to hold together the Eiffel Tower. Basically, I'm seventy percent scar tissue and five percent metal and plastic. I travel with X rays these days just for the airport security systems, and I have my own money-back guarantee. Better yet, in another five to ten years, I'm going to have surgery again. Fake knees don't last forever. And then—'' she scowled "—then I'll get to reenter PT and play with puzzles!''

"It won't be as bad," he tried diplomatically.

"I hate puzzles," she told him clearly.

"Then we'll find something else for you. Maybe a game to play. See how long you can stand and beat the socks off of me in Monopoly. Playing against an invalid may be the only way I ever win at that game."

Her face fell. "Don't. Don't promise things you can't deliver."

"What can't I deliver, Tamara? You don't like Monopoly? You think after decades of being one of the top-selling games it suddenly won't exist?"

"You alluded to the future. That's a very dangerous thing."

"Well, we're naked and wrapped in a blanket together. Call me old-fashioned, but I've been thinking about the future."

"No. No, you're not. I've heard all about you, C. J. MacNamara, and you're not a 'future' kind of guy. So don't lie to me and don't mislead me. Don't think that because I've been through a few things, you have to handle me with kid gloves. I've brought junior account managers to tears before and don't you forget it!"

"Tamara, I don't think you're fragile."

"I'm not some injured woman for you to save." Abruptly, she was struggling with the enshrouding covers, kicking at them vehemently. "The accident was ten years ago. I've moved on."

"No. Dammit!" He snapped his hand around her wrist just as she broke free from the covers. She didn't want him to treat her like she was made out of glass? Fine. He flipped her onto her back, straddled her thighs and pinned her on the bed. Her eyes turned to pure gold menace.

"Let me go!"

"So help me God, Tamara, you run so fast, pinning you on your back is the only way I can keep you in place long enough to finish a sentence. One of these days, I'm going to buy handcuffs just for you.''

"I am not enjoying this!"

"Then, listen to me. Cut me some slack. You just accused me of manipulating your feelings and lying to you. I don't deserve that."

Her breath escaped as a muted hiss. Her eyes glowed with dark promises of retribution, but she didn't refute his statement.

"Dammit, I'm more than a little bit interested in you. No man in his right mind would put up with everything I've put up with if he was just looking for sex."

"Conquest," she muttered. "Challenge."

"Well, you are challenging—no argument here."

"Compensation."

"Compensation? What the hell are you talking about? I make a good living on my own."

"Your mother." She fired the words out. "You didn't save your mother, C.J. So now you're trying to save the rest of us. You're not the only one who can play psychoanalyst."

Her voice was injured, raw. For a moment, he was too stunned to speak. He felt a lot of things. Anger. Outrage. And beneath all that, fear. He had wanted to save his mother. He had *believed* that he could. If he was just smart enough, clever enough, strong enough... But he hadn't. And now it was laid out in black and white, C.J.'s secret failing. The failing so big that even late at night when he was all alone and protected by the shadows, he didn't bring it out and contemplate it. It made him feel too small, like a fraud.

"I...I thought I could keep her well," he said quietly.

"You were just a kid." Tamara's voice had softened.

His gaze latched on to the patch of pillow next to her head. Abruptly, his jaw hardened. He shook his head. "No. I wanted to save her, Tamara. And maybe that made me naive or arrogant or something, but I tried and I failed and I feel like I failed. *But—*" he looked her in the eye "—I don't confuse you with my mother, Tamara. When I look at you, I don't see my frail mother dying in a cheap apartment. I see a strong, vibrant woman with incredible wit and passion. I see good values, I see a sense of honor and pride and dignity. I see someone who interests me very much, someone who attracts me very much. I see someone I want to get to know a helluva lot better."

"C.J.... I'm going back to New York."

"Why?" he demanded fiercely.

"I've got a good job there, I've got a good life!"

"Really, Tamara? So why did you come back to Sedona at all? Why now, after all these years?"

Her mouth opened, but she hadn't a good defense, and they both knew it. The answer was just there: Her life wasn't so great. Her career wasn't so wonderful.

"I've been there, too, Tamara," C.J. said quietly. "I lost my parents. I know what it's like to be that sad. And I know what it's like to be that angry. My grandma helped get me through it. But you haven't had anyone help you deal with everything. And that's why you came back."

"There's nothing to deal with," she whispered mutinously, but her heart wasn't in it.

"Nightmares, right? That's why you're not getting enough sleep. Anger at odd moments. The inability to plan ahead. Moments of stupefying terror when you're in the middle of doing something simple like climbing aboard an airplane, or car, or boat. And an unbelievable sense of guilt, because you're alive and they're not. Then more guilt because you are angry at them for leaving and that makes you feel even worse."

"Stop it! I don't want to talk about it. It doesn't change anything. They're *dead.*"

"But you're not, and you have to learn a bit more to get on with the business of living!"

"I am!" she insisted. "I have a job, a car, a co-op. I have friends and a social life."

"Yeah, Tamara, and you're so damn repressed you can't even accept a stranger's offer of assistance when your car goes off the road! Worse, you've got a pretty great guy in bed with you right now telling you how much he cares about you, and you're calling him a liar! You won't even allow yourself to enjoy sex, because that's about life, isn't it? And you can't let yourself be that alive."

"I want out." She twisted her hips, her heals digging into the bed. The movement arched her against him provocatively, but he was too busy being frustrated to be aroused.

"That's it. Run away, Tamara. Just keep running, even though some part of you must know better, because you do eventually come back."

"Sure, fine, whatever." She fought more vehemently, her face a fierce, unreachable mask. Abruptly, he released her. He could tell by her expression that he wasn't going to make any progress now.

She practically bolted from the bed. In the shadowed room, the sun fighting the blinds for entrance, she began to hastily retrieve her clothes and yank them on. C.J. remained naked on the bed.

"Sooner or later," he said softly, "you're going to have to trust someone."

"Stop it! Stop analyzing me, stop crawling into my head. For God's sake, you've only known me five days. You don't know as much about me as you think."

"I know enough. Tamara… Dammit, you're in a much bigger mess than you realize."

"I'm not in any mess at all." She had her slacks on. Now she forcefully stuffed her shirttails into the waistband. "I came to Sedona and volunteered my PR expertise for Senator Brennan's campaign. End of story."

"So you really are PR?"

"Of course I'm PR!" She sounded exasperated. Her hands swept up the thick strands of her hair, and she ruthlessly tied the swath into a thick knot. Already, she reached for hairpins on the nightstand.

"You've told me several different stories."

"And now I'm telling you the truth. Listen, it's none of your business—"

"Don't insult me." His voice dropped to a growl. She flinched, not quite as sure as herself as she pretended.

"It's not important," she insisted at last, having gotten her hair up. Her transformation was complete, from naked, passionate woman to composed executive in five minutes or less. C.J. still didn't bother to cover himself. He was feeling belligerent on the subject. Her hands settled on her hips. Composed now, she squared off against him.

"I made a mistake, C.J. I was looking for someone to blame. I *wanted* someone to blame. I honestly believed it might be the senator who hurt my family. But I checked it out. It's not him—he had no need for a red sports car. And after all these years, there are no other leads." Her voice dropped, steady and blunt. "I don't think I'll ever know who drove that other car."

C.J. looked at her just as levelly. "Well, whoever it was, they called to tell me to mind my own business. And if I did—then maybe they'd tell me what really happened to my father. Then to prove their point, they slashed the racing tires of my Scirocco."

She paled visibly. "What?"

"I don't know what, Tamara. I don't know what, who, why or how. But I would guess that you haven't been as discreet as you thought and you've been a lot closer than you realized, because someone sure as hell knows what you're up to and wants it stopped."

"No," she began weakly.

C.J. cut her off with one narrow glance. "The holes in your brake line, Tamara. The scorpion in your room."

"No, no." She clenched her hand against her stomach. "I'm a PR executive from New York. I'm a real average, boring human being. Conspiracy theories do not apply to people like me."

"Then, who called me, Tamara? Who the hell would know about my father?"

"I don't know." Her gaze swept up. For a moment, her eyes were pleading. "C.J., honestly, I have no idea who might have called you. I didn't think anyone knew I was back or what I was doing. I've spent most of my time in the senator's war room, surrounded by volunteers—most of whom aren't even from Sedona and didn't know me ten years ago, let alone recognize me now. To everyone, I'm just an executive from New York. Honestly, I've kept a low profile."

"Who knows you're back?"

"Just my best friend, Patty."

"Would she have any reason to tell anyone about your return?"

"Patty? Are you kidding? She's been terrified that someone would find out. I told her just this morning that I was heading back to New York, and frankly, she was relieved. In her opinion, I should be heading back today instead of closing out my volunteer work."

"What about someone else at campaign headquarters?"

"Who? I don't socialize with anyone, I don't really talk to anyone. I do what they ask me to do, which is a lot of writing and editing of press releases, speeches, and so forth. Most of the people there probably don't even know my first name."

"Well, someone knows something, Tamara. And from the call I got this morning, it's someone powerful, someone with connections. Someone who knows someone who knows about my father. Maybe you weren't so wrong about the senator, after all."

"But…but how? He has drivers, he has chauffeured cars. Dark, American-made sedans."

"Do you know that he actually had driver service that evening?"

"Mrs. Winslow said he always uses a service when he's in town."

"Do you know that he actually had a driver service that evening?" C.J. insisted.

"No," she admitted. "I don't know specifically about that evening. I thought of calling the service, but would they really have records of one night ten years ago?"

"Probably not," C.J. agreed. He finally swung his legs over the edge of the bed and picked up his jeans. "We'll have to figure out another way."

"We?"

"We. Like it or not, Tamara, you got me involved in this. If Brandon knew I had an opportunity to learn more about our father and wasn't taking it, he'd personally strip off my hide."

"C.J., why don't you take it? You don't have to help—"

"Stop it," he said angrily. He yanked on his pants with more force than necessary. "Neither you nor Brandon get it. You're both too lost in your grief to move on the way you say you are. My father is dead. I don't care what he did or didn't do. I care about today, and, dammit, I care about you. You may not be willing to believe it, but I think you're in a whole hell of a lot of trouble, Tamara. I think someone knows you're looking for the truth. And I think the brake lines and scorpion were not accidents. Now, come on. I'll take you to your car."

Tamara didn't say anything more. She didn't seem to have any words. C.J. left her to her silence, too frustrated and wound up himself to feel like talking. Too many things didn't make sense. He didn't like things that didn't make sense. And the phone call had upset him. No, it had ticked him off. Hell, maybe a little of both. Worse, it had made him afraid.

He hated being afraid.

When they arrived at the Ancient Mariner, he pulled in next to Tamara's car and killed the engine. She was already popping open the door, anxious to bail out, of course. At least she was consistent.

He watched her wordlessly. Her hands, when she fumbled for her keys, were shaking.

"This isn't over, Tamara."

"I need...I need time to think."

"Fine. Take an hour. I'll pick you up for lunch at one. I want to make some calls."

"C.J.—"

"One o'clock, Tamara."

Her lips thinned, and she looked as if she would argue. Then she dropped her keys and swore. He waited while she bent down to retrieve them. She took a very long time to straighten back up. When she did, her features were ashen.

"C.J.," she whispered. The tone of her voice made his blood run cold.

"What?"

"I think there's a bomb. A bomb, fastened to the bottom of my car."

Please."

Chapter 9

"Okay, sweetheart. Step back real slow."

Tamara remained frozen like a statue. "Do you have a
cell phone?" she whispered. "Call 911."

"Just a minute." C.J. eased out of his car and passed
around to her side. She stared at him with wide, panicked
eyes.

"What are you doing?" she exclaimed harshly, then
abruptly bit her lip as if the volume of her voice might
activate the bomb.

"I have some training in this kind of thing." He got on
all fours and peered beneath the car. "Please stand back."
Sure enough, he could see a brown-paper-wrapped brick
with protruding wires sticking out from between the
shocks of her front driver-side tire.

Tamara had actually moved closer. "What can I do?"
she murmured by his shoulder.

"Dammit, get the hell behind my car. Do you have a
death wish or something?"

"Frankly, that's quite possible." She bent down beside

him, her brown eyes somber. "I need to do something. Please..."

"Stubborn, stubborn fool." He eyed her a minute longer, but it was obvious she wasn't going to run screaming in the other direction. She was too much like him— needing to fight her own battles, to prove to herself that she could. "All right, fetch me the flashlight from my car."

She moved away wordlessly, and he heard her fumbling around in the back of his Mustang. She eased the flashlight into his waiting hand just a moment later. "C.J., you get yourself blown up and I will kill you."

"I'll keep that in mind." He studied the bomb. "All right, sweetheart, what we have here is a solid block of C-4."

"C-4?" She sounded chilled. "Please, let's just call the police."

"It's okay, Tamara. C-4 is pretty stable, so there's no immediate danger. As my sergeant liked to say, you can set the damn stuff on fire, just don't try to stomp out the flames." C.J. parted the black and red wires. The next thing he knew, Tamara was beneath the car right beside him.

"Tell me," she said.

He studied her for a moment. He hadn't lied to her—as long as the car was stationary and they didn't have an earthquake, both of them would be fine. And he could tell by her gaze she wouldn't be put off. She was an intelligent person, a rational person, and this was the way she fought her fear—through knowledge.

"Okay." He outlined the brick of plastic explosive with his fingernail. Beneath the brown wrapping, it was white. "This is C-4, a pretty stable explosive. But this is what they've done.... They've wired it here—" he pointed to the black and red wires "—connecting it to the engine. When you start your car, the sparks will carry down and catch this brown paper on fire.'' He rubbed it between his thumb and index finger. The pads on his hand came away damp. "Some kind of accelerant. Probably lighter fluid. Yeah, this is strictly a Mickey Mouse bomb, could've been assembled by a twelve-year-old. Probably with a little bit of information downloaded from the good old World Wide Web. I can handle this.''

"I don't understand. The lighter fluid helps it catch on fire, but you said that wouldn't set it off.''

"It won't. Not just the fire. But look here, where they've placed it. Right in your shocks. Now glance at your tire.''

"It's low,'' she supplied. "I didn't see that before.''

"Yeah. The first time you hit a big bump with that tire, the shocks compress the burning brick and—''

"Kaboom.''

"Kaboom,'' C.J. agreed.

Tamara shut her eyes. Her throat worked. "What do we do?''

"We take it out.''

"Just pull it out?''

"Just pull it out. I'm going to clip the wires first, then we'll gently ease it out. It's not that tricky—don't be scared. This stuff can even handle a small fall.''

C.J. clipped the wires with his Swiss Army knife. Then, flat on his back, acutely aware of Tamara lying beside him on the pavement, he drew out the wrapped brick. "Why don't you crawl out,'' he suggested softly, "and I'll hand it to you? Will that be all right?''

"Just don't drop it?''

"Oh, it's probably not the best idea.''

She licked her lips, her gaze going from the explosive to him. Then her jaw tightened and a hard glint shone in her eyes. "I can do it.''

"Let's just get this thing out of here. I'm beginning to lose that fresh feeling.''

She pushed herself out from beneath the car. He waited

until she was balanced, then he passed the explosive to her. His hands were shaking a little. He knew C-4 was stable—that's what made it so popular as an explosive. But the knowledge of what kind of damage that brick could do was still sobering. Tamara's hands were also trembling. She accepted the wrapped brick with the same intense care people used when handling newborn infants.

She stood quietly, though, without a trace of hysterics. He admired that. He didn't know many women—many people—who would discover a car bomb, then crawl under the car to help dismantle it.

They stood in the middle of the parking lot with their precious package, neither of them moving.

"Okay," C.J. said after a moment. "Let's walk to the edge of the parking lot, to the dirt, and set it down. Do you want me to take it?"

"I don't think we should pass it back and forth."

"Tamara, it's stable. Unless you throw it down and jump on it, we're fine. Its power was catching you off guard when you went over a bump. It's over."

"Let's just take it over to the dirt and set it down." She walked very carefully, each foot placed slowly in front of the other, as if she were on a tightrope. He let her go, not saying a word because he didn't want to distract her. A minute later, she was placing the C-4 in the dirt. When she straightened, her hands glistened with the greasy residue of the accelerant.

"Come inside. We'll wash up and call Sheriff Brody."

"No."

"Tamara, whatever's on your hands is not a good thing." He turned without further discussion and led the way inside.

At the bar's industrial-size metal sink, they both rinsed their hands. Tamara scrubbed hers with the intense ferocity of Lady MacBeth. When they were red and swollen, he pulled them from the hot, scouring water.

"Enough."

Tamara looked at him. She was trying to play it tough, but he could see her fear.

"We'll move you out of your hotel. You'll stay with me."

"No. I won't put you in jeopardy."

"Tamara... I think that ship may have already sailed."

She backed away, drying her hands briskly with paper towels. "I'll return to New York. Now. Right now. I'm almost packed."

"Do you really think that will make a difference?"

"I'll go to the Brennan war room, say Lombardi's really needs me back for a new client, and I have a lot of work to do."

"You saw someone ten years ago, Tamara, and you've started following up on it. These days, you are a liability to that person whether you're here, in New York or Timbuktu."

"I didn't see that much."

"But obviously he doesn't know that."

Her hands suddenly pounded against the sink. "Dammit, I don't even know who it is!"

C.J. remained silent, and after a moment, she crumbled.

"But how can it be the senator?" she cried softly. "I can't find any trace of a red car. Any evidence against him."

"You saw his face."

"I was dazed and disoriented."

"He doesn't know that."

"I was ready to drop it. I was ready to go home."

"He didn't know that." C.J. placed his hands on her shoulders. "Think about it, Tamara. Ten years ago, the man was involved in an accident. He had the resources to cover it up. Frankly, he covered it up so well it actually incriminates him—only people with a lot of power and influence can disappear as easily as the driver of that red sports car did. For years, he's probably wondered what you were going to do about it. He was probably even keeping you under tabs. But you were in New York, right?''

She nodded.

"You were going through rehab, then getting a job, launching a career. You were all the way across the country, and you didn't seem to be thinking about the accident at all."

"I needed to get on with my life."

"He begins to relax. Thinks you didn't remember him, or maybe you didn't get a good-enough look. He moves on with his life, too."

"Then suddenly I'm back in Sedona."

"Yeah, the man is planning on running for president of the United States, and he discovers not only have you decided to return to Sedona, but you're asking about the accident. After all these years, you're asking all the questions that keep him awake at night."

"He panics."

"Damn right. He can't exactly call you up and ask you how much you know."

"But C.J., I don't have any proof! Even if I ranted and raved at the top of my lungs, I would be just a hysterical woman chasing phantoms. There's absolutely nothing that ties the accident to the senator."

"That you know of yet."

Tamara was shaking her head. She broke out of his grip, walked back a few steps, then rubbed her temples. She was pale and thin. Her week in Sedona had taken a bigger toll on her than the senator could have imagined.

She wrapped her arms tightly around her waist. The shadows beneath her eyes seemed to have grown darker. "I'm going away."

"Dammit, it's not safe for you to be alone. Stay at my place tonight. Get some rest. I'll dispose of the C-4, call the sheriff, and we'll pick a new game plan in the morning.''

"No. I don't want you involved. I don't want the cops involved. This whole thing, it's too crazy. Too far-fetched—''

"De Nile ain't just a river, sweetheart.''

"Dammit, I am a public relations executive! I go to meetings. I repackage garbage truck drivers into sanitation engineers. I tell mattress warehouses that they are selling sweet dreams and good sex. I...I write press releases and I stay up way too late most nights trying to think of events, celebrations, gags, so my clients can get more press! I don't exist in the center of some twisted, horrible political cover-up. And I will not depend on you. I will not need you! And I will not drag you into this!''

"What scares you more, Tamara? Being the center of a 'twisted, horrible political cover-up' or possibly needing me?''

She stabbed her finger at him, her face drawn and fearful. "You call the sheriff, C.J., you tell him someone stuck a bomb beneath my car, and by the way, we think it was the fine, upstanding Senator George Brennan, and you see how fast they throw me in the loony bin.''

"We have the bomb. We have a package of C-4 sitting in my parking lot right now. Plus, I have a pile of slashed tires. That's evidence, Tamara. Someone is doing something.''

"They won't believe it," she insisted. "Ten years ago, when the trail was fresh and the Senator didn't have half the clout he has now, the police didn't believe me. They'll accuse me of planting the bomb myself or slashing your tires myself. They will!''

"Dammit, Tamara, Sheriff Brody knows me. We've worked together—''

"Can you swear I didn't plant the bomb, C.J.? Were

you with me all night? Can you swear I wasn't the one
who slashed your tires?''

"Why are you so convinced they'll focus on you?"

"Because a pale, sleep-deprived woman who's in Sedona under false pretenses makes a much better suspect
than a U.S. senator. I've been around the block. I am not
an idiot!''

"Tamara—''

But she was already whirling away from him. He could
see it all on her face. She was scared, confused and overwhelmed. Worse, she'd worked herself into a state of
thinking no one would believe her, no one could help her.
Dammit, he believed her. He wanted to help her. She was
already stalking toward the door.

"You can't stay by yourself!'' he yelled behind her.
"It's not safe.''

She didn't miss a step. "Are you kidding? It's the only
way to be safe.''

She headed straight into the parking lot, inspected her
car for more booby traps and climbed inside. Minutes later,
she was pulling out in a cloud of red dirt and dust. No
apologies, no goodbye.

C.J. turned abruptly. He gave into the anger and frustration, the feeling of helplessness he hated more than anything, and slammed his fist into the bar. The blow popped
three of his knuckles, scuffed up his bar and made absolutely no difference.

Tamara didn't know what she was doing. She drove too
fast, feeling exposed and vulnerable beneath the vast Arizona sky. She swore eyes were upon her, the whole world
staring at her, watching her. The rising slabs of red sandstone were no longer majestic or grand. Now they were
bloodred boulders, ringing her in, pushing ever closer. She
would be trapped once more on the dusty, arid soil of
Sedona, with only the crickets to hear her cries.

She grabbed her suitcase from her hotel, checked out and began driving again. She didn't want anyone to know where she was going. Not Patty, not C.J., not anyone. She would do this alone, one hundred percent alone. It was the only way to ever be safe.

Her hands were shaking when she checked into the new hotel under a false name. It took her four tries to count out cash for the night because her fingers wouldn't cooperate. She felt out of sync, outside herself. Maybe she was finally having a nervous breakdown.

At three in the afternoon, she entered her new hotel room. She pulled all the shades. She locked the chain lock and the bolt lock. She left her suitcase in the middle of the tiny, pastel-colored room and curled up in a corner chair with her gun on her lap. The beige carpet spread out around her like a sandy sea. The desert mauve-and-green trim seemed cartoonish and overdone, while the swirling pink-and-red patterned comforter made her ill.

She squeezed her eyes shut and clutched her gun against her chest. Her .22 didn't bring her comfort, though. It felt lighter than she remembered. Not quite right. Nothing seemed right.

She rocked back and forth, and the unbridled emotions hit her like a storm.

She wanted her mother. She wanted to curl up in her mother's arms the way she used to when she was a child. She wanted to wrap her arms around her mother's neck, inhale the soothing scent of gardenias and cry out all her troubles. She wanted to feel loved again. She wanted to feel safe.

You left me, you left me. I needed you. I cried your name and you died out there, dammit. Why didn't you fight harder for me? Why didn't you cling to life the way I did? How could you just leave me like that? Why?

She pressed her hands against her temples, trying to push the thoughts away. She was angry. No, she was scared. No, she was composed. No, she was a little girl, lost and horribly, horribly lonely. She missed her family.

Oh, God she missed her family. How could they die on her? How could they leave her like that?

Why had God let them? Why had God taken them and left her behind? Why couldn't she have gone with them?

I hate you, I hate you, I hate you. I hate all of you.

But she didn't hate them. Somehow her shoulders were shaking, her chest heaving. For the second time in a matter of hours she was sobbing and she didn't understand why. She never cried. Crying got you nowhere. Crying changed nothing.

You had to hold yourself up at the parallel bars and endure the pain if you wanted to learn how to walk again.

She sobbed. She curled up in a ball, her forehead pressed against the gun on her lap, and she cried until she had no more tears. Then she slept.

But her dreams took her to the Arizona roadside. She floated above the car wreckage, looking down with curious dispassion. Her father, slumped over the compressed wheel, only his hair visible. Her mother, flung half-out of the car. Tammy and Shawn, thrown out of the back but pinned by the wreckage. Shawn holding Tammy's hand. Her mother reaching for them both even though moving made her moan with pain.

Her mother's fingers, inching toward her in the red, Arizona dust.

Then the wreckage was gone. The scene flashed back to four healthy people laughing in the car.

"Look at the moon, Dad. Look at the moon."

"Robert, look out!"

The nightmare faded to black. She hovered in a void with no images, just the sound of crickets and the weight of her own guilt.

I'm sorry, I'm sorry, I'm sorry.

"Don't be." Suddenly Senator Brennan was behind her,

his conservative gray suit skewed, blood staining his tie. *"It was all my fault, little girl. Isn't that what you want to hear?"*

He smiled at her kindly. Then he raised his arm and hurtled the brick of C-4.

Tamara bolted awake. It was only four-fifteen in the afternoon. She'd slept for twenty minutes. Her eyes felt grainy and dry. Her throat was so sore it hurt to breathe. Her hands wouldn't stop trembling on her lap.

She moved without thinking, reaching over and picking up the phone. Her fingers began to dial C.J.'s number.

Then she caught herself and snatched her hand back as if she'd been burned.

Call him, a little voice pleaded. You need help. He will help you. You can trust him.

And then what? the rest of her cried. You drag him into your problems, you learn to depend on him, and then the senator or whoever it is, gets him, too? One more person to care about. One more person to lose. No. She wouldn't do it.

She would take care of herself. She'd let herself go, cried too much, gotten lost in the labyrinth of self-pity. No more. She was stronger than this.

She got up. She took a long hot shower, hoping to relax her bunched neck. She ordered a large pizza with fresh vegetables and a tossed salad, and forced herself to eat. She drank a whole glass of orange juice for the vitamins. Then she slipped outside and swam fifty laps, making her body function long after it would've given out.

When she returned to her room, she fell instantly into a light slumber, gaining precious hours of rest.

By 5:00 a.m., she was feeling calm, grounded, composed.

Maybe it *had* been the senator all along. Who else would have the power to watch her? Who else would have the resources to find out about C.J.'s father? Who else would have so much to lose that he would contemplate murder?

If that was the case, she was in a vulnerable position. She couldn't hide forever, and yet she couldn't come forward. She'd found no evidence tying the senator to that night ten years ago. She had only her hazy memory, and if something happened to her...

She made her decision. By the dim light of the bedside lamp, she wrote out everything she remembered from ten years ago. She stated why she thought the senator might be involved. She recorded what happened with her brake lines, the scorpion, the bomb beneath her car.

There wasn't enough information to stand up in court, but if something happened to her, at least it would raise the right questions. Maybe it would be enough to get an ambitious journalist or D.A. digging.

Maybe it would give C.J. a lead to get the senator once and for all.

She sat alone in the middle of the tousled bed. She folded the two-page letter carefully and sealed it inside an envelope. Her hand wavered for a long time.

Who to send it to?

C.J. would listen. C.J. already knows what's going on. He has credibility, he has expertise. He cares.

You will not need C. J. MacNamara.

With a quick, forceful flourish, she wrote Patty's name on the letter and called a courier. Thirty minutes later, fifty dollars poorer, it was done. Patty would be receiving the letter within the hour.

Once more, she'd taken care of herself.

She curled up in a ball in the middle of the bed and tried to sleep without dreams.

At 7:00 a.m., a knock on her door roused her from the bed. Her first thought was that it was Patty. Her second thought was C.J. Then she peered out the window.

Two brown sedans sat in the parking lot of the tiny hotel, the gold stars on their doors proclaiming them to be from the sheriff's department. The rapping on the door continued while she stood there, fighting the sinking feeling in her stomach. Something had happened to C.J. Something had happened to Patty.

She knew why cops came to people's houses. They stood at the foot of your bed, their young faces somber, while they told you what had happened to the people you loved.

The rapping continued.

She undid the locks like a woman in a dream. She drew open the door very slowly, knowing her face was too pale, her eyes too stark.

Sheriff Brody and two young deputies stood in her doorway in full uniform. The sheriff stood in front. His broad, ruddy face was grimmer than Tamara remembered. His small brown eyes were as sharp as a hawk's. He'd unsnapped the top of his holster, and his hand was poised on his hip, his fingertips brushing the handle of his gun. The two deputies stood to the side. Their holsters were unsnapped, as well. Their hands hovered above their hips.

Their faces were very serious.

A low buzzing filled her ears.

"Tamara Allistair?"

"Yes."

"Tamara Allistair, you're under arrest for the murder of Spider Wallace. You have the right to remain silent...."

Chapter 10

Sedona did not boast a large sheriff's department. A small town that existed mostly for tourists, its law enforcement officers were accustomed to a steady supply of petty theft, fender benders, and drunken and disorderly charges. Sheriff Brody hadn't arrested a murderer in five years, and he wasn't taking any chances.

He'd read the Miranda to Tamara promptly and cuffed her hands behind her back. Now she sat in the department's one interrogation room, her hands finally freed, but with two deputies stationed at the door. Sheriff Brody had left her a small cup of coffee, which she refused to touch even though her system craved caffeine. She'd watched TV; she knew how this worked. The fuzz brought you in, pumped you up with coffee and cigarettes until your bladder was so overloaded and your nerves so tightly strung you'd agree the pope was Protestant just to use the bathroom.

She was smarter than that. And she was determined to keep her wits about her even while sitting alone at a wood table with a metal fold-down chair cold and hard beneath her butt and the room stark and bright white around her. This whole thing was a big mistake, and if she just remained intelligent and lucid, it would all be cleared up.

Sheriff Brody had informed her she could make one phone call, but she hadn't used it yet because she didn't know who to call. She didn't have a lawyer, and she didn't have many connections in Sedona. She could call her office in New York—certainly Lombardi, the senior partner, knew some heavy-hitting lawyers, but it would take at least twelve hours to get someone out here.

She was hoping she could resolve the matter before then. After all, she hadn't killed Spider Wallace. She'd never even heard of the man until three hours ago.

From the hallway came the sharp snap of two deputies pulling themselves erect. Obviously Sheriff Brody was returning. He'd been gone for forty-five minutes or so. Maybe he thought the solitude would wear on her conscience and make her snap.

The door opened. The sheriff walked in, pulled out his chair and settled his imposing bulk on the thin metal frame. Methodically, he set his little spiral notebook on the table, unclipped his black disposable pen from his shirt pocket and pulled off the cap. Tamara was becoming accustomed to this little game. Sheriff Brody moved like molasses, never in a rush. He even spoke slowly, as if he was on the verge of falling asleep. It created long moments of silence, which no doubt she was supposed to fill with sudden confessions of guilt.

Tamara kept her gaze on the sheriff's eyes. He had a hunter's eyes, and that assured her of her place—she was the prey.

"Tell me about Spider Wallace," Sheriff Brody drawled.

"I don't know who that is."

"You shot him."

"I did not."

"We found him dead in the cemetery, in front of your parents' grave. Cognac at his feet."

"I didn't shoot him."

"You said you went to the cemetery that night."

"I did!" Tamara's nerves frayed a little. They'd been over this before. Three, four, five times. She didn't remember anymore. But she hadn't shot Spider Wallace. Not even New Yorkers went around shooting poor, innocent cemetery caretakers.

"So you went to the cemetery, but you didn't shoot Spider Wallace?"

"Exactly, there you go. I visited my parents' grave, I left the bottle of my father's favorite cognac as I do every year on the anniversary of the accident—"

"And you shot Spider Wallace."

"And I walked away."

"And kicked Spider's dead body out of the way."

"I did not shoot Spider Wallace! I did not see Spider Wallace! I was there alone, saw no one, spoke to no one and left without meeting anyone. Why are you doing this, Sheriff? So the man was shot in front of my parents' grave. That doesn't make me the killer!"

"Got a witness who says he saw a woman walking away from the sight. A woman in an expensive black suit and fancy heels."

"I don't wear heels. Haven't you watched me walk? Women with grafted ankles and plastic knees have no business on spikes."

"Maybe he was wrong about the heels."

"Maybe you're grasping at straws!"

"Spider was shot with a .22," the sheriff said evenly.

"Lots of people have .22s."

"Yup." Abruptly, the sheriff tossed a file onto the table. It landed with a slap. "But only one .22 matched the ballistics report on the slug we took from Spider's body. That would be yours.''

Tamara felt the blood rush from her face. ''Wh-wh-what?''

Sheriff Brody leaned over, his thick arms crossing on the table, his wide shoulders filling the space. He spoke in rapid, clipped tones she'd never heard from him before. ''We got a full ballistics match. We got a witness who saw a woman walk away from the scene. We got a man dead in front of your parents' grave and a bottle of cognac with your prints. Now I hear you've been asking questions about your parents' accident ten years ago. I hear you're asking about the senator. Was he next, Tamara? Were you going to shoot him next?''

''I...no! Of course not!'' She couldn't think. She stared at the sheriff like an idiot, her eyes blinking, her mouth open.

Dammit, pull yourself together. He's confusing you and you're letting him.

''Why'd you kill Spider? He never harmed anyone. The man was just a cemetery caretaker. It was cruel to kill a man like him.''

''I didn't,'' she whispered.

''Now, the senator, he's made some enemies. I hear stories about him from time to time. Politicians get a lot of power, lot of influence. Maybe you held him accountable for something. Maybe you didn't like his politics. But I could see why you might have reason to go after a man like him.''

''I'm not after the senator.''

''He likes to chase women. You ever been involved with him? He break it off with you?''

''I've never even met him!''

''Yet you come all the way from New York to work on his campaign. And you asked around about him. I hear you even kept tabs on his schedule....''

"I want my phone call," Tamara said.

"Were you obsessed with the senator? Maybe you stood at your parents' graves and told them you were plotting to kill the senator. Folks do crazy things like that. Then you realized Spider overhead you, so you shot him."

"I want my phone call!"

"Did Spider hear too much? Is that why you killed him?"

Tamara pressed her lips together in a thin, white line. She stared at the sheriff with all the outrage and mutiny she could muster. Minute turned into minute, the silence growing, stretching, becoming taut.

Tamara didn't give in. She was in over her head. She didn't know what had happened, but her arrest was no longer a matter of simple mistaken identity. She'd been foolish to answer any questions at all, she realized. Well, she'd never been arrested before. She'd chalk it up to experience, and move as fast as she could to correct her mistakes.

She was very scared.

"Why'd you shoot Spider Wallace?"

She stared at the sheriff mutely.

"Why are you after the senator?"

Tamara locked her gaze on the far wall.

"Did the senator hurt your family? Is that why you wanted him?" And a minute later he added, "Why hurt a poor man like Spider, Tamara? Hell, he never hurt anyone."

Tamara didn't say a word.

Finally, Sheriff Brody hefted his bulk from the chair. He looked at her with frank disapproval, the way a father might stare at his rebellious daughter. His fingers stroked his luxuriant mustache. "It would make it easier on everyone if you'd just tell us why you did it."

"Get me the phone, Sheriff."

"Well...if it has to be like that..."

He lifted his heavy shoulders and got to the business of exiting. It seemed to take him a full minute just to close up his spiral notebook and slip the cap onto his pen. A whole minute, when the bright lights of the sterile room pressed against her and her backside grew sore from sitting on such an uncomfortable chair. Her shoulders were too tight, her eyes too tired. She started to eye the coffee seriously.

The sheriff moseyed to the door as if he had all the time in the world. The silence begged to be filled. Tamara refused to comply.

It took five more minutes for the sheriff to reappear with an old rotary phone. He paused before the table, his gaze sharp on her face as if he were giving her one last time to confess and beg for clemency. Tamara wondered how many teenaged children he'd raised to develop such skills in interrogation.

He planted the phone on the table. It gave a small clang of protest.

"I'll be back in a bit. Holler to Dennis or Rod if you need anything."

Tamara was tempted to say thank you, but somehow that sounded too hospitable, given the circumstances.

The door of the interrogation room had been closed for thirty seconds before she could bring herself to lift the receiver. She still wasn't sure who to call, but there was one person who knew the truth, one person who could vouch for her actions. One person who'd pledged to be her friend forever.

Tamara called Patty. The ringing phone filled her ear. One, two, three rings.

"Please be home, Patty. Please be home." Suddenly, the line picked up.

"Patty! Oh, Patty, I'm so happy you're there." She was babbling. She was too desperate to care. "Do you have the envelope, Patty? Please tell me you have the envelope."

Patty didn't immediately reply. Instead, a long, troubled silence filled the line. Tamara began to sweat.

"Patty?" she whispered.

"You went too far," Patty said abruptly. "When you were just asking questions, it was one thing, but, Tamara, I heard about the arrest."

"I didn't do it—"

"Spider Wallace never hurt you. He never hurt anyone. He was just a sweet old man who took care of the graveyard. How could you turn on him like that?"

"I didn't hurt Spider! Didn't you read the letter? Patty, please..." Tamara was begging. She heard herself beg, heard the desperation hitch up the words until they came out high and falsetto. She was leaning forward, clutching the phone with whitened knuckles as if it would somehow help.

"You've changed a lot more than I realized, Tamara. I'm sorry I ever helped you."

"Patty—"

"What kind of person would kill Spider Wallace? What kind of person sinks that low?" Her voice broke. She sounded as if she was crying again. "Don't call me again, Tamara."

The phone clicked. The dial tone filled Tamara's ear. Fine use of a phone call. Today was just not her day.

Dammit, I didn't do it, I didn't do it! How could you believe something like that about me, Patty? How could you not trust me anymore?

Tamara stared dully at the beat-up wood table. Her hands no longer seemed to belong to her. And the room was unbearably white, unbearably cold, unbearably bright.

What did she do now?

"Tamara?"

She looked up and C.J. stood in the doorway, his blue eyes shadowed.

She looked like hell, C.J. thought. The cool, composed woman in designer suits was gone. This woman sat in the same pants and shirt she'd worn yesterday, and they appeared wrinkled enough to have been slept in. She was pale as a ghost and ragged as a frayed sheet. Sitting on the edge of the chair, she looked like she hadn't a friend in the world.

He'd been surprised when Sheriff Brody had shown up at his place this morning looking for Tamara. The sheriff had refused to say why, of course, but his tone and the presence of both of his deputies had indicated that it was pretty serious. C.J. had spent the rest of the morning trying to weasel the information out of the sheriff's receptionist. When Yvonne had finally admitted Tamara had been booked for murder, C.J. had been stunned.

Tamara was many things. She had many secrets to hide. But C.J. didn't believe murder was one of them.

He pulled out the vacant chair.

"We don't have much time. I'm not even supposed to be in here, but Dennis owes me. Of course, when the sheriff decides to check in on you again, he'll probably tan my hide and fine me to hell and back, that is, if he decides not to book me for obstructing justice."

Tamara looked at him wordlessly. Her eyes had turned into huge, dark pools. Dilated. Shocked. He reached across the table and took her hand, rubbing her icy fingers as he spoke.

"Did you kill Spider Wallace?"

"No," she whispered.

"Do you know who did?"

"No."

"Do you understand why you were arrested?"

"They said the ballistics report on my gun matched it to the bullet."

"Is it your gun, Tamara, or did someone give it to you?"

"I bought it. In New York."

"Has it been in your possession the whole week you were in Sedona?"

"No. When I work I leave it in my hotel room. I didn't think it would be good to be seen in the campaign war room with a gun."

"Did you take your gun with you when you went to the cemetery that night?"

"Yes. I think so."

"Was it really your gun? Did you check the registration number on the barrel?"

"No, of course not. I had no reason to."

"Huh. Well it's a start. Someone could've stolen your gun, leaving a dummy in place while using your weapon to shoot Spider, then swapped back."

She blinked her eyes several times rapidly. He didn't try to pretend the theory wasn't far-fetched.

"Tamara, do you know how they found you? Do you know how they knew to come arrest you?"

She shook her head.

"Yvonne told me they pulled a pair of prints for Tamara Allistair off the cognac bottle. Then they got an anonymous tip that Tamara Allistair and Tamara Thompson were the same person. They've been looking for you since last night. Word of advice, Tamara—don't order pizza or personal couriers when you're trying to hide."

"Oh." Her fingers had curled slightly. Tentatively, unconsciously, she'd begun to grip his hand.

"Sweetheart, do you know who would've called in with that kind of tip?"

"No."

"Well, I do. My guess is that it's the same person who shot Spider Wallace."

Abruptly, her eyes filled. She gripped his hand in earnest. "I don't know what's going on," she wailed, her voice raw. "I swear I didn't kill Spider Wallace, C.J. I swear I wasn't plotting to kill the senator, not even if he did turn out to be the person who hit my parents' car. I wanted real justice—legal justice. I don't even know how to shoot a gun!"

"Sh, sh, sh. I know, I know. Someone's set you up, Tamara. Someone has set you up since the beginning, and when I started helping you, they did their best to make me back off, as well. Well, I don't run from a fight, and I'll be damned before I sit back and let them railroad you for something you didn't do. Have you had the arraignment yet?"

"No. Two o'clock."

"Okay. I'll be there. Whatever bail is set at, I'm sure Brandon's good for it."

"I'll show up at the trial," she said immediately. "You won't lose the money."

"If we play our cards right, maybe there won't be a trial."

"C.J..." Her voice grew quiet. Her gaze searched his. "Thank you," she whispered at last. "For everything. You were right yesterday. I should've...I should've listened to you. I'm sorry."

C.J. stilled. It had hurt him when she'd run away from his bar. Hell, it had ticked him off. But he'd already discovered it was impossible for him to stay angry with her—he understood her actions too well. He squeezed her hand one last time and gave her a crooked smile.

"Ah, sweetheart. Now, those are the words every man loves to hear."

Her shoulders came down. She finally offered a tremulous smile. He could hear fresh noise in the hall.

"Two o'clock," he whispered, winked and strode for the door. As silently as he came, he disappeared.

Tamara sat alone at the table. She replayed his words in

her mind, the feel of his hand gripping hers. And she did her best to believe in him, even if she wasn't very good at believing in others.

For C.J., she tried.

At two o'clock, Tamara was delivered to the courthouse, where she was met by an overworked, underpaid public defender who only had time to ask her how to pronounce her name before the judge called the brief proceedings to order. The district attorney pointed out that Tamara had no roots in the community and was wanted for cold-blooded murder, making her a high flight risk. Her public defender mumbled that she'd once lived in Sedona, ten years ago, and with a bang of the gavel, the judge set her bail at $500,000. Tamara began to realize it was a good thing she made a lot of money—she was about to spend it all on a good defense lawyer.

Just as the court officers were leading her away, she spotted C.J. in the back of the room. He gave her a thumbs-up and a wink.

An hour later, two corrections officers delivered her to him. Immediately, he guided her to his car.

"Sorry about the delay. Brandon had to liquidate some stocks, and you wouldn't believe the paperwork they made me fill out."

"Your brother paid the full $500,000 to post my bail?"

"Wired it thirty minutes ago."

"That...that was incredibly generous of him."

"That's what family is for."

"He'll get the money back, C.J. I promise."

"Well, I don't know if I should tell you this, but Brandon will hardly care. He's...uh...well actually, he's doing his damnedest to lose money. Of course, the poor guy has the Midas touch, so generally his sure-to-fail investments end up making him more money. Talk about a curse."

Tamara decided she must be in a greater state of shock than she'd realized. "He's trying to *lose* money?"

"Well, Brandon worked too hard as an investment banker. His wife was always trying to get him to slow down, spend more time at home. He kept insisting he would—when they had more saved. Next thing he knew, she was dead and he was rich—her life insurance was worth a million. Brandon doesn't appreciate irony. He's been fighting it ever since."

Tamara just nodded. The story seemed to run in circles around her head, and she was too overloaded with other matters to try to make sense of it. Instead, she said with all the meager dignity she could muster, "I'm innocent, C.J. I am. And I have no intention of jumping bail or becoming a fugitive from the law. If worse comes to worst, I'll hire the best defense lawyer Lombardi can find to beat this thing."

"Lombardi?" C.J. opened the passenger-side door of his Mustang for her.

"He's the founding partner of the public relations firm."

"No romantic interest?" He slid into his side of the car.

"He's seventy."

"Oh, okay. Then Lombardi sounds like a great guy."

"He knows lots of lawyers."

"We'll give Lombardi a call, but tomorrow morning. It's after five in New York now, and frankly, you look like you're on the verge of fainting. Fasten your seat belt, sweetheart. I'm taking you to my place and putting you in bed."

Tamara had never really thought about where C.J. lived, but when he finally pulled up to a small cabin on the outskirts of town, she realized this was exactly where she'd pictured him. A white Volkswagen Scirocco was up on blocks in the front yard. Its hood was propped open, and she could see the interior roll cage through the windows. A pile of four slashed racing tires rested beside it.

C.J. walked past the tires as if he didn't see them, but she saw a muscle jump in his jaw.

"Here we go. Nothing fancy, but, well, it's home." For the first time, Tamara realized that C.J. was a little bit nervous.

She walked through the front door to discover a house of sunlight and wood. Windows of different sizes and shapes dotted the walls like a crazy quilt of sky and wind. Above her, exposed beams arched up twenty feet, while thick gold pine planks glowed beneath her feet. The cabin had no interior walls. The old beat-up sofa and oddball collection of chairs seemed to be the living room. The kitchen was straight ahead, defined by a relatively new blue counter and bar stools. To her left, a Chinese screen sectioned off an area she supposed was the bedroom. Next to it, a small-sized room was boxed in and packaged with a door. She figured that had to be the bathroom.

"Forgive the mess. I don't have visitors often."

Obviously the man wasn't into housecleaning. As Tamara watched, he self-consciously snatched up the navy blue towel puddled in front of the kitchen counter, the white T-shirt thrown over the Chinese screen, the pair of jeans wadded in a corner. Other miscellaneous items were quickly scooped up and unceremoniously piled behind the screen. The dirty dishes were dumped into the sink.

Tamara used the time to roam. There were fragments of people's lives in their homes. She knew this, because she had no such fragments in her apartment. She had glass, chrome, works of art—the kinds of things a successful PR executive of an exclusive firm should have. She didn't have pictures. She didn't have crystal her grandmother had given her, or a doll handed down from her mother, or a baseball glove used to play catch with her father. Those items lived in boxes she only dragged out on Christmas morning, when the darkness was already crushing her chest.

C.J. had fragments. She found pictures, a huge collection of them, unframed and jumbled together on his mantel. A large black-and-white portrait shot of an older woman in barn clothes. A small color photo of three kids sitting on the back of a parade float, dressed up in straw hats and blue jeans and dangling bamboo fishing rods. The middle child was a charming girl with a beaming smile and red Pippy Longstocking braids. Here was a wallet-size photo of C.J., the young marine, wearing full dress uniform and looking at the camera with his sternest expression. There was C.J. on some tropical beach, waving a fruit-festooned coconut and dipping a scantily clad woman. Writing on the back stated "We'll always have Maui." Tamara put it back quickly. Most of the shots, however, were of C.J. in fatigues with his marine buddies, or C.J. in blue jeans with his siblings. Except for his formal marine class photo, he always looked happy.

She found a kachina doll at the end of the mantel. Above the mantel, he had a samurai sword mounted in its intricately carved sheath. A wood-carved chess set with crude peasant figures, reminding her of sculptures she'd seen from South America, sat in front of a window. Bamboo weavings covered one wall.

"Here. You can change into these."

C.J. held out a pair of gray sweats and blue chambray shirt for her. He still looked nervous.

"Your cabin is very beautiful."

He shrugged. "I like it."

"You collected all these things while traveling?"

"The marines. You know, travel to exotic place, meet exotic people, and kill them." He smiled abruptly. "I miss the marines."

"Why did you leave?"

"Time to move on. After a while, always following orders—and bureaucracy—gets to a man. I like it here in Sedona. I'm happy with the Ancient Mariner. Racing all year round is pretty good, too." His expression grew curious. "Do you ever miss Arizona, Tamara? Do you ever think of coming back?"

"No. The land...it has a beauty unlike any other in the world. But for me... There are too many sad memories here, C.J. Even the crickets remind me of my parents dying."

C.J. opened his mouth. She thought he'd push the subject harder, but abruptly he changed his mind. He shoved the clothes in her hands. "I thought you might like to clean up and change. There are fresh towels stacked in the bathroom. The bedroom is behind the screen. I promise not to peek...maybe."

She arched a brow skeptically.

"I'm not much of a cook. I kind of think Chinese takeout was one of the greatest advances of the twentieth century. But I do make a mean pot of chicken noodle soup—"

"Fresh?"

"Yeah, right. I add some 'personal touches,'" he insisted. He brought up his nose in perfect imitation of a haughty connoisseur. "Just you wait until you've tried my soup. You haven't had nothing till you've tried my soup."

"I'll take your word for it."

Abruptly, he brushed her cheek with his fingers. The touch lingered. "I want you to eat," he said softly. "I want you to relax and sleep. You'll be safe here, Tamara. Do you believe me when I say that?"

"Yes." She spoke the truth and it surprised her.

"I don't expect anything from you. I'm not going to jump your bones the first time you close your eyes—"

"I know you wouldn't do that."

"I understand you've been through a lot. I understand you probably need some space, some room, to sort it all out. I can be a sensitive nineties guy. Just don't let the word get out."

"C.J....you've been unbelievably kind."

"Yeah." He made a face, then shrugged ruefully. "Just don't let the word get out."

Tamara smiled. She liked the cute side of C. J. Mac-Namara. Their gazes met and held for a moment. Neither of them said anything. The silence stretched, not taut, not sparked, just...comfortable. Real. Nice.

"I'm...I'm going to go shower now."

"I'll cook soup."

"Okay."

"Okay."

She finally got her feet to move. Her gaze was still on his. He had a half smile around his lips, soft, earnest. She liked that look. It fit the wave of golden hair curling down his forehead. She almost tripped, finally drawing her attention back to her feet. She pulled herself together and showered.

Afterward, she put on his clothes. She was acutely aware that the soft, worn fabric smelled like him. She caught faint whiffs of soap and spice. She bunched the warm fabric between her fingers and imagined it against his skin.

She padded into the kitchen, the wood floor smooth beneath her feet. She was just rolling up the sleeves of the chambray shirt—which seemed to fall to her knees—when she spotted C.J.

He was seated at the small round kitchen table, looking ridiculously proud of himself. A big Dutch oven sat on a pot holder in the middle of the table. English muffins steamed from a recent toasting. He'd set two places with big blue ceramic bowls and hastily polished plastic spoons. The pièce de résistance, however, was the single pink rose he'd placed across her bowl.

"I bought it yesterday," he said. "Thought I'd give it

to you when I hunted you down this afternoon, maybe get a smile from you. Oh, wait. There we go. You're smiling."

"I'm not smiling. My lips itch."

"Your lips itch?" He arched a brow, then waggled it devilishly. That made the corners of her mouth curve more, and he grinned in triumph. He waved her toward the chair and she came.

She did feel better. More relaxed than she had for a long time, more…at ease.

She ate his soup. It was thick with noodles and fresh carrots and celery he'd added himself. She slathered honey on English muffins and polished off two slices. She drank cool glasses of iced tea and stroked the velvety petals of her rose. The sun was beginning to set. It sent rich, vibrant hues of pink, mauve and amber through the crazy quilt of windows. It bathed them both in gold.

When she'd polished off the last bite, scraped the bottom of the bowl, and retrieved the last crumb, C.J. pushed back his chair. He held out his arms.

She went to him, wordless, thoughtless. In baggy sweats and his oversize shirt, she curled up on his lap and slipped her arms around his waist. He held her against him. She inhaled his scent. She listened to his heartbeat. She closed her eyes and let his warmth seep through her.

"Relax, Tamara." His fingers lifted, settled on the back of her neck. "And let me do this. I want to do this for you."

Chapter 11

He had such great hands.

Those long, powerful fingers dug into the corded muscles of her neck, kneading, kneading, kneading. They crept into her hair, massaging little circles and sending pinpricks of pleasure up her spine. They squeezed her shoulders, his strong thumbs rubbing her collarbone and finding more knots. Her head sagged against his chest.

Traveling down her spine, he searched out her tension and knuckled it away. The small of her back, the indent of her waist, the curve of her bottom, all turned into a pliant, supple mass.

Her eyes drifted shut.

He threaded her thick hair behind her ears. He lifted coiled strands and ran them through his fingers. He feathered his fingertips down her cheek, over and over again, as if she were a kitten to be stroked into purring. She shifted more tightly against him.

He circled his fingers around her upper arms, squeezing slightly, then releasing. Warmth flooded through her. Her breathing grew shallow. Her world narrowed down to the exquisite sensation of his hands working her body. She became acutely aware of his fingertips brushing the side of her breast.

He moved his left hand to her leg, his thumb channeling deeply into her thigh. He pinched just above her knee, where tendons and ligaments knotted, and when he released his hand, goose bumps bloomed across her skin, and she expelled her breath in a rush. He kneaded the taut muscles of her calves. He found the bottom of her foot and pinched with such delicate pressure she bit her lip to keep from moaning. He even rubbed her toes, her poor, unpainted toes. Then he started back up her legs.

She began to squirm.

She didn't mean to. He was willing to give her space, and she should take it. She wasn't good at passion. She was frigid, half a woman, ashamed. C.J. deserved better.

She pressed her cheek farther into the curve of his shoulder. She inhaled his fresh, spicy fragrance. She wished she had more to give.

His hands were still moving on her body. She wanted to push up his T-shirt and taste his skin.

"Relax," C.J. murmured in her ear. "I just want you to relax."

She squirmed again. Suddenly, she discovered him against her hip, hard and rigid. Large and hot.

She curled her hands into fists at his waist. She wanted to stroke him, to taste his skin, explore his flesh. She wanted to show him the sensations he so generously shared with her. She wanted to pretend, for one moment, that she was a real, sensual, giving woman.

Her fingers twitched. She found her hands creeping beneath his shirt, tentatively touching his bare skin. Warm. Smooth. Like hot satin. She pressed her lips against his neck.

His hands had stilled on her arms. Now she could hear

a ragged undertone to his breathing. He was thinking about her, too. She sat there with her hands against his back and her lips against his throat, waiting to see what he would do.

"Are you sure?" C.J. whispered.

"No."

His arms tightened around her. His hips moved a bit, his groin pressing instinctively against her. She liked the feel of it. "I want you, Tamara. I do. But only if it's what you want."

She squeezed her eyes shut. She didn't know what to do. She hungered, she feared, she wanted, she rejected. She pulled back a little. She gazed at him, knowing her need must be in her eyes and willing him to make the first move because she couldn't do it. She just couldn't do it.

"Gold," he murmured. "Pure gold. God, Tamara..."

He swung her up in his arms, and she wrapped her arms tightly around his neck. In four long strides, they were in the bedroom.

"You have to tell me if you change your mind," he said thickly. "I can be patient."

"Please."

He dropped her in the middle of the bed, his fingers already struggling with his clothes. As she watched, he grabbed the hem of his T-shirt and ripped it over his head. Muscles gleamed and rippled. His skin spread out over his spare frame like a tawny lion's; while satiny swirls of wheat blond down covered his chest. She stared at the hewn lines of his ribs and the washboard undulation of his stomach. She memorized the thick swaths of muscle binding his shoulders and curving his upper arms. When his hands curled around the top of his jeans, tendons snaked up his forearms.

Slowly, he popped the first button of his jeans. Then, gripping the material tighter with both fists, he ripped open the button fly, shoved the denim down to his ankles and kicked it free. Clad only in red plaid boxers, he climbed onto the bed.

The mattress dipped strategically, rolling her into him. She thought he would take her into his arms. Instead, he surprised her, trapping her shoulders and rolling her onto her stomach.

"Let me," he whispered. "Trust me. Relax for me."

His hands curved around. She arched up enough to give him access to the buttons of her shirt. His fingers lingered on the swell of her breast, finding the hard nub of her nipple. He squeezed gently, and she closed her eyes against the sharp, bittersweet sensation. The buttons slipped out one by one. Very slowly, C.J. stripped the oversize shirt from her body.

The air was cool. Not cold, but crisp enough to stir her skin and send a fresh wave of ripples up her arms. He leaned over her, pressing his warm, bare skin against her back, tangling his legs with hers. She couldn't see him. She was flattened against the mattress, unable to move and unable to hold him. He nuzzled back her hair, then suddenly closed his teeth around her earlobe and suckled hard.

She nearly bucked off the bed. Her whole body shivered. Nerve endings screamed to life, passion poured into her belly. She wanted to cry out, she wanted to yank away. She remained pinned to the mattress, his mouth wreaking havoc with her senses, sucking, sucking, sucking. Then his mouth whispered down, gnawing on her neck, covering her with love bites. His lips trailed around her shoulders to her spine, leaving a shuddering trail of prickling flesh in his wake.

He kissed the back of her neck. His mouth was hot. She felt it acutely on each exposed inch of her skin. Her nipples were hard, her body achy. It would be so easy to surrender to him. And yet some part of her still fought to maintain control.

His lips traveled down to her waist, his tongue trailing

around the elastic waist of her sweatpants. His leg lifted
long enough to permit her to arch her hips, then his hands
dipped inside.

She squeezed her eyes shut, she bit her lip to keep from
moaning.

Control, control, control. Don't surrender too much.

He pulled her sweats down to her ankles, then yanked
them to the floor. Her underwear quickly followed suit.
She heard a small rustle as he pulled off his boxers. Then
he was over her, the fine hairs of his legs prickling the
backs of her thighs, his arousal stiff and hot against the
soft swell of her bottom. His hands slipped between her
legs. She opened for him wordlessly.

He stroked her. Those callused, capable fingers delved
into her folds, eased inside. She was hot, moist. Her hips
arched back. She fisted the coverlet and twisted it urgently.
She bit the pillow to keep from crying out.

Want, but don't need. Enjoy, but don't surrender.

She hovered on the brink of a nameless precipice. The
fall terrified her.

"Let it go," C.J. whispered. "Trust me, Tamara. Trust
yourself."

He flipped her over, and before she knew it, his hands
were bracketing her hips and his mouth was upon her. He
found the small, pearly nub of her desire and sucked it
hard.

She cried out, the sound of her hoarse voice shocking
her. He devoured her, and the sensations were so intense
they almost pained her. Her fingers tangled in his hair. She
gripped his head and held him against her shamelessly.
She wanted... She needed... She was dying.

He tongued her, slow and hot and wet. She writhed
against the mattress, squirming, wiggling and moaning his
name. She could feel the heat building inside her. The
prickling pleasure razor-sharp against her skin.

Her hips arched helplessly. She'd lost sanity. She was

going to shatter into a million pieces. And she was scared. She wanted to pull back. She wanted to go forward. She opened her eyes and gazed at him with agony.

C.J. rose up. His eyes were dark and steady. His arms were strong as he planted them beside her head on the mattress. Abruptly, he plunged into her. She cried out, unprepared for this fresh onslaught.

"Take it," he commanded. "Go with it, Tamara. I have you. I have you."

She shattered. She burst around him, digging her fingers into his flanks, welting his skin, screaming his name. The fire rolled through her in wave after wave after wave.

Far off, she heard his triumphant shout. She felt his body arch, watched his magnificent neck cord and bend. Then he snapped, bowing above her, crashing upon her.

They collapsed on the bed like broken dolls, limbs tangled, bodies meshed. She was covered in sweat and tears, bathed in glory and shock. She wrapped her arms around him and held him as hard as she could.

"It's okay, it's okay, it's okay," he murmured over and over again.

She couldn't let him go. She was too raw and turned inside out. She clung to him desperately as her breathing slowed, her heartbeat slowed, and the exhaustion hit her as hard as the passion had. Her eyes drifted shut. Her overloaded senses declared defeat.

Bit by bit, C.J. felt her fade away into badly needed slumber. He pulled away from her slightly, arranged her more comfortably against him, then wrapped his arms around her bare shoulders and held her.

"I love you," he murmured, and kissed her sleeping forehead. "And I'm going to tell you about it, too. In a bit. When you're ready."

He closed his eyes and also went to sleep.

* * *

"We got English muffins, we got orange juice, we got raisin bran. Pick your poison."

Tamara opened her eyes drowsily. C.J. stood in front of her, wearing only the red plaid boxers and bearing a breakfast tray. She thought it should be dusk or late evening, but bright morning sun streamed through the cabin windows. She yawned, disoriented.

"All three it is." C.J. deposited the tray on the oak nightstand.

"What time is it?"

"It's 10:00 a.m."

"Ten! As in the next day?"

"Yep."

"I've been asleep for sixteen hours?"

"Seventeen. You really needed the rest."

Tamara bolted upright. The sheet promptly fell down, bearing her naked body and earning C.J.'s full attention. Belatedly, she snatched the sheet back up and tucked it primly beneath her arms. C.J.'s gaze lingered on her exposed shoulders. She blushed, a rather silly reaction given how much of her body he'd seen...touched...tasted. She blushed harder. She was not cut out for the morning after.

"I would seduce you," he murmured, "but unfortunately, we have work to do."

She nodded vehemently, trying not be disappointed when she was staring at his bare chest. She remembered how fine and silky that matting of golden hair felt against her fingertips.

"Come on, let's eat. Then we need to devise a battle plan."

While C.J. cleared the dishes, Tamara took a quick shower and pulled back on the clothes she'd borrowed yesterday. When she came out of the bedroom, she discovered C.J. sitting at the kitchen table, armed with pen and paper and wearing a fresh pair of jeans.

"We need a strategy," he said without preamble.

Tamara pulled out a wooden chair and plopped down. "I don't have any great ideas," she said bluntly. "At this point, I think I'm up the proverbial creek without a paddle."

"Never. How much time do we have before you go to trial?"

"Preliminary date is three weeks from today. We might be able to postpone it, though. I'm not sure. I need to get a lawyer."

"Right. You should call that Lombardi guy today. We'll let the lawyer tackle the legal angles. In the meantime, I think we should mount an offense."

"An offense? C.J., with all due respect, what kind of offense? I've been checking around. If the senator was the one involved ten years ago, he covered his tracks very well."

"I know. I didn't say this would be a piece of cake. But let's start with what we do know." He dragged out the pad of paper and a pen. "Now, what kind of car was involved?"

"The police deduced that it was an old red Firebird, based upon the type of suspension and kind of tires. I don't remember all the specifics, but I have a copy of the police report back in my hotel."

"Good. We'll stop by your hotel and pick up your stuff this afternoon. What did the police do?"

"They checked with the local junkyards, auto shops and car rental agencies for any car that had been returned with substantial damage. They also followed up with local hospitals in case the driver had come in with injuries."

"Nothing?"

"Zip."

"We'll need to widen the search, then. It could be the senator drove up to Scottsdale, or down to Phoenix, or what the hell, maybe even to Nogales on the border. A lot of things disappear in Nogales. We can use the phone book, call around.''

Tamara shook her head. "You're forgetting the time span. A lot of shops listed in the yellow pages today might not have existed ten years ago, and there were ones then that probably aren't listed today. We'd have to go with an old list from the Chamber of Commerce or something like that. But even then, C.J., can you imagine how long such a list would be? Plus, we're asking about a single car that appeared for repairs or salvage ten years ago. Not even a race car junkie can remember every car he saw ten years ago.''

C.J. frowned. A ten-year-old trail did make life difficult. "Okay, let's try it from a second angle. What's the other thing we know?''

"I don't understand.''

"We know someone is watching you, right?'' She nodded. "For that matter, we know someone is watching me. But more to the point, whoever did this had to know a lot about you, Tamara. He had to know about your yearly visit to the grave site, and that you were back in town. How many people knew about your ritual?''

"I didn't think anyone knew,'' she said honestly. "I would fly in the day before, visit the grave site and fly out. I didn't want to linger. I just...I just needed to do something.''

"And the cognac. Was it always the same kind?''

"My father's favorite brand.''

"You bought it here or in New York?''

"Here, before I went to the cemetery. I bought it from the same store he always visited, toasted with one glass and left the rest of the bottle.''

"So the same store owner saw you each year?''

"There were different people working from year to year. I didn't exactly stop and make small talk. I just purchased the cognac and left.''

"What about Patty?" C.J. asked abruptly. "Did she know?"

"Patty? Eventually she did. I called her six months ago. It was the first time I'd called her in ten years. We talked about my parents, Shawn. I think I told her about my...tradition."

"I see."

Instantly, Tamara shook her head. "It's not Patty, C.J. Patty is not the weak link. She's wanted to find out who killed my parents as badly as I did. They were like her parents, too."

"Then why didn't she stand beside you, Tamara? Why didn't she come to the sheriff's office when you were arrested? Why didn't she go to the arraignment hearing?"

"Because she's Patty," Tamara said weakly. She leaned forward, wanting to explain it and not knowing how. "We were best friends, C.J., but that was a long time ago, when we were just girls. In those days, Patty was wild, fun, fierce. Then her mother got breast cancer. First there was the mastectomy. Then the radiation therapy. Then a second mastectomy. Then more treatment. Then the news that the cancer had spread to her bones. Her mother died shortly after that.

"It was horrible. Patty was only twelve, and suddenly her mother was gone, her father was a mess, and she felt like she had no one. So she came over to our house more and more. Sometimes she sat at the kitchen table and cried. Once, she went into a rage and broke half our plates. She could be really sweet, then suddenly, hell on wheels. But my parents never complained. They understood—I understood—and we kept loving her, anyway. That's what she needed. To feel like someone still loved her. And then just when she's coming out of it, just when she's starting to settle down and feel in control of her life once more, there's a night with a full moon and a driver in a red sports car. I woke up alone in the hospital. But Patty was in her own house, sleeping soundly in her own bed, without any reason to believe anything was different. Then her father is knocking at the door.''

Tamara grew quiet. She said, ''You lost your mother, C.J. You know how hard it is to get over that. It was your grandma's love, your brother and sister, that helped heal you. What if something had happened to them just a few years later? How would you have felt?''

''I see your point,'' he said shortly, his face troubled.

''She doesn't get close to people, C.J. Not even to me. She never came to visit me in the hospital. She never looked me up in New York. Honestly, I don't think she even liked it when I finally called her. Maybe a part of her did, for old time's sake. But it's been awkward for us. Worse, it's been painful. She just…she needs her distance from me, from the past. It doesn't mean she's bad. It just means she's human.''

''Well, someone knows, Tamara.''

''If it is the senator, maybe he has had me watched. Maybe a private investigator? He would have the money for it.''

''Perhaps,'' C.J. mused. ''Then the question becomes, how do we find the private investigator?''

''There would be records,'' Tamara thought out loud. ''Money exchanging hands. Maybe checks in the investigator's name?''

''No, the senator's a savvy guy. He'd pay in cash to avoid the paper trail.''

''Then we're back where we started.''

''Maybe not.'' C.J. stared at her hard for a moment. ''What if we set a trap?''

''What kind of trap? We're not even sure we know who we're trying to lure.''

''Oh, sure we do. It's the senator, Tamara. Everything simply points to him. One, you saw his face. Two, who else would have the resources? And three, who else would care why you are back in Sedona, asking about George Brennan?''

"I know, I know." She sighed and dragged her hand through her hair, genuinely troubled. "We've had this conversation before, and you'd pretty much convinced me. But that was before Spider Wallace, C.J. I can believe the senator hit my parents' car, but why would he shoot Spider Wallace?"

"To frame you."

"But a witness saw a *woman* walk away."

"Perhaps he hired someone."

"Well, if he could hire someone to shoot Spider, why didn't he hire that person to just shoot me?"

"Someone's been trying to kill you."

"Then, why kill Spider?" Tamara insisted. "It makes no sense! Was the senator trying to kill me or trying to frame me? There's no reason to do both, and an extra murder is hardly a small thing. I mean, hitting my parents' car could've been an accident followed by panic. Hiring an assassin to shoot a poor, unarmed cemetery caretaker—that's just unbelievably cold and cruel. And incredibly risky."

C.J. opened his mouth, then clamped it shut. His glum expression said he agreed. "All right, all right. So we haven't figured it all out. It is far-fetched, but maybe he did plan both. When you went to the graveyard, you didn't see Spider, right?"

"Right."

"You opened the cognac, toasted with one glass and left it. Yes?"

"Yes."

"All right. So either Spider came to investigate the bottle of cognac and was shot, or he was already shot and the stage was set. Either way, the person wanted the bottle of cognac with your prints on it found. It ties to you. Your gun ties to you. The police will put the pieces together—

if they're too slow, an anonymous tip will help them out. They'll come looking for you. Now, if you're alive, you'll argue your case. But what if you were recently killed in an automobile accident, or fatally stung by a scorpion? Suddenly, it's open, shut. Spider Wallace's case is closed, and with you dead, no one asks about a ten-year-old auto accident again.''

Tamara just wasn't convinced. "That sounds so preposterous! Think of all the assumptions we're making and without a shred of proof.''

Abruptly, C.J. perked up. He leaned across the table. "So let's test our theory, Tamara. Let's pretend we have proof.''

Tamara quieted. "I'm listening.''

"You asked around for witnesses, right?''

"Yes, Mrs. Toketee. But she hadn't seen anything.''

"Let's pretend someone did. Listen, we'll contact the Chamber of Commerce and get a listing of auto shops, and so forth, from ten years ago. We'll conduct the noisiest search in the free world, calling repair shops, driving services, hospitals, the locals. We know someone is keeping tabs on us, so let's give them a show. And then—'' C.J.'s voice dropped to a conspirator's whisper "—in a day or two, we'll suddenly stop calling. We'll hole up in here, cast furtive glances over our shoulders and pull the blinds. We'll have a car pull up. I'll appear and hustle the person inside with a coat over his face. The next day, we'll leak word that we have someone who saw George Brennan driving that night. If he's guilty at all, that'll drag him into the fray.''

Tamara sat up straighter. Real research, theatrics and pure pressure rolled into one. Surely it would make the senator sweat. "But who? If we have someone claim to be a witness, they could also become a target.''

"Gus,'' C.J. said instantly. "Gus would do it. And believe me, honey, she can take care of herself.''

Tamara turned the idea over in her mind again. "It could be worth a try."

C.J. smiled. It wasn't his usual smile, however. This was a predator's grin. "We'll get him, sweetheart. Just you wait and see."

Night fell. The sun sank behind bloodred rocks. The waxy moon rose into orbit. The crickets began their mournful cry. In C.J.'s tiny cabin, all the lights blazed, as two people hunched furiously over their work.

Tamara had been on the phone most of the afternoon. She'd had to explain her situation to Lombardi, request a leave of absence and get a list of lawyers. She told C.J. that Lombardi had been supportive, but C.J. could tell the conversation had taken its toll. Tamara was a person who valued her privacy and her professional image. Murder charges had a way of stealing that from a person—even an innocent person.

Afterward, she'd started in on the list he'd gotten from the Chamber of Commerce with a vengeance. Using his cell phone, C.J. had contacted Gus and gotten her agreement for the plan. Then he'd called Sheriff Brody. While Brody was satisfied with his arrest of Tamara, he was a fair man and he did respect C.J. After hearing about the punctured brake line, scorpion and homemade bomb, he agreed to have his deputies dig a little deeper. They would talk to employees at the hotel Tamara had inhabited for most of her stay in Sedona. Perhaps someone had seen someone sneaking into her room or tampering with her car. In a perfect world, they'd discover a witness who saw a woman in black steal Tamara's gun and temporarily replace it with another.

C.J. didn't believe the world was perfect, but he couldn't stop from hoping.

A little after two, C.J. had made tuna fish sandwiches and heated up the leftover soup. Tamara barely ate two bites. After five, he'd cleared the soup from the corner of her elbow and replaced it with an apple. That had gone completely untouched. Now as he watched, she dragged her hand through her hair for the fourth time, then pinched the bridge of her nose. She sat cross-legged in the middle of the living room floor, surrounded by a sea of papers. They had retrieved her clothes from her hotel, but she remained clad in his old sweatpants and oversize shirt. The large, bulky garments made her appear even smaller and more fragile.

The shadows seemed to have magically reappeared beneath her eyes. She had the tight look of a woman sporting one helluva migraine.

"How are you doing?" he asked after a minute.

"No one remembers anything from ten years ago," she stated flatly. "The whole world has Alzheimer's."

"It's seven o'clock. Most places are closed. Why don't we call it a night?"

"We can try the hospitals. They're still open."

"You haven't eaten all day, and I'm tired of soup. We'll go out, grab a quick meal. The hospitals will still be there when we're done."

"Just a few more calls."

"Tamara—"

She was already reaching for that list, waving him away. C.J. had had enough. He crossed the room and took the list from her.

She finally looked up. For a moment, she appeared simply rebellious, then her gaze broke. "I have to do this," she said abruptly. "I just...have to do this. Otherwise I'm just going to sit here, losing my mind. C.J...."

"I know, sweetheart, I know. But you're wearing yourself out. You can't keep doing this to yourself. The human body isn't infallible."

She chewed her lower lip. For a moment, she looked

curiously vulnerable. "Am I too intense?" she whispered. "Too much?"

C.J. sat down beside her and placed his hands on her shoulders. The muscles in her neck were already rock hard with tension. He thought about what she'd said earlier regarding Patty—how after her mother's death she'd needed to feel loved again, accepted again, because it was impossible to lose a parent and not wonder if it was somehow your fault.

"Tamara, you are absolutely perfect just the way you are. In fact, you are so perfect, I want to make sure you eat and sleep so you will live perfectly forever."

She finally granted him a small smile. "All right. You made your point."

He tilted up her face. "Tamara, I care about you very much."

He said the words softly. He contemplated saying even more, but the uncertainty on her face was enough to quiet him. It was hard to keep the words in, though. He felt this big warmth in his chest, an unbelievable tenderness. He wanted to crush her against him and protect her forever, and he loved her precisely because she would never let him do that. She would always push, always challenge, always need to stand on her own feet. At the same time, she would need to know he was there beside her, because even if it was hard for her to admit, she did need him. And she did care.

"What if I go pick up food and let you make just a few more calls?" he suggested. "In return, when I come back with food, you have to stop and actually eat it."

She eyed the long list. "Do you think...do you think it's safe to split up?"

He considered it for a moment. "Yes. At this point, you've already been arrested for murder, and frankly, the evidence against you is pretty good. Your untimely demise would actually raise questions and leave the senator worse off. So yeah, since you're probably going to jail as a murderess, you're safe.''

"Lucky me."

"We'll figure it out."

She sighed. "All right. If you return with food, I'll take a break. It's not like the calls are producing anything, anyway."

"Oh, yeah? Wait until I get my phone bill."

"I'll repay you," she said immediately.

"Sweetheart, I can handle the phone bill." He picked up his coat lying over the back of one of the chairs. "You have about twenty minutes. Make it good." Then he was gone.

The twenty minutes didn't make a difference. But she did manage a couple of bites of the General Tsao's chicken he ordered. Afterward, they curled up on the couch and just sat in silence for a long, long time. He could feel the tension still in her. He could tell that her thoughts were a million miles away, but when he asked her, she just shrugged.

At nine o'clock, they turned off the lights and went to bed. He didn't try to make love to her. He just held her against him, trying to will her to sleep. It took her several hours to relax. Then he woke up to her jerking limbs, as she twitched in the throes of a nightmare and called her parents' names.

He held her against his chest as she sobbed quietly in her sleep. He kept holding her when she whispered, "I'm sorry, Donald."

And when she climbed out of bed shortly after that and didn't return, he stayed in the dark shadows of the bedroom and did his best to let her go.

Chapter 12

"**T**hat was Sheriff Brody."

C.J. hung up the phone as Tamara raised her head expectantly in the living room. It was 9:00 a.m., but from what he could tell, Tamara had been awake ever since leaving his bed at three in the morning. She wore only his white T-shirt, her long, slim legs framing the map she had spread out before her. Her scars stood out prominently on her left ankle. More thick, smooth skin marred her knee. Her thick sable hair was a disheveled mess.

"Did he learn something?" Her hand was frozen in midair, bearing a little blue flag she was using to mark the map.

"He said his deputies made the rounds. No one in your hotel saw anything."

Tamara stabbed the dark blue flag into the map with more force than necessary. "How the hell does that work, anyway?" she said sourly. "In this day and age, Big Brother is always watching. We are knee-deep in fellow humanity, having to constantly memorize rules of engagement so we don't offend our neighbors, while computers compile databases on every facet of our lives. For God's sake, I go to the grocery store and those damn bar codes tell some market researcher whom I've never met what brand of feminine hygiene I buy. And yet, when you truly need assistance, nobody has seen anything.'' She stabbed the map with a second blue flag and twisted. "That's ridiculous!"

C.J. hunkered down beside her. This close, she appeared even more frayed around the edges. He ducked his head until he could catch her gaze. "What are you doing, Tamara?"

"Narrowing our search." She pounded the Chamber of Commerce list beside her. "Places that don't remember anything or don't know anything get a blue flag." She slapped the map of Arizona. "So lookie here, Scottsdale is almost obliterated, Phoenix almost obliterated. Maybe you're right about Nogales. He could've just driven the car into Mexico and junked it there. A couple of teenagers probably fell on it like a pack of wolves and ripped it down into salable components. Better than tossing a corpse into a wood chip machine."

"Okay, Tamara, that's enough." He grabbed her hand and, before she could argue, pulled her to her feet. "You're coming with me."

"I have work to do!"

"No, you don't. You're exhausted, grumpy and about as entertaining as the Grim Reaper. You call a hospital now and they'll patch you through to the psycho ward without a second opinion."

"I have been arrested for murder. What kind of humor should I be in?"

"Throw these on." He tossed her a fresh pair of black sweatpants. "We're going outside, and I don't want our shadow staring at your bare legs. Then I'd be forced to beat him up. I am the jealous type.'' He grinned as charmingly as he could, though he was also tense.

Tamara yanked up the sweatpants. ''I want to make my calls!''

''In a minute, dear, in a minute.'' He dragged her outside while she continued to shoot daggers at him with her eyes. He didn't really know what he was doing. He was a former marine, a man more comfortable with action than words. He didn't read much that wasn't related to racing cars or guns and ammo—he didn't even watch TV talk shows—but he was a bartender, and he supposed all bartenders learned some proficiency in counseling. He hoped so.

He stopped in front of the punching bag hanging from the towering pine tree in his backyard. It was old, covered in places by gray duct tape and brick red from years of absorbing Arizona dust. The sky yawned clear blue above them. The fall sun was hot and fierce.

''Here you go. Let it rip.''

Tamara stared at him blankly. ''You want me to hit a bag?''

''Yep. I'll hold it, you smack it for all you're worth.''

''C.J., I have much more important things—''

''Tamara, hit the damn bag.'' C.J. got behind it, planting one leg behind him for balance and positioning the bag against his neck and shoulder. ''Come on, young lady. You're in a foul mood. You want to be able to control everything, to hold your life in perfect order so it will never fall apart again. Instead, the senator has ruined everything, once more. He's yanked your life from you, left you framed for murder and without a leg to stand on. You're smart, you're good, you tried so hard to be careful, and none of it mattered. The senator has you right where he wants you and you are *angry*.''

''Yes!''

''Hit the bag.''

She scowled, then finally gave the bag a little slap. Weighing more than a hundred pounds and anchored by C.J.'s body, it didn't even rock. "Yeah, you're a tough girl. The senator destroys your family and you hate him only enough for a baby slap?"

"Damn you." She jabbed her fist harder. The bag still didn't move, but she popped three knuckles. Her face gained color. Her eyes went gold. Sweat bloomed across her forehead, and her loose hair waved wildly around her face. He could feel the intensity building inside her.

"Curl your fingers into a fist, thumb on the outside. Now try again, step into it."

"I don't want to hit a bag—"

"The senator framed you for murder. Killed an innocent man. Destroyed your reputation."

She hit the bag with a solid thwack. This time, the force traveled through the bag, and made C.J. grunt.

"That's it. Up on your toes. Dance like a butterfly, sting like a bee, baby."

"This is stupid." She hit the bag again, then again. Despite her words, he could see her homing in on the punching bag with the intent to kill.

"Come on," he murmured. "Don't hold back. You can't hurt the bag, you can't hurt me. So go ahead, beat the crap out of it. Show it how you really feel about losing your family, being left alone, having no one to even visit you in the hospital."

She hit the bag harder than he would've thought she could. Better.

"You're angry, Tamara. You have so much anger, you never let go, do you?"

"I do not!" Thwack.

"You're angry at the man who killed your family."

"Yes!" Thwack.

"You're angry at yourself for surviving."

She didn't say anything. She lashed out with her fist.

"You're angry at your family for dying."

Her face fell. Her lower lip trembled. She hit the bag hard.

"And you're even angry at me, aren't you, Tamara?"

"No," she whispered, but she was pummeling the bag.

"Yeah, sweetheart, you are. Because I love you and you know that I do. It scares the living daylights out of you. And it makes you feel even guiltier, because with me, you're actually living, and you've done a pretty good job of avoiding that until now."

She didn't say anything, but he heard her gasping for breath. Her face contorted. She beat at the punching bag in a small torrent.

"Tamara, tell me about Donald."

"No," she cried. She stopped hitting the bag and kicked instead. Then she really lit into it, like a small child having a temper tantrum. C.J. kept nodding, encouraging her all he could. He didn't know if it was healthy or mature or sensible. He just knew that on bad days, the punching bag worked best for him. And each year on the anniversary of his mother's death, he woke up, came outside and beat the crap out of this bag until his arms could no longer move and his lungs could no longer breathe. Sometimes, when he woke up in the middle of the night having dreamt of Iceland, he came out here at two or three in the morning and did the same.

Tamara was still swatting the bag. Her breath had become labored, her movements sluggish. Still, she kept fighting. He dug in his heels, held on to the bag tighter and weathered the storm.

Finally, she fell into the bag, hugging it for support. Her breath came in heaving gasps.

C.J. took her sweaty, exhausted form into his arms. She leaned against him completely, her limbs shaking, her red cheeks covered in moisture.

"Come on," he whispered. "Sit with me. Let's talk."

Tamara followed him to the ground wordlessly. She felt drained, like an exhausted child, searching for a safe, dark place to curl up and pretend the world didn't exist. C.J. cradled her against his body. She would pull away from the big lout, but she didn't have the energy.

"How are you doing, sweetheart?"

"I'm tired."

"I bet you are. Honey, how long have you had the nightmares?"

"Forever."

"They're worse in Sedona, aren't they?"

"I work a lot in New York," she said weakly. "There isn't much time for sleep, anyway."

"Ah, that's how you do it."

"Do what?"

"Avoid," he said matter-of-factly. "Repress. Did they ever talk to you about grief counseling?"

She pushed away. She was tired. Her arms hurt. She didn't want to talk about the past. Why did everyone want to rehash the past? "They recommended it," she said curtly. She tried to rise to her feet, but her leg muscles wouldn't cooperate. She ended up just sitting a little ways back from C.J., who didn't try to pull her closer. Why did that disappoint her?

"But you didn't think you needed it?"

"I wanted to move on, darn it. Physical therapy, all the surgeries, took so long. Sometimes it seemed like the car accident had lasted forever. When I finally had the last operation on my knee, I just wanted out. I got on with my life."

"You threw yourself into school, then work. Built a pretty fancy life and decided that was good enough."

"I've done well," she insisted. She had. She didn't want to lose sight of that even if she was discovering all sorts of new potent emotions these days. Even if some dark,

feral part of her had truly *wanted* to beat the hell out of
the punching bag. Had needed it.

"You've done very well, Tamara. Maybe too well."

"Don't say that. That's not fair. I worked hard for my
career. I could've given up on life, instead."

C.J. was quiet. It took her a second to realize that he
was uncertain. She was used to him seeming to know exactly what he was doing. "I bought two books yesterday,"
he announced abruptly.

"Books?"

"Books. And trust me, I don't read books very often. I
leave that sort of thing to Brandon. But the Chinese res-
taurant was next to a bookstore, so while they cooked the
food, I paid a visit. I...uh...well, I picked up one book on
surviving and one book on post-traumatic stress disorder."

Tamara didn't move. She felt shocked, hollow and, for
some reason, guilty, as if she'd just been discovered doing
something bad. C.J. knew too much about her. Even the
weak, ugly, vulnerable places she tried to hide. Her gaze
latched on to the ground.

"Why...why did you do that?"

"Because I love you."

She swallowed heavily. My God, she was being ripped
apart. She turned away.

C.J. suddenly cradled her cheek with his fingers. "Tamara, I'm no good at this. I know you've been through
something traumatic, and I understand a bit because I lost
my family, too. But you are going through something more
complex. I'm watching you tear yourself apart, run yourself down, self-destruct, and I want to help you, but I'm
not an expert in these things. I thought...I thought maybe
we'd go through the books together. Would you be willing
to do that?"

She couldn't speak. She was going to cry. And not angry
tears or frustrated tears or sad tears. Good tears. When had
she last shed good tears?

"Tamara, I love you. Please say something."

"I'll go through them," she said, expelling the words in a rush, some part of her suddenly afraid he'd rescind the offer. She clutched his hand. "C.J...." She couldn't get any more words out. Her throat was too tight. "C.J.," she repeated, then sighed.

His blue gaze was steady. He cupped her face with his callused palms. "Do you care about me?"

"Yes."

"Do you want to be with me?"

She whispered, "Yes."

"Good, good."

Her grip on his hand tightened. "My life is a mess," she said abruptly, earnestly. "I have nightmares. Sometimes I am really angry for no good reason. I'm probably going to go to jail for a murder I didn't commit. My job is in New York. This is all insane."

"Sh." He broke off her tirade by settling her cheek against his throat and rocking her back and forth. "One thing at a time. I know what I'm getting into. I'm willing to take the plunge, anyway."

"You give me too much."

"That's love, sweetheart. That's just love."

She closed her eyes and wrapped her arms around his neck. For a long time they remained holding each other beneath the vast Arizona sky, and it was enough.

Later, after showering, she pulled on one of his flannel shirts so she could be surrounded by his scent. She padded across his home, touching his Chinese screen, his table, his sofa, as if they were all extensions of his body and she was seeing them for the first time. She cooked pasta in his kitchen while he discussed next steps with Gus. She set the table with her gaze drifting more and more often to him.

She watched the way his lean, blunt fingers tapped the

receiver while he talked on the phone. She admired the way he would pace the Navajo rug as he spoke, his whipcord body barely holding its own power in check. She liked the way he would glance up, catch her gaze and automatically smile, the corners of his eyes crinkling.

They ate in companionable silence as the sun set, the map sitting on the coffee table in the living room and covered with enough blue flags to indicate the futility of their search. Later, Tamara curled against C.J. on the sofa, and as she watched the sky fade to black and the stars twinkle to life on a velvet matting, she told him about Donald and the friends she didn't have and the holidays she'd never learned how to survive.

He traced small patterns on the back of her hand and held her as she talked.

"Have you ever thought of joining a survivors' group?" he asked quietly when she was done.

"I've never looked into it."

"I know there are grief groups, survivor clubs. My grandma looked into them for Brandon after his wife died. He was too stubborn to attend—not that you would ever be stubborn."

"I don't know. I'm not sure sitting in a room talking about the past really helps. What happened was tragic. Sad. No one will disagree with that. No one has anything to add. So how does talking about it help?"

"It's not just the talking, Tamara, it's learning how other people cope. It's people like me, who've found punching bags to be the most effective way of handling bad days, and it's people who may feel starting an agency in memory of the person they've lost is the best way. That sort of thing. You have a lot of stuff held tightly inside. Maybe by talking to others, you can find the best way to let some of it go. I'll go with you."

She pressed her cheek against his shoulder.

After a bit, she got out the list of hospitals and they

continued their calls, to no avail. At eleven o'clock, C.J. took her hand and led her to bed. She was tired, she was sore all over from having attacked the punching bag. She felt genuinely exhausted.

C.J. stripped off her clothes slowly in the moonlight. He didn't touch, he didn't caress. He slipped an oversize T-shirt over her body and a pair of boxers onto his. He arranged her against him on the bed, her hips tight against his groin, her back against his bare torso. She could feel the length of him grow and swell against her bottom. She knew he wanted her and she knew he wouldn't try anything.

She lay in the darkness for a long time, feeling his body against hers, listening to the silence around them.

And then she rolled over and seized his lips. His answering kiss was immediate and fierce. She didn't wait, she didn't play passive. He'd given so much to her, and she'd done so little in return. Now she gave him the most she had to offer—she opened up, she demanded, she craved, she touched, she devoured.

She pushed him back on the mattress, ripping off his boxers. She rose above him and stripped off her T-shirt. Then, naked and vulnerable, she clamped her legs around his hips and lowered herself onto him slowly. Moist folds stretched and engulfed, tiny muscles contracted exquisitely, pulling him in. She watched him grit his teeth. His hands dug into her hips.

She didn't take her gaze from him. In the shadowed room, the moonlight like a fine, gossamer film around their entwined bodies, she took him deeper into her and told him with her eyes how much she loved it, how much she needed it. Her teeth dug into her lower lip. Her body found the tempo and his hands gripped tighter.

Suddenly her fingers fisted on his chest. She could feel the building pressure. Her body was stretching, stretching, stretching. He was large, thick. She felt him impaling her, consuming her, driving into her womb. She wanted to close her eyes. She wanted to let her head fall back. She kept looking right at him, watching the sweat bead his face, seeing the intensity grit his teeth and cord his neck.

She couldn't think. She couldn't stop. She couldn't look away. The pressure exploded, the climax slapping her fiercely. She came while staring into his dark blue eyes and his gritted cry answered her. His hips ground into her. His back arched triumphantly. He spilled into her and she collapsed over him and his arms were already around her, clasping her against his sweat-streaked chest.

She fell asleep with her legs straddling his hips and his heartbeat in her ear.

Thursday morning, they put their plan into high gear. They each called four or five locals, including Gus. Suddenly, they swept out the door and drove to the closed Ancient Mariner where Gus's car was in the parking lot.

Sheila came down to help with last-minute plans. They wrote out Gus's statement and bundled her into a large trench coat while she mumbled about theatrics. Sheila wrote out a sign declaring the bar was closed until further notice and hung it on the door.

"Don't worry," C.J. said. "It'll be just for a night or two, and I'll still pay your wages."

Sheila shook her head. "You've helped me enough, C.J. I want to do this."

"Lock all the windows and doors. Don't take any chances."

"Maybe she should come with us," Tamara whispered. She worried about Sheila. She still remembered sitting with her on the edge of the bed.

But the young waitress gave her a small smile. "I'm fine here. There's no reason for anyone to think about me. Gus is the witness. Besides, I'm getting better at taking care of myself. You should see all the lamps I moved into my room.'' She winked slyly.

Tamara took her hand. ''Thank you. For helping. For...believing, you know. You don't even know me that well.''

''You wouldn't shoot Spider. You just wouldn't. Women know about these things better than men. Okay, are you guys all set?''

''I feel like a dressed-up turkey,'' Gus grumbled, ''the day before Thanksgiving.'' She scowled, but her eyes held a gleam Tamara hadn't seen before. Gus was having the time of her life.

''We're outta here,'' C.J. declared. ''Step two of Operation Cry Wolf is underway.''

He cracked open the door, motioned with his arm, and Tamara and Gus made a great show of scampering out to the car. C.J. gave Sheila one last wink, then a mock salute. He strode out with his fiercest ''I am a Marine!'' expression. Somber and grim, he checked his Mustang for bombs, looked over his shoulder half a dozen times, then climbed behind the wheel.

''We're being followed,'' Gus declared three miles later. ''Perfect.''

That night, with Gus sitting in the living room sharpening her bowie knife, C.J. made the calls to the local press. He talked about the accident ten years ago. About the driver that was never caught. About the new witness, saying the driver was Senator George Brennan.

They went on full alert. The blinds were closed, lights turned out so forms would not be backlit by lamps and turned into targets. Every hour, C.J. sneaked out the back and patroled the perimeter. Gus remained in the living room, balancing the tip of her bowie knife on the end of her finger. Tamara watched the clock as hour ticked into hour without anything happening.

Surely the senator had been contacted by now and asked for a quote. A public relations executive, she imagined he had his lawyers and spin doctors on the job, devising a reply, formulating damage control. Would he take a more forceful step, as well?

More C-4 taped into shocks? Sniper fire? Setting the house on fire and picking them off one by one as they ran from the front door? Her imagination produced pictures too easily. She squeezed her fingers against her forehead and tried to keep a grip.

Hour turned into hour.

Gus began to pace. She took a piece of wood from the kindling pile and soundlessly whittled. C.J. drifted along the perimeter like a ghost, clad completely in black.

At 2:00 a.m., Tamara brewed more coffee. Then it was three. She put on another pot at four, she grew tired of going to the bathroom every fifteen minutes. She splashed cold water on her face.

By six, the sun began to rise in Sedona and another night was done. C.J. waited till seven, then called his friend at the *Sedona Sun.*

He hung up after only a few words.

"We have our reply," he said shortly.

Gus and Tamara looked at him expectantly.

"The senator's office has issued a statement that he was being honored by the American Legion that night and has a roomful of witnesses. Any paper irresponsible enough to print the story based on one unreliable source will be hit with an immediate libel suit. The papers won't run it. It's dead."

"He has nothing to fear," Tamara whispered. "He's that powerful."

"The man can play hardball."

"What do we do now?"

"I have no idea."

Gus napped on the couch, then woke up at noon and announced she was going home. No amount of reasoning would change her mind. She could take care of herself. She wanted her own bed.

"Gotta open tonight."

"The bar can handle being closed for another night," C.J. said impatiently. "Get some rest."

"You get enough rest when you're dead. I want to open the bar. Sheila needs the tips."

She'd run the bar alone enough times for that to hardly be an issue, and she was right about Sheila needing the tips. "I don't want to read your obituary," C.J. grumbled. "Old bat."

Gus grinned, clearly taking that as a term of endearment. "It's Friday night. Good money on Fridays."

That seemed to be as good a closing line as any for her, and she huffed her comfortable bulk out the door, still fingering her bowie knife. C.J. kept shaking his head.

"Stubborn women. That's what that double-X chromosome thing is also about—double dose of stubbornness."

"What do we do?" Tamara asked. She'd really hoped their plan would work. She didn't know how to look beyond it.

"Calls," C.J. said shortly. "Let's finish out the list. Maybe we'll get lucky."

They didn't get lucky.

At 10:00 p.m., C.J. rose from the living room. He disappeared into the bedroom, and Tamara figured he was getting ready for bed. She pored over the map; most major cities were now covered with blue flags. It was hopeless. After ten years, the trail was too cold. Most shops they called didn't even have anyone working there who was around ten years ago. The driving services didn't keep records that old and refused to divulge information about their clients, anyway. The hospitals claimed to have records, but most inactive files had been archived and were about as easy to access as the peak of Mount Everest.

She'd been foolish to return to Sedona, Tamara thought. And she would pay for that foolishness.

C.J. reappeared in the living room. He was dressed in black jeans, black combat boots and a black T-shirt. He'd streaked charcoal over his face until only his blue eyes remained. He unlocked a cabinet and pulled out a gun, followed by clips of ammunition.

"What are you doing?"

"Going on a field trip."

"Over my dead body!"

"Tamara, hear me out."

"You're going to get into trouble. No one dresses like that unless they're headed into trouble!"

"No one will see me. That's the whole point."

Tamara was off the couch. "What the hell are you doing?"

"The senator's not due into town until tomorrow, right?" C.J. fastened a utility belt around his waist as he spoke. "So for tonight, his home outside of Sedona is empty. Maybe I can find something in his personal records, private correspondence, I don't know. I need to do something. This situation is killing me."

"Fine, I'll go with you." She strode for the bedroom. He caught her wrist.

"No."

"Yes."

"Tamara." He twisted her body until she faced him. "I'm trained in this kind of thing. Reconnaissance, infiltration, evac and evade—that's me. Most likely the senator's private residence has a security system. No problem. I go alone, I'll slide in, slide out, smooth as butter. I'll be back in a matter of hours and no one will be the wiser. Honestly, this is the best way to handle it."

She scowled. She hated the fact that he was right.

"I'm scared," she said abruptly. "I don't want anything to happen to you."

"I know." He wrapped his arms around her shoulders. "I won't take any unnecessary chances, I won't try anything stupid. Trust me, Tamara. I'm not your family. I'm not going to die on you now. Just give me a few hours. In the meantime, start thinking up plan C, because I have no idea if this will actually work."

He slipped on a black windbreaker, grabbed a flashlight and pulled a dark gray wool hat over his gleaming blond hair. He was ready.

"Be careful." She tugged a bit at his jacket, then smoothed the wrinkles away.

"I will. See you soon."

He whispered his lips over hers. She clung to him for one more minute, then she let him go.

He opened the back door and disappeared into the night.

It's okay, it's okay. Everything is going to be all right.

She missed him already, dammit. And for no good reason, she was afraid. She sat down at the kitchen table and forced her mind to think of plan C while the night grew thicker and the goose bumps prickled her arms.

Chapter 13

At eleven, Tamara started pacing. She closed the blinds on the windows. She turned off all the lamps, lighting just a single candle on the fireplace mantel. Even then, she felt exposed and vulnerable with the ceiling yawning above her and the sound of the wind whining behind the walls. The candle cast long shadows across the hardwood floors.

She was nervous and fearful and trying hard not to be.

Focus, focus, focus. How to prove the senator's involvement? How to prove her own innocence? She had no alibis and no witnesses. Her own gun was tied to the scene. But what woman would've shot Spider? A professional? Someone else?

Was there a paper trail to hire a hit woman? She had no idea.

Was C.J. all right?

The phone rang. The piercing shrill made her jump, then curse her own nerves. There was nothing sinister about a telephone ring, Tamara. Nothing at all. She eyed the black receiver for another two rings before warily picking it up.

"Hello?" she said cautiously.

There was a small pause. "Tamara?" a man's voice asked.

"Ye-yes..." She dragged out the word. Her hand was fisted at the hollow of her throat.

"Peter Foster. Patty's father."

"Oh," she said stupidly. She hadn't heard Mr. Foster's voice in more than ten years.

"Tamara, I know it's late. I've debated making this call ever since I saw the article on your arrest and learned you were back in town. The article mentioned C. J. Mac-Namara had posted your bail. I hope you don't mind me calling."

"No. No, that's all right. It's been a long time. How are you?" She grappled with the polite phrases, suddenly feeling like a silly eighteen-year-old just caught staying out late with Patty. The power of voices from the past...

"I'm fine. And yourself?" His voice cut off, then he laughed ruefully. "I'm sorry. Stupid question after reading the article. I'm afraid I'm feeling a bit awkward."

Tamara finally relaxed. "Me, too. It has been a long time, and in all honesty, I'm not sure why you are calling. Is it about Spider Wallace? Mr. Foster, I didn't kill him."

"No, that's not why I called. I don't know what to make of all that, to be honest, Tamara. A part of me says I should just butt out. On the other hand...I've wanted to contact you for ten years now. I owe you an apology, Tammy. There hasn't been a year when I haven't thought I should pick up the phone and hunt you down. Then I saw that you were here. And though I know the circumstances aren't the best, that it's been a long time, I felt...it's better now than never."

Tamara waited quietly. She could hear him composing his thoughts in the silence. She didn't know Mr. Foster very well. He was always the reticent academic, Patty's tall, quiet father with thick glasses and taupe wool sweaters. He never said much to either one of them. Patty's mother did the talking. Then after Patty's mother's death, Mr. Foster would disappear into the library. Sometimes Tamara came over to their house and never saw him emerge at all. Mostly, Patty came to Tamara's house.

"Your parents were very kind," Mr. Foster said abruptly. "I wanted you to know that, Tamara. What they did for Patty, taking her in, helping her during a time I couldn't be there for her—that was very generous. I'm not sure how we would've gotten through everything without them. And I wanted...I wanted to thank them. It's one of those things you know you should do, but at the time I just couldn't get the words out. Then it was too late.

"When I heard you were still alive, that you'd been flown out by Medivac, I knew Patty and I should be there for you the way your family had been there for us. But you were in critical condition for so long, I didn't know if we should come. Patty took the news of the accident very hard. For the first week, she was virtually catatonic. I couldn't get her to eat. She had horrible nightmares. For a while...for a while I had her under a suicide watch."

"I...I didn't know."

"Then there was the funeral for your parents. You were in the New York hospital then. The church told us you probably wouldn't be out of the hospital for at least six months, so it was decided to go ahead with the services. Your parents were well loved, Tamara. Most of Sedona showed up to lay them to rest. I took pictures to mail to you. I thought it might help to see how much everyone cared for your family."

"I would like to see the photos."

"I should've mailed them. But I kept thinking Patty and I would come to visit you. But..." His voice grew heavy, then quiet. "I am sorry, Tamara. It was a difficult time for us, too. Patty had already lost her mother, and she considered you as her second family. She was devastated, just devastated, and every time I mentioned visiting you, she became more upset. Your condition, your surgeries, frightened her. I think she was afraid if she saw you, something bad would happen.''

Tamara was still in the middle of the living room. The candlelight flickered over her face. She had been angry at Mr. Foster, but she hadn't realized it until he'd started talking. Yes, she'd needed him to come to the hospital. Yes, she'd been hurt by the fact that he'd never so much as written. Now she heard his voice, the true emotion, the genuine regret, and she discovered her anger wasn't that strong. He'd done the best he could. Patty had done the best she could. Tamara had done the best she could. It was all anyone could ask for in life.

"It's okay," she said quietly. "I understand. It was a big-enough shock for me to wake up in the hospital. I can't imagine what it must have been like for Patty to go to bed at night, then wake up the next morning in her same bed in her same room and hear you say that the people she cared about—her second family—were dead."

Mr. Foster sighed. "It wasn't even that simple. She wasn't in her bed. You know how Patty was back then—angry, rebelling, trying to get me to notice her. Well, to make a long story short, she didn't come home until the night after your accident, Tamara. Then she dragged herself through the doorway with her head bowed, waiting to see what I would do. I was frantic, of course. I'd spent eighteen hours trying to find her, with visions of Armageddon in my head. I...I didn't handle it very well. I yelled at her. I told her angrily that you were in serious condition and your whole family was dead. She went pale as a sheet, Tammy. Then she looked at me with the most horrible expression of guilt. She'd been playing hooky, and look at the punishment she got—your family was dead. She collapsed. Fainted away. I've often...I've often thought the death of your family hurt her more than her mother's. She at least rebelled against her mother's death. After hearing about your family, something in her just gave up. She never broke curfew again. She threw away all her short skirts. She stopped wearing makeup. She became this quiet, serious, fearful girl. Sometimes at night, I'd actually hope she'd ask to go to a concert again and stay out all night. Funny, huh? Life keeps you guessing.''

Tamara couldn't think of anything to say. She nodded into the telephone.

Mr. Foster cleared his voice. "I'm sorry. I didn't mean to lay it on you that thickly. I just wanted...I just wanted to say I'm sorry, Tamara. Patty and I both should've been there for you. I wish we had been. Your parents were wonderful people, generous neighbors, good parents. I miss them a great deal.''

"Thank you,'' Tamara murmured. Her throat had become thick, but she didn't feel like crying. "It was very nice of you to call, Mr. Foster—''

"Please, call me Peter.''

"Peter... I...I would like to see those pictures sometime.''

"I'll bring them over to the Ancient Mariner and leave them for C.J.''

"Thank you, that's very kind.''

"And Tamara...as for the rest of this...well, good luck. I know I haven't seen you in ten years, but the girl I knew would never be capable of murder. I hope the trial goes...goes well.''

"Thank you.'' The awkwardness had returned. Obviously, there was no good way to talk to someone about your upcoming murder trial. They exchanged a final round of pleasantries, saying all the expected things, then Tamara hung up the phone with relief.

Tamara crossed to the mantel and watched the flickering flames. Her throat was still tight, but it was different. She felt sadness, a yearning for the days that had been. But she felt comforted, as well. Mr. Foster remembered. Mr. Foster held the image of her parents in his mind, too. He understood. He mourned.

Her grief was no longer hers alone. It was part of the community here in Sedona.

Perhaps it *had* been a good thing to return.

She turned away from the candle, trying to get back to the business at hand. Halfway across the Navajo print rug, however, she halted midstride. Mr. Foster had said Patty didn't come home that night. Patty had told her that her father had come to her room. Why would Patty lie about a silly thing like that? Did she truly believe that by staying out all night in a stupid act of rebellion she'd caused the accident?

The thought hit her all at once. Her expression fell in the dimly lit room. Her pain was genuine.

"Oh, Patty, how could you?"

C.J. was no longer breathing. He inched his way along the side of the house with his gut sucked in and his bones pressed against the wooden siding. Wearing night goggles, he clearly saw the crisscrossing red beams that made each step an adventure. The senator's security system had been a bit more than he bargained for.

He stepped up over one beam very carefully, while ducking down to avoid another. A third passed by his navel so close it looked like it was drilling a second hole. Finally, he came to the French doors leading to the patio.

With his fingers, he searched out the wires of the electronic system, then cut them with his Swiss Army knife. Life got a little easier. He smoothed packaging tape over a small pane next to the doorknob, then used the tape to fasten a small handle on the glass. With a sharp rap of his knife, the glass splintered as a fine web, held together only by the tape. He pulled out the section neatly and dropped it on the ground. Then he simply reached in, unlocked the

latch and opened the door. Breaking and entering really
wasn't as difficult as people thought.

The house was pitch dark, the air stale. The thin beam
of his flashlight illuminated a large, king-size bed, sheet-
swathed chair and covered bureau. The senator didn't stay
in this house often or for long.

C.J. crept through the master bedroom into the hallway.
He entered a foyer with a vaulted ceiling and a crystal
chandelier. The curved legs of Queen Anne antiques
peeked from beneath protective sheets. The floors were
covered by thick Persian rugs. He saw the first signs of
disturbances. Marks on the floor from the door being recently opened. A slim briefcase sitting next to the elegant
brass coatrack.

His footsteps slowed. The senator wasn't supposed to
be in town until tomorrow. He listened for sounds of other
intruders, but the house was quiet. Whoever it was had
come and gone. But there was no knowing when they
might return. He would have to move faster.

He crept to the back of the house and found the senator's
study. Large mahogany bookcases rose up like looming
beasts. The air carried undercurrents of aging leather and
bound parchment paper. The windows were heavily cur-
tained.

C.J. went straight to the large, cherry-wood desk that
dominated the room. Its covering sheet had already been
ripped off and dumped casually in a puddle on the floor.
A huge computer filled most of the space. A fax machine
rested next to it. All the modern toys for an office away
from the office.

C.J. went straight to the locked desk drawer. A steel
lock. Good quality. The senator didn't fool around. But
apparently, neither did his guests: the lock bore recent
marks of being opened.

C.J. got busy. Fifteen minutes later, he opened the

drawer to reveal several stacks of paper and a generous sum of cash.

"For emergencies," C.J. murmured, and started reading.

Halfway through the pile, he stilled in the hushed silence.

"Oh, Tamara," he whispered. "I'm sorry. I'm so sorry."

She didn't know what she was doing. She did it, anyway. First she unburied C.J.'s black sweatpants. Next she pulled on one of her own black silk turtlenecks. Then she called a cab. She had it drop her a quarter mile from Patty's house.

She should just go up to the front door, she kept thinking. Patty was her best friend. She could knock on the front door and demand answers to her questions.

She approached the house like a thief, her stomach tight with nausea, her hand pressed against her belly.

It couldn't be Patty. It couldn't be Patty.

Don't be such a fool.

Lights poured from Patty's window. A little after midnight, Tamara's best friend obviously wasn't sleeping.

Tamara made it to the wrought-iron fence before drawing up short. What are you going to do, Tammy? What are you trying to prove? She could see her friend's back patio, the porch lights reflecting off the soft waves of the kidney-shaped pool, the thick, waving branches of the mesquite tree. No one was moving at the back of the house. The bedroom window remained a hollowed-out shadow in the night.

When they were little girls, Patty had kept a diary. Every night, she'd made an entry. Then she'd slip the diary beneath the mattress of her bed.

Five minutes, in and out, that's all it would take. She'd find the diary and be out the door. Very, very simple. Patty wasn't expecting anyone to break into her home, after all. At this point, she probably thought she was safe.

The anger rose up in Tamara's throat as bitter as bile. She eased open the gate and approached the back of the house. Pressing her ear against the sliding glass door, she could hear the low murmur of voices. The sliding glass door was too risky; it would dump her into the kitchen with a clear line of sight to the living room. She ducked low and headed to the left side, where she could see a French door leading to the master bedroom.

She discovered the door unlocked, which didn't surprise her. In Sedona, people had a tendency to leave back doors open. There just wasn't much crime.

Tamara eased inside.

Patty's room was large. Moonlight poured through a skylight, illuminating a modern wrought-iron bed with a desert-print comforter. Six pillows in designer cases fluffed up the back, while a huge painting of Indian figures, no doubt from Patty's gallery, covered the wall behind the bed.

Patty had done well for herself. So well. Tamara's hands were shaking again. Rage, pure rage. She had no pain or understanding left in her heart.

She stepped forward and plunged her hand beneath the mattress. She could hear the voices clearer now. Patty's voice, nervous and high, a deeper voice, trying to soothe. Tamara dug for the diary. In and out. Just get the proof. Just read in black and white what your *friend* did to you.

Abruptly, she heard footsteps. She ducked behind the bed, sucking her lips against her teeth. The sharp rap of heels on hardwood grew louder, then abruptly veered away. A door opened. She heard someone rummaging through a hall closet. Then the door shut and the footsteps faded back to the living room. Cautiously, Tamara looked up. The light beamed from the hallway.

Sweat beaded her brow. Her breathing was ragged.

Leave, Tamara, just leave. She couldn't. She had to know. She had to find that damn diary.

She didn't care anymore about the risks. And at this point, what the hell did she have to lose?

She plunged her hand back beneath the mattress and searched in earnest. Nothing, dammit, nothing.

Her gaze fell on the nightstand. She eased out the lower drawer and pawed through it. Still nothing. Her gaze fell on the closet.

Get out of the house, Tamara. It's too risky. You're being stupid.

She told her common sense to shut up and attacked the closet. It was a walk-in, lined on both sides with conservative suits and elegant dresses. Shelves rimmed the top. She spotted several books and went after them.

"Now, what do we have here?" The light snapped on.

Her arm arched over head, Tamara froze. That wasn't Patty's voice. This was a distinctly male voice. She turned and found herself face-to-face with Senator George Brennan.

C.J. left the senator's home via the front door, no longer worried about activating the security system. He grabbed his cell phone in the car and dialed his house. The answering machine picked up on the fourth ring.

"Come on, Tamara. Wake up. Wake up and answer the phone."

He waited as second turned into second. Then his own answering machine cut him off.

"Damn." He dialed and let it ring again. Tamara wasn't exactly a heavy sleeper. She'd pick it up this time.

But she didn't.

And then he knew.

"Damn, damn, damn." He put his Mustang in gear and peeled out into the night. He was already dialing Sheriff Brody's number.

* * *

"Wh-wh-what?" Patty sat on the edge of her fine leather sofa, her hand gripping a tumbler of Scotch for dear life as George dragged Tamara into the living room.

"I told you I heard something in the bedroom." The senator pushed Tamara forward. She stumbled slightly. "At least she dressed appropriately. Patty, get your gun. We'll make it look like you shot her breaking and entering."

Tamara glanced immediately at her best friend. Patty seemed to have turned to stone. Her fine features were still, her green eyes blank. Just her red hair tumbled down her back with a hint of fire. Tamara remembered French-braiding that hair as a child.

"Patty..." she whispered urgently.

"Get your gun," the senator said firmly.

Patty's hand began to shake.

"Don't!" Tamara countered. She leveled her gaze on her friend, trying to get her to meet her eyes through sheer force of will. "Patty, what are you doing?"

"I...I..." Patty turned to the senator, her expression silently beseeching.

"Gun," he said simply. "One shot, that's it. Then it will all be over."

"All be over? Killing me will not make it 'over,' Patty! You'll still have to get up every morning and face your own reflection. You'll still have to go to sleep every night, picturing your best friend's body on the floor. You know that's no kind of 'over,' don't you? Haven't you spent the last ten years living with the image of my parents' crushed car?"

"Shut up!" the senator growled. He backhanded her cleanly, and she fell to the ground.

She could taste blood in her mouth. Her lips throbbed. Slowly, from her hands and knees on the plush Berber rug, Tamara looked up at Patty. "Tell me about it," she whispered. "Tell me everything you did that night ten years ago, all the things you've wanted to admit, but you were too ashamed. I'm your best friend. I'll understand."

"I'm not your best friend," Patty said dully. "I don't deserve a best friend."

The senator was moving behind them. He was opening a drawer. After a moment, Tamara realized he was trying to find Patty's gun. She leaned forward.

"You were with him that night, weren't you? The senator must have told you how beautiful you were, how sophisticated. Did he tell you that he loved you?"

"I'm not that dumb," Patty said flatly. "We were having an affair. It was wild. Dangerous. It had nothing to do with love."

"Were you the one who rented the red sports car?"

"I made the arrangements. We had a rendezvous spot, after the American Legion speech, so no one would see us."

"Were you the one driving?"

"No!" Patty said sharply. For a moment, her eyes blazed to life. She jabbed her finger toward the senator. "*He* was the one at the wheel. *He* was the one not paying attention. Oh, my God, Tamara... We didn't mean to. It was an accident. Such a horrible accident."

Behind them, the senator ripped open another drawer, his movements more frantic. Tamara began easing back on the rug, toward the front door. She kept her gaze on Patty, wondering at what point her friend would say something, at what point her friend would try to stop her.

"The senator wouldn't let you call for help," Tamara filled in as she crept back, trying to keep Patty distracted. "He couldn't afford to be caught with an eighteen-year-old girl. He said if you came forward, he'd deny everything. It would become all your fault."

"We took the car to Mexico. He knew people. A doctor. I don't know what happened to the car. Someone in his office rented it. I just picked it up. He said he would take care of everything if I would just trust him, if I would just keep quiet. I didn't...I didn't know who we'd hit." Patty's voice broke.

"Shut up. She might be wearing a recorder." The senator crossed the room abruptly. Although an older man, he was still fit. He caught Tamara's shoulder just as she reached the edge of the rug. He hauled her to her feet roughly, and shook her. "Going someplace, sweetie?" He hauled off and slapped her hard. Her head whipped back, pain exploding in her cheek and firing up her eye socket. She tasted blood again.

Then abruptly, the senator dropped her like garbage on the rug, where she lay stunned, her eyes tearing up from the force of the blows. She couldn't see. Her ears were ringing. Her mind was fuzzy.

Pull yourself, together, Tamara. Focus, focus, focus.

The senator took the tumbler from Patty's hand and held out the revolver as its replacement. "Take it."

Patty recoiled slightly, but she didn't shake her head. She stared at the senator wordlessly.

"Don't, Patty! Don't let him do this to you. That night was an accident. You were just a kid going through a rough time. The senator is the one to blame. He took advantage of you, he chose to cover things up instead of letting you come forward. He wouldn't let you call for help."

"Don't waste your breath," the senator said. "Patty was hardly the victim, and she knows it. If she was such a good little girl, she never would've had her head rooting in my lap while I was trying to drive. Tell your friend about it, Patty. Tell her how you earned a reputation as the girl who could suck a golf ball through a garden hose."

The senator thrust the gun forward. His gaze on Patty was hard. "Just like Spider," he said.

Tamara was going to vomit. Far off, she heard Patty

whisper. "I had to. He overheard me talking to my mom...."

"I know," the senator said soothingly. "You did the right thing, Patty girl. You took care of everything, just like I asked. And I've taken care of you. The house, the car, the gallery. Who's been there for you through everything, Patty? Who's the one person who's never left you?"

"You."

"That's right, Patty girl. That's right. And now it's almost done. You did well with Spider, switching the guns, taking him out with one shot. You had problems, though, with the brake lines and the scorpion and the bomb. Remember?"

"I grew up with Tammy." Patty closed her eyes, her throat working. "She said I was like her sister."

"She left you and never looked back, Patty. Nine-and-a-half years it took for her to call you *sister.* Then she just wanted to use you to get at me. Don't let her treat you like that. Don't fall for that kind of manipulation. Take the gun. Pull the trigger. One shot, and it's over. You'll be able to sleep again at night. You'll be safe. No one will ever know the truth."

The senator forced the gun into Patty's hands. Her fingers wrapped around it.

Tamara tried to get up. She tried to run. The senator backhanded her again and sent her flying. Her elbow cracked against the glass table. Her arm went numb, her vision swam. As if peering through a long tunnel, she saw Patty raising the gun.

"He's going to kill you!" Tamara cried desperately. "Don't you see it, Patty? Once I'm dead, you'll be the only other person who will know the truth. He can't afford for anyone to know the truth."

"You should've stayed in New York," Patty whispered. "I tried to get you to stay in New York. Why didn't you

listen? Why, after all these years, did you have to come
back?''

The gun was steady in her hand. Her pale face was
composed.

"My parents loved you. Patty, for God's sake, they believed in you, like I did. If you'd just come forward, I
would've forgiven you. I would've known you would
never intentionally harm them any more than I would.''

"I killed them.''

"The senator killed them....''

"I...''

"Enough!'' the senator roared. "Shoot her. *Shoot her!*''

"I...I...''

The senator grabbed the gun from Patty's hand. His face
a mottled red, he turned on Tamara.

She lashed out with her foot, catching him squarely in
the kneecap and toppling him down. "Run, Patty, run!''

Tamara scrambled to her feet, tripping over the coffee
table and barely catching herself. Her arm felt invaded by
an army of red ants. Her cheek was on fire. Behind her,
she heard the senator's roar as he launched himself up.
"Dammit!''

She dove behind the overstuffed leather trail. The gun
exploded, the bullet burying itself in the pillow. Patty cried
hysterically.

"Shut up! Shut up!'' the senator yelled.

Tamara scampered for the front door. Plaster exploded
above her head, the dust stinging her eyes.

She heard another cry. She turned to see Patty swipe at
the senator with her Scotch-filled tumbler. He yelped as
the whiskey burned his eyes, then pistol-whipped Patty
hard. She fell back as her nose gave with a sickening
crunch.

"Patty!''

The senator raised the gun, aimed it at Patty's seated
form and fired.

"No!" Tamara screamed and the pillows turned red. She saw the haze of rage contort the senator's face. She saw him turn, already aiming. She dove for the front door and bullets rained over her head.

She slid behind the dividing wall, finding meager cover. She was trapped, pinned down. He was going to kill her. And from the living room, she heard Patty's faint moans as the life drained out of her.

No! No more waiting for someone else to save her while her friend and family died. She was sick of it. She'd had enough. She wanted to fight and she wanted to win.

She rose with a cry. From far off, she saw the senator raise the gun. She lunged for the door, her finger curling around the knob, her hand twisting the handle. His finger squeezed the trigger.

She flung open the door and leapt into the brilliant embrace of the sheriff's headlights. Gunshots exploded around her. She was falling down, down, down. The crickets cried for her.

C.J. yelled her name.

The world went black.

Epilogue

Tamara didn't wake up in the hospital. There were no nurses poking her with IV needles, no cops standing at the foot of her bed with somber faces, no doctors asking her if she could wiggle her toes. She opened her eyes to C.J.'s anxious face and the sound of sirens splitting the air. Red lights danced over his lean cheeks from the approaching ambulance. Men shouted in the distance, *Over here, over here*. Night washed over the scene thickly.

"Don't move," C.J. ordered. His arms cradled her against his seated form. She couldn't have gone anywhere if she tried.

"The senator."

"Brody has him."

"Patty…"

"The medics are here. Are you hurt? Can you move? Are you shot?" He relinquished his hold long enough for his hands to dance over her body. When he was convinced all body parts were accounted for, he scooped her up again.

He was rocking her back and forth. It made her dizzy, but she didn't feel like telling him to stop.

His chest felt strong and warm.

Her ears rang from too many gunshots. Her ribs hurt from the force of her landing. Her mind remembered what Patty had said—what Patty had done—and she suspected she'd sustained some injuries much deeper down, in the dark places where she still mourned her parents and now had to add the loss of her best friend. She would get to deal with those wounds later and over time. Maybe she'd haul out C.J.'s punching bag for the occasion.

"Patty shot Spider," she said simply now, "because he overheard her confessing to her mother's grave."

"I know, sweetheart. I went to the senator's house. I found a letter Patty had mailed to him just a few days ago saying she couldn't take it anymore. She wanted to confess everything. It appears the senator caught the first flight here after receiving it."

"She was my best friend."

"I know," he whispered with genuine feeling.

"C.J., don't let me go."

"I won't."

He kept his word, too, until the paramedics finally arrived and took her away.

At the hospital, they treated Tamara for shock and exhaustion, monitored her for a possible concussion and bound her bruised ribs. Patty wasn't so lucky. The bullet had rattled around inside her ribs, doing a great deal of internal damage before finally lodging in her spine. She was listed in critical condition and the doctors didn't expect her to make it. Two hours later she slid away, her father holding her hand.

The senator took a bullet to the shoulder. The injuries were not serious, but the publicity was. In a matter of hours, Sheriff Brody held a news conference announcing a full investigation into the senator's role in a ten-year-old auto accident, while C.J. leaked a copy of Patty's letter to the press.

The next day, a private investigator came forward under pressure from the D.A. He stated he'd been hired ten years ago by the senator to watch Tamara Allistair. The senator had never told him anything more or anything less. For the first nine-and-a-half years, the P.I. had simply issued reports every six months and collected his cash. Then she'd come to Sedona and his surveillance had stepped up to minute-by-minute monitoring with nightly briefings to the senator.

But he just watched, the man swore. That's all the senator asked.

The real testimony came from Patty's letter and tragic death. The D.A. swore to pursue the senator on charges of Murder One.

C.J. and Tamara left that for the bureaucrats to work out. They understood enough. They'd been through enough. It was time to heal.

A little before five, they released Tamara from the hospital. An orderly wheeled her downstairs, where she found C.J. waiting for her. He leaned against the wall with his hip jutting out and his arms akimbo. His hands were stabbed deeply in his back pockets, and his hair waved over his forehead. He saw Tamara and his face split into a grin, crinkling the corners of his blue eyes.

"Oh, my," sighed the female orderly with clear reverence.

Tamara agreed wholeheartedly. She held out her hands wordlessly, and C.J. took her home.

For one week, they shut out the world. They slept together, ate together, made love together. They told silly jokes and stayed up late with rented movies and fresh popcorn. They invited Sheila and Gus over for dinner. They played house.

C.J. never pushed, never probed, never alluded to the future. But sometimes Tamara caught him watching her from across the room, his blue eyes intent, his face somber. Sometimes she woke up in the middle of the night and discovered him propped up on one arm, watching her sleep.

He didn't ask, but the question hovered in the subtext of everything they said, everything they did: *Would she stay in Sedona or return to New York? Would she love him forever?*

She didn't know the answer. Until the night she found herself up on one arm watching him sleep. The afternoon she caught herself gazing at him from across the room. The moment when she leaned over and kissed him simply because she had to.

Monday, before he was due at the bar, she handed him his coat and picked up his car keys. Wordlessly, she drove him to the Chapel of the Holy Cross. And for the first time in ten years, she stepped inside a house of God.

They sat at the front pew. Through the arching window, the sky was the color of bone. The sun didn't come out today. The rock monuments remained a muted amber. Not even Arizona was beautiful every day of the week.

After a bit, she rested her head against C.J.'s shoulder. The silence settled over them.

She'd come to this church as a child. She'd sat with her parents, risen with her parents, prayed with her parents. In the misty shadows, she could almost see her mother singing Hallelujah while her father mouthed the words. In her mind, they turned toward her and smiled.

Something inside her loosened, broke free, let the memories in, the good, the bad. Her family was in this church, in the values they'd shared, in the traditions they'd taught her. If she closed her eyes, she could reach out her hand and touch them.

She kept her hand on her lap and replayed the memories,

instead. It felt right. The images filled in the hollow places, offering a soothing balm for her wounds. You never realized how far you had journeyed, until you returned home.

After a while, she raised her head.

"I could open a public relations office here."

"Yeah?" C.J. stretched out his legs. "That would be nice," he said noncommittally. "Otherwise, I was going to spend a fortune flying to New York."

She stared at the Arizona skyline. "I'm going to marry you."

"Well, it's about time someone made an honest man out of me."

"Can I use your punching bag?"

"Whenever you like."

"Can I wear your clothes?"

"When I'm not hell-bent on getting you naked."

"Will you read the books you bought with me? Will you come with me to a survivors' group?"

"I think I should."

She slipped her arms around his waist. Her mother was smiling. She could feel it in the softness of twilight.

"I love you, C.J." she whispered.

"I love you, too."

* * * * *

But what really happened to Max?
Watch for the conclusion of
Maximillian's Children in BRANDON'S BRIDE,
coming in February from
Silhouette Intimate Moments.

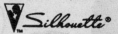

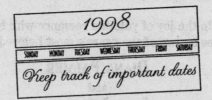
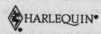

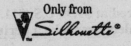

SHARON SALA

**Continues the twelve-book
series—36 HOURS—
in October 1997
with Book Four**

FOR HER EYES ONLY

The storm was over. The mayor was dead. Jessica Hanson
had an aching head...and sinister visions of murder.
And only one man was willing to take her seriously—
Detective Stone Richardson. He knew that unlocking
Jessica's secrets would put him in danger, but the rugged
cop had never expected to fall for her, too. Danger he could
handle. But love...?

For Stone and Jessica and *all* the residents of Grand Springs,
Colorado, the storm-induced blackout was just the beginning
of 36 Hours that changed *everything!* You won't want to miss a
single book.

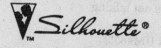

®
TM

Look us up on-line at: http://www.romance.net

36HRS4